DIRTY
SECRET
RHYS FORD

Dreamspinner Press

Published by
Dreamspinner Press
5032 Capital Circle SW
Ste 2, PMB# 279
Tallahassee, FL 32305-7886
USA
http://www.dreamspinnerpress.com/

Dirty Secret

Cover Art by Reece Notley
reece@vitaenoir.com

ISBN: 978-1-61372-775-1

Printed in the United States of America
First Edition
September 2012

eBook edition available
eBook ISBN: 978-1-61372-776-8

To my grandfathers,
John Kaleimomi Notley and Louis "Primo" Pavao

You might have left us, but I have carried you with me always.
Love you both. Hope I make you proud.

ACKNOWLEDGMENTS

SO MUCH haato and love for the other four of the Five—Jenn, Penn, Tamm, Lea—also Ren and Ree. There is a giant thank you and snookies to Lisa H., Bianca J., and Tiff. T. for weeding through the dregs of my drafts, and I'd like to thank my friends on Twitter who so thankfully supplied me with a glut of sex shop names. You degenerates know who you are.

I cannot go further without extending my gratitude to the wonderful staff at Dreamspinner, including Elizabeth for taking a chance on me; Lynn, who guides me through the rapids; Ginnifer for being so great to work with; and all the other editors who worked on this project. A special shout out to Julili, who is rocking the world now.

Lastly, a heartfelt celebration of thank yous to JYJ, Big Bang (especially G-Dragon), Tool, VAST, Vamps, AC/DC, and a slew of the blues rock for keeping me company and going forward while writing this book. You guys make a great soundtrack.

CHAPTER ONE

MEN are—by nature—stupid creatures.

I think I can speak with some experience on this. Both as a man and, well, a gay man. It's bad enough to be one of the stupid creatures. It's quite another to be attracted to them. Cursed at both ends: brain and dick.

My older brother, Mike—a fine example of a man doing a stupid thing—was sitting next to me in the new Range Rover I'd bought. He wordlessly grumbled as he sipped from the burnt, bitter coffee we'd gotten from a convenience store down the street. An open bag of Funyuns sat between us, keeping my stash of Twinkies company. I thought fondly of the young Korean man I'd rather have keeping me company than my brother, but Jae-Min was probably hard at work in my living room, where I'd left him.

We were sitting across from a sex shop called Back Door Lover. It wasn't a high-end shop, not like one of the perfumed, delicate places on Sunset named things like Pandora's Box, or Chocolate Starfish. The shop was a cinder block square building set among other low-rent businesses. A twenty-four hour taco stand sat on one side of a tiny parking lot it shared with the shop, and a computer repair shop sat a few feet away, on the other side. There wasn't a five-dollar cup of coffee place for miles. This neighborhood ran to greasy donuts and quick oil changes, with a scattering of cookie-cutter apartment complexes.

We'd parked across the street, so we could clearly see the shop, and the alley that ran between it and the computer store. The taco shop did a steady business. Pity it was mostly between a drug dealer and his customers in the parking lot.

Surprisingly, the Back Door Lover Sex Shoppe did a hell of a lot of trade, up until it closed at three thirty in the morning. Mike and I watched as the last customer shuffled out, clutching a plain paper bag of magazines to his chest. The moonfaced college kid who worked the night shift rolled a thick metal gate down over the front doors, cutting off our view of the shop's interior. Moments later, the shop's neon sign flickered, then went dark.

It was hard to get comfortable, even in the Rover's lush seats. The scar tissue from where Ben shot me kept clenching up, painfully twisting the nerves along my shoulder, chest, and rib cage. My more recent gunshot wound was a picnic in comparison. *That* just throbbed, and mocked me with twinges whenever I lifted something heavy.

"I can't fucking believe I'm sitting here at 4:00 a.m. watching the front door of a porn shop." Mike gritted his teeth, grinding them loud enough for me to hear him across the seats. "God damn it. Why do I let you talk me into these things?"

His hair, a hedgehog bristle on his square head, stood up even angrier from the hours he'd spent running his hands over his scalp. He took after our dead mother more than I did, having inherited her thick black hair and Asian features. Taking more after our Irish father, I envied Mike's hair. Its fury at the world was something to behold.

"'Cause Bobby had a date," I reminded him. "And technically, this is a sex shop. It says so on the side of the building. You can't miss it. It's in bright pink fluorescent letters. We're here on a case for a client, remember?"

"Your *client* has an inventory loss problem." Another slurp of coffee, and Mike's almond-shaped eyes became slits. "I have better things to do on a Saturday night than babysit my brother on a stakeout, so he can catch someone ripping off dildos."

"You're sitting here because you replaced your kitchen's cork floor with Spanish tile." I brought the binoculars up to my face to check out the couple walking by the sex shop, but they were more interested in checking each other for tonsillitis than breaking into the now closed business. "Wet Spanish tiles are hard to walk on when you've got feet. Imagine what a bitch it is if you're missing the bottom halves of both your legs."

"I was supposed to know that?" Mike slumped down in his seat. "I thought it would look nice. Be a surprise for her when she came home from New York."

"Yeah, well, maybe she'll think that once she forgives you... and rips out the fucking tile." I reached for my coffee, and swallowed as much of the hot, sweet, bitter brew as I could. "Right now, you're stuck here with me, watching a *sex* shop. And for your information, a *client* is someone who pays you. I'm doing this gratis, as a favor for Bobby."

"Who's on a date," he grumbled. "Nice best friend."

"I do not stand in the way of a man getting laid," I replied.

"Car One, come in. Over." The walkie-talkie I'd set on the console squawked with a harsh hissing noise. I reached for the handset before Mike could grab it. "Car One, are you there? We've got a situation at Car Two. Over. Kkkrrrawwr."

"Did he just hiss into the mic?" My brother's disdain was as sour as the coffee. "Are you shitting me? What is this? Are we in the fourth grade?"

"Not everyone plays real-life Army Soldier like you do, remember?" I clicked the send button before Trey could spit into the speaker again. "Trey, what's going on back there? Do you see someone?"

Trey, the recipient of said favor for Bobby, and owner of the Back Door Lover, was in charge of watching the rear entrance. It was a strategic move on our part. Trey was a bit of a pig, and even sitting across the street in a beat-up Toyota Camry, he'd cruised the men coming out of his own sex shop. I'd partnered him with Mike, while I sat in the back with Trey's current fuck-bunny, a frosted blond twink inexplicably named Rocket. I thought separating the lovers was a good idea. After twenty minutes of Trey's lascivious comments about men's asses and cocks, Mike threatened to cut off my balls if I didn't do something about it.

We'd switched places, moving Trey and his car to the back. Mike jumped in with me, reasonably more than half-afraid Trey would look for something else to do with his mouth besides talk in the dark alley behind the store.

Unfortunately for us, Trey had three *situations* while covering the back door, including the panicked reporting of a possum, digging through the dumpster he shared with the taco shop next door.

"Stop me if I'm wrong," Mike interrupted by poking me in the ribs. "But it looks like someone's coming out of that sleaze shop with some of your client's shit."

I'd never played with dolls of any kind, so it came as kind of a surprise when an oddly shaped balloon poked out a small opening set high up on the Back Door Lover's outer wall. It convulsed, then shot out, catching air. The brunette blow-up doll's freed limbs unfurled, and it pinwheeled in the air, then floated down to the ground.

A blond version popped out next. Its bright, nearly pink vinyl body floated upward momentarily, catching the faint breeze before it drifted down to land beside its brunette sister. Even in the shadows, its creamed-corn-yellow hair shone, and its wide, surprised mouth was obscenely bright in the darkness.

What came next was even more of a surprise. The doll was followed by what looked like a size nine red Converse en pointe.

"Son of a bitch must have been hiding inside." I was in awe, really. The man was scarecrow skinny and able to contort himself into a pretzel to get out of the shop's exterior air vent. It couldn't have been more than a two foot square, but he slithered free of the opening like he was made of gelatin. He landed awkwardly on a pile of boxes stacked in the tight alley between the Back Door Lover and the computer place, but recovered before he could fall. Mike and I were out of the car before the thief's feet could hit the concrete.

That's when the gunfire started.

A quick shove from behind, and I was tasting the pebbles and oil on the street. Mike's heavy weight landed on my back, and what little air I had left in my lungs rushed out, leaving me gasping. I was more than mildly insulted when Mike pushed me down onto the asphalt and covered me with his body. I didn't need my older brother to protect me. Besides, he was a lot shorter and smaller than I was, so he wasn't really much use as a body shield.

"Get the fuck off of me." I shoved Mike away. The walkie-talkie in my jacket pocket screeched with Trey's screams. I was up as soon as Mike's weight lifted, yelling at my brother as I headed to the back of the store. "Go after the guy. I'll check on Trey."

Throwing himself to the ground apparently made my brother deaf, because he ran behind me, as fast as his stumpy little legs could carry him. I was still spitting grit out of my mouth, and the road rash on my hands was beginning to sting. I wasn't in the mood to be generous.

I was even less generous when I came around the corner of the building to find Trey sitting next to a battered green dumpster with his pants and underwear down around his ankles. Trey twisted slightly to look at us coming toward him, and what I could see of his skinny, bony ass wasn't a pretty sight. I had no idea what the hell Bobby saw in the man's stick-figure body and hooked-nose face. Trey's cousin and resident twink seemed more like Bobby's style.

The twink, Rocket, stood between Trey and the car, twitching nervously next to the remains of a shot-out headlight. His T-shirt had disappeared sometime after they'd moved to the back of the store, and his mouth looked suspiciously swollen. If anything, he was skinnier than Trey, nearly cadaverous, and pale. I could count the bones of his spine, and I was half-afraid the weights on his nipple rings would topple him off balance, pitching him forward. He held a brick in his hand, clutching it like it was a Bible.

Freddy, the store's clerk, stood in front of him, looking surprised to see us. His mouth gaped, mimicking the blow-up dolls' orifices. Unlike Rocket, he wasn't clutching a brick. He had a wicked looking .357 pointed straight at Trey.

I skidded to a stop, and Mike slammed into my back. Freddy screamed, flailed, and the huge gun in his hand went off.

Several things happen to people when a gun goes off around them. Some scream. Others dive for cover. I, for some reason, did something my brother just did to me. I grabbed Rocket and covered him with my body to protect him.

This time, my brother chose instead to raise his hand—a hand with fingers clenched around a mean-looking Glock, which Mike dropped to aim at the sex shop's round-faced, pimply clerk.

Rocket squeaked and tried to squeeze out from under me. The cloying scent of a bad grade of pot, and grimy boy sweat clung to him as tightly as he held onto his pet brick. His squirming turned to near seizures, and he swung his arms, smacking me across the cheek. Of course it was the hand with the brick. I saw stars and rolled over. If Rocket got shot at, maybe he could deflect it with his brick, like Wonder Woman.

"Drop it." You'd think Mike was the former cop instead of me. He had the voice down. He probably practiced it while standing in front of a mirror.

It was enough to make Freddy drop the gun. It clattered when it hit the cement walkway, and I flinched, half expecting it to go off. Standing up, I brushed flecks of cement and boy debris off my jeans.

"What the fuck do you have a gun for?" I went to pick up the weapon. It was heavy, and the powder reek coming off it smelled dirty. Trey uncurled from the fetal position he'd taken on the ground. His skinny frosting-white ass disappeared from view as he sat up, and he gave me a sheepish smile when he saw me frown at his nakedness. "Pull your pants up, Trey."

That's when I noticed he had a glass juice bottle hanging from his dick.

"He's stuck," Rocket mumbled, scratching at a mosquito bite on his skinny arm. "His cock's stuck."

"Yeah, thanks. I kind of noticed that, Rocket." I motioned for Freddy to step back, and he shuffled quickly, his eyes pinned on my older brother. The container was an iced tea bottle, a wider mouthed opening compared to a soda bottle, and Trey's considerable girth was lodged firmly down its long neck. "Well, I guess that's what Bobby saw in him."

"Fucking hell." Mike spat on the ground. "I'm going to go see if I can find the skinny guy with the fake chicks. You deal with this shit."

"That asshole had a gun," Freddy stammered, after Mike stalked off. "He was going to shoot me! He had a fucking gun!"

"To be fair, so did you," I said, holding up the weapon I'd picked up. Shouldering Rocket aside, I approached Trey and looked down at his captured dick. "Trey, what the fuck happened?"

"I needed to pee." Trey shrugged. He also smelled of pot, sweat, and the added bonus of sex. "Freddy locked up and came outside to get high with us. Then, I needed to pee."

"There's a bathroom inside of the store," I pointed out. "Your store. The one you own."

"Yeah, I didn't think about that," he admitted. "I had the empty bottle, and then Rocket started doing some things, so I got stuck. Freddy was going to try to shoot it off, but he missed."

"He could have shot your dick off, stupid." I looked away as Trey was still sitting bare assed on the filthy cement without pulling up his pants. Considering we were in back of a place where people bought lube and dildos, I'd have kept my naked butt as far away from the ground as possible, but it didn't look like Trey was all that worried.

"He was going to hit it against the dumpster, but Freddy said it wasn't a good idea," Rocket mumbled. "We thought we'd try the gun first."

Rocket's tongue kept wandering through the piercing on the side of his lower lip, turning the skin red. I wondered if I'd ever been that young and stupid. Looking at Trey sitting on the ground with his legs spread wide open and with a glass sarcophagus around his dick, I didn't think I'd been born that young and stupid.

"And the brick?" I was afraid to ask. "What were you going to do with that?"

"Oh, yeah. Right," Rocket looked down at the brick, surprised to find it in his hand. "Trey told me to do this before Freddy said he could shoot it off."

For a skinny, twitchy stoner, Rocket had great aim. The brick flew tight, hitting its target cleanly: right onto Trey's glass-encased dick.

CHAPTER TWO

"LOOKS like you've got company," Mike said as we pulled up to the old building I'd restored following the shooting.

Such a small phrase—the shooting—for such a fucking implosion of my life.

The sky was turning to a light dusky blue by the time we reached the massive Craftsman-style building that held both my home and my business, McGinnis Investigations. I'd given over the front bottom half to the office, and I'd turned the rest into a place to live. The landscaping had taken a beating from an incendiary device left by a former client's daughter, so the front was a bit barren. A cement drive on the right side of the building led to my front door, and the dual-car port where I parked my Rover. The other side of the open air garage held Jae's white Explorer, so Mike'd left his squat Porsche at the curb.

Sucking up the rest of the concrete curb was a long black town car with its customary accessories, a pair of square-jawed, thick-bodied Korean men dressed in black suits. The car was parked so they could clearly see the side of the building and where the front door to my home was. From what I could tell, the Koreans only had two purposes: chauffeuring and protection. They answered to a staunch Seoul-born man with shady connections to the Korean embassy. Since the businessman commanding their allegiance never visited me, they could only be here for one reason, to protect his lover.

Scarlet.

I'd met Scarlet years ago while working a vice sting at Dorthi Ki Seu, an elegant gentlemen's club that catered to gay Asians, mostly Korean. She performed a torch song act there, slinking across the stage while singing smoky classics. Tall for a Filipino, her slender body seemed made for little blood-red dresses and sips of whiskey. Her beauty was timeless, with gorgeous features, a lush mouth, and skin the color of fresh milk with a dash of Kahlua to make things interesting. Without a doubt, Scarlet was the most beautiful woman I'd ever seen.

And she was also a man.

I'd probably met one, or maybe even both of the Korean men hovering near my house. Sadly, they all seemed to be hired not only for their deadly aim and hard fists, but also for their stony faces. I couldn't tell any of them apart. It was even worse in the daytime when they wore sunglasses. I'd been worried about it until Mike told me he couldn't tell them apart either, and he dealt with them a lot more than I did.

"Hey." Mike paused before he got out of the Rover. "You going to bring Jae to the dinner with Mom and Dad?"

"I haven't asked him yet." I was tired, and there was a burning hole in my stomach from all of the bad coffee I'd inhaled over the past few hours. "It's not like Dad wants me there, Mike. We haven't talked in years."

My father and Barbara, the woman he'd married after my mother died, put off their initial visit after I'd been shot by Jae's crazy cousin, Grace. It wasn't so I'd have time to heal before they visited me. It was because Barbara tore the ligaments in her ankle and needed a month before she could travel. I'd called Barbara "Mom" once. That was before she stood silent while my father railed on about me being a faggot and then did nothing when he tossed me out of the family.

"Cole." Mike would be a good father one day. Not only had he mastered *cop*, but he also mastered *dad taken to the line* voice. "Tasha wants you there. Maddy wants you there."

One thing about my brother, he never failed to pull out the big guns: the half sister I knew and his wife, two women I didn't want to disappoint. I'd never met my other two sisters. This was the first time I'd been invited to see them.

Sighing, I rested my head against the steering wheel. "Fine, I'll be there. I'll ask Jae if he wants to come with me. Just tell Mad Dog not to count on him being there. He's got his own family shit to deal with. He might not want to deal with mine too."

"It's in a couple of days, so don't forget." Mike got out and slammed the car door behind him. I got out and nodded to the Korean guys. Not surprisingly, they didn't wave or smile back. "I'll call you."

I stood there in the rising sun as my brother got into his little sports car and headed back to his corner of suburbia. My neighborhood was just beginning to wake up. The coffee shop across the street already had its lights on, and someone was moving around behind the counter, filling up the pastry display cases for the morning rush. There were other old buildings near mine, many of them turned into boutiques or their insides chopped up into tiny apartments. A bottle-blonde woman jogged past, her breasts bouncing with every stride, but the Koreans didn't so much as glance her way, their attention fully pinned to my building.

"Well, good night, guys." They said nothing, watching me head to my front door. "Try not to burst into flames when the sun comes up."

My front door was locked. It was a habit Jae had, locking the world out. Fitting my key into the knob, I opened the door to my home, and stepped in to be greeted by a tiny black demon screaming at me from the top of the stairs. She was a small cat, barely five pounds of black chinchilla fur and fangs, but Pearl Harbor envied her air-raid vocalizations. Jae didn't need to lock the door to keep intruders out. The cat's banshee screams did the job just fine.

"Morning, oh evil one." Neko ignored my greeting and dashed off, a furious ebony streak bent on hell and the destruction of the upstairs bedrooms.

Most of the downstairs was wainscoted, with cherrywood paneling and cream plastered walls. I'd stripped the wood, sanded it smooth, and restained it. She couldn't do much damage there, other than the occasional eyeing of the massive comfortable couches spread about the living room that took up much of the first floor.

Upstairs was a different matter.

I'd papered the smaller bedroom with a silk damask print the cat loved to strip off the walls. I'd bought her a gigantic scratching post with enough holes and levels to house most of the city's homeless. The wallpaper continued to suffer until Jae fitted her claws with something he called nail caps. They worked, so she couldn't claw out anything, and looked pretty against her thick black fur. They also pissed her off something fierce.

Now I had a small black furry pissed off cat with glittering gold claws staying with me four days out of the week when Jae slept over. I feared she'd move on from clawing up my wallpaper to chewing off my testicles as I slept.

"Hello, *hyung*." The locker of doors and owner of demonic black cats padded into the foyer from the living room, and my heart skipped. I didn't blame it. My brain seemed to have taken its own vacation, because words failed me.

My dick, however, knew exactly what it wanted to say, and was as pissed off as Jae's cat that we had company.

Kim Jae-Min was nothing I ever wanted in my life, nothing I ever expected. He was beautiful and enigmatic, a gorgeous Korean man trapped between his sexuality and his family's traditional expectations. He shouldn't have caught my attention. I'd never looked at an Asian man. Never imagined sharing a bed with one, much less having another man after Rick died. Once I'd found him, I didn't want anything... anyone else.

Jae was a loose-hipped, sensual creature, a little shorter than me, but with long, lean legs I couldn't get enough of. His mouth was kissably full, and his dark-brown eyes were hard to see through the fall of black hair framing his face, but I knew there were light honey specks in them that caught gold when he was out in the sun. He dressed with little care to how he looked, preferring low-slung threadbare jeans or drawstring cotton pants that hung low on his narrow hips. His feet were always bare when he was home, long toes that bore more than a few scratches from his cat's vicious playing. He preferred T-shirts, usually mine when he slept over, and tank tops that left his muscular arms free. They were nice arms. They went with his broad shoulders, built up from lugging photography equipment around.

It was a shame we had issues. I was having a hard time getting over my dead lover, and he wrestled with being gay and coming from a culture where being homosexual would get a man excised from his family. I was never certain if he understood his beauty, or even was aware of the attention he attracted when he came into a room. It was a pity he couldn't stay mine.

I was working on that.

"*Nuna* is here." The kiss he gave me was light, a brushing of our mouths, but it was enough to short circuit my brain the rest of the way.

I wasn't paying attention to what he was saying. Not when his arms slid around my waist and his body fit up into mine. I slid my hands down, cupped his ass, and ran my fingers along the rise of his rear, filling my palms with the feel of him. Since there was company in the living room, the couches were off-limits. Heading upstairs was also out. She'd hear our feet on the steps and would wonder why we'd left her alone downstairs. The laundry room was looking good. I could see Jae balanced on the washer, his pants pulled down just enough for me to spread him apart and work myself into his warmth.

"Cole-ah, listen," Jae said, flicking me on the end of my nose with his fingers. The -*ah* at the end of my name was a term of affection, but the flick stung. He'd let go of my waist, and pushed me away gently. I reluctantly let go, telling myself I was too tired for a romp on the washing machine anyway. "I said, *nuna* is here."

"I know. I saw the kim chee mafia outside," I replied, leaning over to bite his neck gently before he could pull away further. He let me, and I briefly worried at the skin before letting him go. "Is she okay?"

"She wants to talk to you. She brought someone for you to meet. They want to hire you for something," Jae murmured. His high cheekbones went pink, a blush over his skin, and he rubbed at the spot where I could still see the dimples left by my teeth. "What took you so long to get home?"

"I had to go watch a doctor pick glass out of some guy's dick." I shrugged. "Is there coffee I can warm up in the microwave? I'll need something to keep me awake for a little bit."

"I'm not enough?" His smile was brief, a flirtatious smirk that left me no doubt I could have dragged him away to the laundry room if I'd tried hard enough.

"Jae, you aren't something to get me into the living room to talk," I murmured, hooking my hand behind his neck and pulling him into another kiss. "You're inspiration for me to head upstairs and see if we can make enough noise to get the cops called on us."

"*Aish.*" It was a guttural sound, a rasp of a rattle in his throat. "There's coffee. I'll get you a cup. And something to eat. Go talk to *nuna* so she can go home and we can get some... sleep."

OTHER than the office space in the front of the building, I'd spent the most time renovating the living room. The enormous fireplace fought me every step of the way, and it'd taken me the better part of two weeks to get rid of decades of paint and smoke. What I got out of it was an elegantly carved mantelpiece and a place I could hang my flat-screen television. Most of the long wall and bookcases were set around and below the windows. I'd tried to find furniture to match the clean lined fireplace, but I'd missed the gay designing gene, and finally settled on buying long, wide overstuffed sofas and a low, squat apothecary chest I used as a coffee table. It was big enough to host a small family if they didn't mind kneeling.

Jae'd declared the chest was off limits for sex. We ate off it all the time. I had to give him that.

I didn't like it, but sometimes, common sense did win out.

"Hello, baby," Scarlet purred, standing to give me a kiss on the cheek.

Despite the late night waiting up for me to come home, she looked incredible, her skin luminous against an untucked white men's shirt. Her trim legs were showcased in black skin-tight leggings, and she'd taken off her flats at the door, leaving her tiny feet bare. Her fingers were naked except for a plain gold band on her left hand, and the jade and gold ring on her right index finger. The band was from her lover. The jade was a gift from me. She'd been there for Jae during the hardest times of his life. I'd have bought her the moon for that if I could.

"Hello, *nuna*." I used the Korean honorific Jae used for her, an intimate word from a young man to an older woman he was close to. It meant the world to Scarlet that he called her that. The first time I did, her tears threatened her makeup, and I'd earned a slap on the arm for teasing her about it. "You should have called me. I'd have come home sooner."

There was a young Korean man about the same age as Jae-Min sitting next to her. He stood as I came in, giving me a slight bow. His black hair was cut tight to the sides of his head and only a little bit longer on top. He was shorter than I was by about a head, but his arms bulged with muscles when he extended his hand for me to shake. A slight tan darkened his skin, and his palm was dry and rough from physical labor. We shook hands briefly as Scarlet introduced him.

"Cole, this is Park Shin-Cho. He is my friend's son and *hyung*'s nephew. Shin-Cho-ah, this is Cole McGinnis, the man I was telling you could help you." She let us shake hands once more, then slid back onto the larger couch, tucking her legs under her. Reaching forward, she retrieved a cup of tea from the table and cradled it, taking a sip. "Unless you want to use your American name?"

"Jason?" Shin-Cho sounded a little bit like Jae when he was tired, his English rounded at the edges and softened with a blurred accent. "I haven't used it in a long time, not like Shin-Ji... David. I don't know if I'd answer."

"Shin-Cho is fine unless you like Jason." The smell of something delicious came out of the kitchen, and my Twinkie-stuffed stomach grumbled in protest. Remembering my manners, I asked, "Did you guys eat?"

"*Musang* fed us earlier." Leaning forward, she patted the couch, urging me to sit. "You eat. He'll take care of you too."

"I'm pretty sure he's sick of taking care of me," I joked, but I'd wondered when Jae would finally say he'd had enough—but then, I put up with his cat, so it was an even trade.

"You're not that hard to take care of," Jae scolded me, his voice husky from lack of sleep. Carrying a tray with dishes and a teapot, he deftly avoided my efforts to take it from him, putting it down out of my reach. "All you want to do is get into trouble, eat, and sleep."

"That's not all I want to do," I said, thinking about the washing machine. My wink was enough to make Jae scoff, and Scarlet laughed. I'd forgotten about Shin-Cho, and his face flushed bright pink from embarrassment. I mumbled an apology, but he waved it off with a shy, crooked smile.

"I believe, Cole-ah, that falls under the *get into trouble*." Scarlet murmured a thank you as Jae refilled their cups with tea.

Jae sat down near me, settling on the other end of the long couch with Scarlet. His knees brushed mine, and we shared a smile. Reaching over, he spread out a small array of panchan dishes in front of me. The little white squares held different pickles and salads, including one of my favorites: thinly sliced daikon, and carrots in seasoned rice vinegar. There was also a deadly looking red-peppered kim chee. It made my eyes water just looking at it.

I'd eat it, because Jae put it in front of me. I'd regret it in a couple of hours, but I'd eat it.

A tall glass of iced coffee and a palm-sized metal bowl of purple and white rice joined the panchan, and then Jae carefully placed a covered ceramic soup bowl in front of me.

"What is it? It smells good." It did smell good, spicy and meaty, with a hint of smoothness I'd come to associate with *dubu*, a silky Korean tofu.

"*Sundubu chigae*." Jae pinched a bit of the kim chee with the back end of a pair of chopsticks and ate it before handing the utensils to me.

"I've had this," I murmured, trying to translate the Korean. I was about to lift the domed cover when I stopped and asked, "Wait, does it have eyeballs?"

There were a lot of changes in my life since I'd hooked up with Jae. One of them was the occasional appearance of eyes in my food, usually from fish heads, and unpeeled whole shrimp. I could handle a lot of things, including tentacles, but having a prawn stare back up at me from my soup wasn't one of them.

"No eyeballs," Jae promised with a small smile. "No legs either."

"Thanks." I kissed his cheek and lifted the cover, inhaling the soup's rich aroma.

I felt weird eating in front of the others, but they reassured me it was fine. Spooning some of the rice into the soup, I cut through the yolk of the egg Jae broke into the hot *chigae* before bringing it out, spreading the thickening threads through the liquid. A big shrimp bobbed up to the surface, its pink body devoid of shell, eyes, and legs. They let me eat, making small talk I now knew was necessary for them to have before they could get to talking about why Scarlet was there. The panchan disappeared steadily with Jae's help, and I reached for the last piece of the cabbage kim chee with my chopsticks, holding it out for him to take.

He tilted his head to bite it free from the chopsticks, his eyes hot with something I couldn't identify. It burned there whenever I fed him, a tingling awareness we never spoke of.

I made a mental note to feed him more often.

The *chigae* was gone before Scarlet turned the conversation to what she'd come over for. Jae brewed us both a strong Vietnamese coffee and condensed milk drip, and moved from filching my panchan to chewing a checkerboard cookie.

"We, Shin-Cho and I, want to hire you, Cole-ah." Scarlet dipped a cookie into her tea, and nibbled on its moistened corner. "It's about his father. He disappeared when Shin-Cho was young… in 1994. We want you to find him."

"Or find out what happened to him," Shin-Cho added. "I need to find out what happened, especially now."

"It's been a long time. Why now?" I mentally guessed Shin-Cho's age, and added a couple of years on for good measure. "You were what? Eight? Nine?"

"Ten," he corrected. Shin-Cho glanced questioningly at Scarlet, and had a silent conversation with her with his eyes.

She nodded once, urging him on. "You can talk to him, Shin-ah. You can be open with Cole."

"My brother, David, is getting married." He bit his lip, obviously fighting with himself over something. "These past few weeks have been hard. I was happy for him. We've known her family for years... she's very sweet. Very nice."

I sipped at my cup. "What does she have to do with your father?"

"It's not her," Shin-Cho said, waving his hand in the air. "Helena is fine. It's *her* father. I found out he used to be my father's lover... about the time he disappeared."

I set my cup down on the table. "Okay, let's back this up. Your brother's marrying your dad's lover's daughter?" Shin-Cho and Scarlet nodded as one. "And you guys don't think that maybe you need a bigger gene pool to swim in?"

"They didn't know. Dae-Hoon's sons didn't know about their father," Scarlet said in a soft voice. "*Hyung*, Shin-Cho's uncle, never told them anything. It's not something that we speak about."

"So why now?" It was an easy question to answer, but from the fidgeting Shin-Cho did all over my couch, I was guessing it was harder than it looked.

"I don't know how much you know about being Korean." Shin-Cho glanced at Jae, who gave him a small shrug. The shrug could have meant anything from *I still have to remind him to take his shoes off when he comes in* to *He's useless, so use small words.* "South Korean men have to serve in the military before they are thirty. I've... I was discharged... for...."

"It is okay to say, Shin-Cho." She reached over and clasped his hand.

"My superior found me and another man in the showers." His facial expression went flat, burying his emotions to get his words out. "The Korean is *dongseongae*... loving the same sex. The *junwi*, our officer, made it sound ugly. It wasn't like that. It was one time… we were…."

His mouth twisted, a bitter curl of shame and injured pride. Looking away, Shin-Cho hid the glittering tears in his eyes, and we all pretended not to notice, giving him time to gain some control. Scarlet stepped in to fill the silence.

"*Hyung* brought Shin-Cho back here when he found out he'd left the military. Their family is not taking it well. Shin-Cho's grandfather told him that he was no better than his father. That's when he found out about Dae-Hoon." Shifting against the arm of the couch, she continued, "I was Dae-Hoon's best friend. We met in Korea. He was married, but unhappy. I'd fallen in love with *hyung*, and we were struggling to find a way to be together. *Hyung* and I came here. Dae-Hoon followed a few weeks later."

"We weren't here long," Shin-Cho interjected. "Maybe eight months? Maybe longer?"

"About a year," Scarlet said. "Then Dae-Hoon disappeared, and Ryeowon took the boys back to Korea. I didn't see them much. *Hyung* visited, but you know…."

I did know. Her lover had a wife and children, a wholly separate life in South Korea that Scarlet wasn't a part of. It seemed to work for them. If it didn't, Scarlet wasn't saying anything.

"My mother remarried. She didn't want us to be… exposed to our uncle's perversions. That is how my family puts it, just not to his wife's face." Shin-Cho had the good grace to look embarrassed. "I didn't know about… *nuna*. I thought… she… I mean he… I didn't know. I thought Uncle was with a woman."

"Yeah," I said, letting him off the hook. "*Nuna*'s a hot woman."

"I consider it a compliment, *dongsaeng*," Scarlet reassured us. Jae chuckled behind the rim of his coffee cup and failed at looking innocent when she tsked at him.

"So your family knows about you liking men, and things went to shit." I nodded. "I know how that is. I'm sorry it happened to you, man."

"It's why I'm in Los Angeles. The Seong family… my mother's family… is very traditional. There's no room in it for someone like me." He pressed his lips together. "My uncle said he would help me. He and *nuna* have been…."

"It's been a rough few weeks, Cole-ah," Scarlet murmured. "All of this has opened up old wounds… old arguments."

"They think I'm this way because of something my father did. One of my uncles even asked me if my dad touched me," Shin-Cho spat. "He says things like that, and they think I'm the one disgracing my family? I thought my father'd been killed in a car accident. So many lies are told to cover up something they hate. I need to find out what happened to him. I need something to make sense now, especially since my family…."

"You have David," Scarlet said. "Your brother is still with you."

"The one marrying your dad's lover's kid." I still had a hard time getting past that tangle.

My brain was spinning a bit. I couldn't read the expression on Jae's face. He'd shut down a few moments earlier, his features becoming a placid mask I couldn't penetrate. What Shin-Cho was describing was Jae's worst nightmare. The pain in the man's voice nearly broke me. I couldn't imagine how I'd feel if I had to watch Jae go through the same anguish. It would kill me. It would kill us both.

"David says he's okay with how I am. He supports me, but the rest of my family refuses to even talk to me." Shin-Cho sighed. "My brother's wedding is Saturday. My mother is here in Los Angeles, but refuses to come if I'm there. I've told David that I'd stay away so she could be there, but he said no, our mother's made her choice."

"What do you need me to do?" I tried to bring them back on track.

"I'd like you to find out what happened to my father. I need to know," Shin-Cho said. "*Nuna* was with him when he disappeared. After that, no one knows what happened to him."

"I think he's dead, Cole-ah," Scarlet said. "And Kwon Sang-Min is the one who killed him."

CHAPTER THREE

"*NUNA*," Jae scolded her gently. She sniffed in response. No one can sniff like a pissed off Filipino transvestite. "We don't know. We can't say."

"It's because she doesn't like him," Shin-Cho added. "I don't like him either. He stares at my brother oddly. Now that I know about him and my father, I like him even less."

"Okay. Let me ask you something." I tried to be as diplomatic as I could. I've sat across from a lot people who wanted to find answers to things before. They didn't really want answers. They wanted to be told there was nothing to be found. Too often, those same people ended up with answers they didn't really want to hear. I wasn't certain what Shin-Cho was expecting to find. "What do you think's going to happen if I find out anything? What do you need to happen?"

"Maybe I can understand my father a bit more? I don't know," Shin-Cho admitted. "I hate that no one looked for him, other than *nuna* and my uncle. He was a problem that went away, and they didn't care. I can't live with that. Not if he went through how I feel. I can't, Cole-sshi. I just have to know."

"Why don't you tell me what happened, *nuna*." I turned to Scarlet. "I can't promise anything. It's been a hell of a long time."

"Trying is enough," Scarlet said, and Shin-Cho nodded briefly, his eyes fixed on his clasped hands. "There are some powerful men involved, *hyung* included. You have to promise that you'll be discreet, honey."

"Discreet is my middle name," I assured Scarlet.

"Your middle name is Kenjiro," Jae snorted. "It means second son who is nosy."

I ignored Jae and dug a notebook and pen out of the stack of work things I left on the coffee table. "Let's start with what happened."

"It was in…." Scarlet paused, counting the time back. "November of ninety-four. Dae-Hoon and I were at a bathhouse here in Los Angeles… in K-town. Bi Mil was more like a club. There was a floor where we could dance, and there *was* a pool of sorts, but it was small, barely big enough to hold twenty men. I would go there to meet *hyung*. We were… younger. Things were harder. It was harder for us to be together."

"This place—Bi Mil—made it easier to meet up?" I made a note to find the address in case I found some older gay men who were around at that time. Too many moved to friendlier climates or died from the disease that ate its way through the gay community. "Lots of people to get lost in? What was the clientele like? Did you have to worry about someone going too far with a scene, or something?"

"It was mostly Asians, like Dorthi Ki Seu, but well, more hidden. Dirtier, really." Scarlet laughed softly, and a gentle blush colored her face. "Not as classy. More like some place men could go to for relief… not love or companionship. *Hyung* and I could take one of the rooms and spend time together… without anyone seeing us. He wasn't as… secure as he is now. Being seen with me would have meant trouble for him. It's different now. So different."

"You and Dae-Hoon were there together? Then what?"

"There was a raid. There were men dressed all in black. They said they were police…." Scarlet's voice dropped, rough and torn from emotion. "This was after the Riots, but the police then, they were still brutal. They blamed us for so many things. Hated us for so many things. We would never go out alone, not to the clubs. Being gay then… was dangerous. Even though things were changing, it was still hard.

"That night," she continued softly. "When the police came in, Dae-Hoon and I ran down the hall. There were doors on the side of the building, and I thought we could get to one and get outside. Those men… those police… followed us. I didn't think about it at the time, but afterward, I thought, 'Why did they follow only us? Why didn't they grab the other men first?'"

"They grabbed you and Dae-Hoon?" I prodded gently.

"No, not me. Just Dae-Hoon. Me, they hit," Scarlet said, shaking her head. She lifted her long dark hair away from her face. The sunlight coming through the living room windows hit the shallow half-moon scar near her temple, throwing the edge of it into shadow. Something sharp had gouged out a tiny piece of Scarlet's skin, leaving behind a memento of that night.

"Was…." I realized I didn't know Scarlet's lover's real name. "Was *hyung* there yet?"

"Not yet. Not then." She leaned back into the couch and looked worn. "There were so many men running out. By then, the cops were hitting everyone. So many of us were bleeding and crying. *Hyung* was outside, just coming in when the police came. I didn't think about it. He was just there, and I was safe. I told him Dae-Hoon was still inside, but he put me into a car and told the man to drive off. Later, *hyung* said no one saw Dae-Hoon… no one could find him. That night was the last time I saw him. I searched. I called everyone we knew… even his ex-wife… but he was gone."

"Ex?" I asked. "They were divorced?"

"Not yet," Shin-Cho said. "My mother said he'd started it, but they were still married when he died."

"He didn't want to hide anymore," Scarlet said, tilting her head. "His family… everything… he walked away from everything, because he said he was tired of lying to protect other men like him. Dae-Hoon was angry about how the family was treating him. *Hyung* told him not to make trouble, but I don't think Dae-Hoon cared anymore."

"Who was he there to meet? Anyone in particular?" I reached for Jae, putting my hand on his. Shin-Cho's dilemma mirrored his own life too closely for him not to be affected, and I was grateful when his fingers tightened on mine in return. "Who was Dae-Hoon meeting that night? Who knew he was going to be there besides you and *hyung*?"

"Kwon Sang-Min," Scarlet whispered. "He'd broken it off with Dae-Hoon, but Sang-Min asked him to come with me, and then they'd meet. I don't think Sang-Min was ready to give Dae-Hoon up. I don't know. We're not close."

"Does his family know?" I asked. "Kwon's family, do they know he's gay?"

"No. He is not like... *hyung*. He goes from... he is not looking for love. For Kwon, young men are just for his... use," she replied. "He's someone *hyung* knows. I hear gossip sometimes, but I haven't paid attention. He treated Dae-Hoon badly. I don't think he's treating any of them any better now."

"Is he close with... okay, what's *hyung*'s real name?" I finally asked.

"Seong Min-Ho," Scarlet laughed.

"Are Kwon and Seong close?" I wrote down the names as best I could. I'd have Jae look over my spelling later when I could be mocked in private.

Scarlet pursed her mouth. "They know each other. Both are second-generation *chaebol*. I don't know when they met."

"They went to university together," Shin-Cho said. "Sang-Min told me that when he met me."

"So both gay and exiled to America?" I drew boxes around their names and dotted a line between them.

"I have something else," Scarlet said. "When Dae-Hoon didn't come back, *hyung* offered to have his things stored. I can get the key for you. I have it in my jewelry case."

"Does Seong know you've come to me?" Seong was at the top of my list of people to talk to. He could have not told Scarlet if he knew something'd happened to Dae-Hoon in order to spare her from any unpleasantness. What I knew of the man, he struck me as someone who'd ruthlessly take care of business, then say it was all kittens and roses.

"He knows," she replied. "He said he'll make time to talk to you if you need it."

"I'll need to," I said, nodding. "So you've had Dae-Hoon's things in a storage unit for almost two decades? You haven't taken a look at it? Or taken Shin-Cho there?"

"No." Both she and Shin-Cho shook their heads. "It hurt too much, but I wanted the boys to have his things when they found out the truth. When I told Shin-Cho about his father's things, he thought you might like to look at it first, in case there is something to help you."

"I miss my father, Cole-sshi, I do," Shin-Cho said. "But *nuna* shared with me what photos and letters she had. I can wait to see the rest."

"Who packed his stuff?" My main concern was someone'd already filtered through Dae-Hoon's belongings. If there was anything incriminating, it could have disappeared long before a single box reached the storage unit.

"I did some. Dae-Hoon's roommate helped. There wasn't a lot," Scarlet replied. "They both used to work for *hyung*."

I had to assume that if Seong had anything to hide, Lee could have taken anything Seong didn't want found, but with Scarlet there, it would have been harder to hide. Seong walked a tighter rope then than Jae-Min did now. "Tomorrow... well, today is Thursday. Can you get me the key later? I'll see what I can find."

"You need sleep first," Jae reminded me. "And if you go, it has to be on Friday. We're going to the wedding on Saturday."

"Eh?" I tried to remember if I'd been asked to attend a wedding, then remembered Jae had a booking for one. He had help in the morning for the formal shots and the wedding, but asked me to help him for the evening reception. The look he gave me was suspicious, as if he'd expected me to forget. "Oh no, don't give me that look. I've got it blocked out on my phone. Even Claudia knows. Big wedding. Help Jae or die."

"You'd wish you were dead if you forgot." Jae gave me an evil eye that would've made his cat jealous. "I would make sure it would take you a very long time to die."

"I'll see you at my brother's wedding, then." Shin-Cho stood up. "Unless you're coming tonight too?"

"What's tonight?" I stood when Scarlet got to her feet, moving out of the way so she could get past.

"The rehearsal dinner," Jae whispered. "Don't worry. Andrew said he'd do that one with me."

"No need to whisper. My feelings aren't hurt." Scarlet lightly slapped his arm as she passed him.

"What? Why would your feelings be hurt?" My lack of sleep was beginning to wear on my brain.

"Because mistresses... even male ones... are not invited to *chaebol* weddings." Scarlet paused near the front door, sliding her flats onto her tiny feet. "But I'll be fine, *musang*, so long as your Cole finds out what happened to Dae-Hoon."

THE bedroom curtains did their best to keep out the morning sun, but they failed miserably. I was too tired to care, and besides, the light made the room bright enough for me to watch Jae as he got ready for bed. We were both exhausted. I'd barely gotten my jeans off and brushed my teeth before falling onto the mattress wearing only my boxers. For all my dick's willingness to give it a good try, I knew I wouldn't get much more than a bit of foreplay before I passed out. The puffiness under Jae's eyes reassured me he was feeling the same.

Still, it was a damned pretty sight to watch him shed the pants and tank top, to crawl into bed next to me. I liked the boxer briefs he liked to wear. They molded the fullness of his ass and left his belly button bare. He'd talked about piercing the skin above his navel, a plan I oddly endorsed.

It felt good when he slid up against my side and traced the alarmingly increasing scar patterns on the left side of my chest. They ached beneath the surface, the nerves being pulled by the puckered skin as I moved. His touch soothed away the tingles, and I grunted when he pinched my side.

"Stop getting shot," he murmured, kissing the newest and smallest of my scars.

His cousin Grace's gun had been a small one, nothing like the police issue cannon Ben used to shoot me, and it left a much tinier imprint on my body. As gunshots went, it didn't do a lot of damage, and I'd recovered from it quickly. Jae and Claudia hovered constantly while I went about trying to regain the strength in my shoulder, so it would take some time for them to break that habit.

From the looks of things, neither one of them were making any progress in that regard.

"I might have to talk to Seong, but I don't want to." I let my fingers trail down Jae's spine. "Especially if I can't find any place else to start. It'll make trouble between them."

He felt warm. Good. His skin heated up under my touch, and I caught a whiff of the green tea soap he used. My body warmed up too. I had to remind it I was too tired to do anything more than talk and cuddle.

"I know," he murmured. His breath ghosted over my nipple, and I had another talk with my dick. "*Nuna* knows too."

"Keep doing that, and we're not going to get any sleep," I warned him. "And I'm too tired to give you a good time. It'll look bad on my report card."

"I'll leave good marks," Jae teased. He lightly bit at the nipple he'd hardened, then pulled back, resting his head on my arm. "Your Korean is bad. It's like your tongue doesn't work. You keep saying who-young."

"You of all people know that my tongue works fine." When he remained silent, I nudged him with my fingers. "Seong Min-Ho. How's that? Am I going to embarrass you if I talk to him?"

"No, you did fine. Scarlet left you his business card. It's got English on the back you can read." He yawned, his jaw cracking slightly. I winced and rubbed at the spot near his chin. "Do you want me to call him for you? He loves *nuna*. He'll help you if he can."

I was debating the stickiness of calling up Scarlet's lover to grill him about a possible murder when a perky pop tune jiggled Jae's phone. It vibrated across the end table, and he sat up quickly to grab it. The bedsheets slithered down around his hips, a soft emerald green framing his back. The frown on his face was thunderous, and his body went taut. There was a brittle, hard set to his shoulders that worried me, and I reached over to touch his back, hoping to reassure him.

"*Aniyo*." He shook his head at me and pulled away, nearly recoiling from my hand. "*Umma*."

I knew the first word, *no*, and the second one only vaguely. It hovered in my mind for a moment then clicked into place. *His mother*.

It was hard seeing him curled up onto himself. His shoulder blades jutted out from his back, framing the line of his spine. The sheets were tented from his knees being pulled up against his chest, and his free hand gripped the linens, kneading them between his fingers as he spoke. I had no way to understand what he was saying, but the thin tightness in his voice hurt me deep. His body was screaming at me, his pain leaking out of every rigid line of his limbs and torso.

Everything inside of me wanted to touch him, to reassure him.

Everything I knew about him told me not to.

I couldn't understand what he was saying. Two months of drive-by Korean wasn't going to give me any understanding of what his mother was pulling out of him. Every time he stopped to listen, he flinched. Her words stabbed him, sharp barbs hooking into his heart and pulling out chunks of his soul. Jae became smaller with each moment, the sheet winding about his fingers and wrist until his knuckles were white and bloodless.

Nearly as bloodless as his face.

He stared through me, his cheek on his sheet-covered knees and his hand nearly invisible as he cradled it against his face. The full mouth I loved to kiss was a flat line, pressed tight against words he didn't want to say… words he couldn't say. His eyes were stones, hard and glittering, with all of the honey gold leeched from them.

It was over before I could think of anything to say or do. One moment he was a porcelain statue and the next a crumbling, fragmented thing full of fury and loathing.

Putting my arms around Jae was like trying to hold a hurricane. He was off the bed, fighting to loosen his legs from the sheets. Clutching the phone, he turned and shook, gulping in large mouthfuls of air to calm himself down. I waited. I had to wait. I'd been with him for two months, and he always needed time to work through his emotions, to find something to grab onto to drag him out of the panic and anger built up inside of him.

"Fuck. Someone told her something… about me… about us," Jae said. The phone flew onto the bed, and he began carding his hands through his hair, pacing alongside of the bed. "My aunt. She speaks to my aunt… maybe…."

"Jae, take a breath." I came up behind him, catching him before he made another circuit of the room. He fought me. I didn't expect him to come to me easily. He never did. I was stronger and calmer, wrapping my arms around his shoulders to pull him tight against my bare chest. "What did she say? What did she want?"

"She needs more money," Jae mumbled. His fingers were cold, nerveless, and still on my skin. "I told her I would try to get her some, and she said… I should ask my rich friend for it. My *hyung*."

Other than Scarlet's lover, I was probably the only one of Jae's friends that could be considered rich. My wealth was hard-won: a city payout for the murder-suicide of my lover, Rick, and my partner, Ben. Six months ago, I'd have said I'd trade the money to have them back alive. Now, I would trade the money to give Jae a little bit of peace.

"She knows about Scarlet. She could have been talking about Scarlet or… shit, Seong." I leaned back and drew my hands up to cup his face. My thumbs smeared the trace of wetness over his lower lashes. He sniffled, but he tilted his chin up. "What about your brother? Can he help?"

I mentioned his brother as a diversion. It didn't work out so well.

"Jae-Su? My brother?" Jae spat. His soft accent grew with his anger and fear, rounding out his words. "If he knew I... how I was, he'd use it to get money out of *me*. Right now, he takes from her. My *hyung*... takes from our mother like he's still a little boy. And she gives it to him. She'd starve my sisters so he can have something new to play with."

"How much does she need? I can...."

"No." It was firm, both his pride and his refusal to let me help him. I understood it. I didn't like it, but understood it. His hands clenched, becoming fists on my chest. The anger inside him begged to be unleashed. I expected him to punch me when he gritted his teeth and shook his head. Jae pulled back, shoving me away with a single push. "No. I don't want your money. This isn't your problem. My family isn't your problem."

I took a breath, a hissing pull to chill my lungs. Jae stalked to the bathroom, his shoulders shaking as he turned the water on. He cupped his hands under the flow and bent forward, but merely stared down into the sink. His hair hid most of his face, but I could still see his mouth, his pink lips trembling with anger and fear. I couldn't understand what he was feeling. I'd made my own choices, walking away when my father decided I wasn't good enough to be his son anymore. Jae didn't need me pushing him.

So of course, that's exactly what I did.

I didn't say anything. I kept silent as I walked over to the open bathroom door and leaned against the door frame. The twisting in my chest bloomed into a fear he'd walk out the door. It was too soon for me to lose him. I hadn't had enough time, not nearly enough time to persuade him that I would catch him if he fell from his family's grace. It hadn't been enough time for me to accept that he might never be mine... not openly... perhaps not even behind closed doors.

Jae shut the water off and rested his palms on the marble counter. Lifting his head, his eyes flicked toward the mirror, momentarily meeting my gaze before dropping back down to study the dark speckles in the stone. The tension bled slightly from his spine, and his hips moved forward, relaxing the line of his body.

We hadn't reached forever then. Not the forever of him walking out of my front door or the forever of our last kiss. My heart lurched and began beating again.

"I'm sorry," he whispered. His face was shadowed, shuttered off, and closed. "I'm… tired. I just… *fuck*."

He let me hold him this time, sliding into my embrace with his usual liquid grace. We'd met halfway. The cold bathroom floor was a shock to my bare feet, but his too warm body more than made up for it. He didn't cry, but I could feel him struggling to keep himself together. I cupped the back of his head and slid my other hand across his shoulders then down his back, stroking away the tension in his body.

"It's okay, baby." When he looked up at me, the pain deepening his eyes broke my heart. Kissing the top of his head, I murmured and stroked him again, "It'll be okay. I've got you."

"I hate wanting you," he said. "I hate wanting… *this*."

This could have meant a lot of things. I knew Jae well enough to know he meant being happy… being gay… being with me, someone who struggled daily to understand him. I couldn't talk. My nights were still filled with memories of blood, gunpowder, and sightless green eyes going dim. We both had our albatrosses. I had Rick's ghost shoveling guilt into my soul like it was feeding a coal furnace, and Jae dragged his family behind him, their claws stuck deep under his skin. He was unable to loosen their grip any more than I could loosen Ben's and Rick's.

It was unfair of me to think that.

I knew that.

Didn't make me hate our baggage any less.

I wanted my fucking forever. *My* forever. Not the one that seemed laid out for me. Certainly not the one laid out for Jae. I just had to have the patience and the strength to fight for him, even if he was the one I was fighting with.

"How about if we get some sleep and talk about this shit later?" I rocked him gently, more of a swaying motion than anything else. "About the money... about *this*."

"The money thing... it's not going to change," Jae warned me, but let me guide him back to bed. He dragged his feet, exhaustion drawing purple shadows under his eyes. The bed dipped when he climbed onto it, and again when I dragged myself up against him.

"Well, *this* isn't going to change either." I covered us, letting him get settled onto his stomach. One of his legs crept over mine, and his arm slid over my chest, his hand resting lightly on my ribs. His breathing slowed, and he shuddered, letting go more of the tension racking his body. "It will just get better, Jae. We'll get better. I promise. We will work this out."

"Getting better is still change," he mumbled into my chest.

I contemplated an argument or two, then went with my gut response. "Shut up and go to sleep."

CHAPTER FOUR

HITTING the bag felt good. The slim gloves were new, a present from Bobby. More like an incentive to get my ass back into the gym. I needed to work out the muscles injured in the shooting, strengthen my arm back up some. It also helped me forget I'd woken up to an empty bed and even emptier house.

The gym was a bare-bones hole-in-the-wall run by Floyd "JoJo" Monroe, an ex-boxer who'd had the bad luck of being a black gay man in the '80s. His career was brilliant... and cut short when, after a match, he'd been discovered in the locker room, getting a blow job from one of the referees, a white man. A few days later, the guy giving the blow job was found floating off the Santa Monica Pier. JoJo didn't fare as well. There wasn't much left of the man who'd pummeled his opponents to the mat. His legs shook as he walked, and his remaining eye was milky from age, but his voice was strong as he yelled at the men in the ring.

I didn't need JoJo yelling at me. Usually Bobby took care of that. I didn't need taking care of. Today was different. I was... different.

The bag jerked with every punch I threw. I didn't hear Bobby's grunts at first, but after a few minutes they grew loud enough to distract.

"Pissed off a bit, Princess?" Bobby was breathing hard when I pulled away from the bag. My T-shirt was soaked with sweat, and I stunk, but I wanted to go another five minutes, maybe even five hours. It felt good to work my body into an aching mess. It matched my insides. "Want to talk about it?"

Even though Bobby was almost twenty years older than me, he was a muscular, beefy guy. The brush of silver at his temples only drew the twinks to him. With a handsome, lived-in face and cut body, he was popular at the bars we went to. He could also beat the crap out of me in the boxing ring, and wiped the ground with me when we went jogging. Except for the liking dick and ass, Bobby was the epitome of an all-American male. Definitely not someone who wanted to talk things out.

"Never thought I'd hear *that* come out of you." I hugged the bag, peeking around the side to stare at Bobby's rugged face. "You want me to *talk* it out?"

"I'm trying to save JoJo's bag. You're fucking pounding the shit out of it." He let go of the bag and came around to help me with the Velcro on my gloves. "Is this about Jae? Was he pissed off about Trey?"

"Shit, don't get me started about Trey. Did he call you?"

"Yeah," Bobby grunted again, this time with disgust. "Asshole said he wanted his money back."

"What money? I was doing it for free."

"I reminded him about that. Trey uses his brain less than he uses that dick of his. And *that* he only uses for pissing and blow jobs. He likes getting fucked. Not the other way around." He tugged on his own gloves and jerked his chin toward the bag for me to hold it. Waiting until I braced myself against its heavy weight, Bobby gave the leather a few jabs.

"Jae caught some shit from his mom this morning," I said. "I don't get why he takes it. It's like they dump all of their crap on him and expect him suck it up."

"I've gotta ask you, man. Jae, is he worth what he puts you through? Not to sound like some emo hipster, but I don't want him to break your heart."

I had to think about it. After losing Rick to whatever demons Ben had chasing him, I drifted around. I didn't like the club scene. Jumping in and out of different guys' beds tired me out more than any pleasure I got from fucking them. Jae did something to me. He touched something inside of me that I thought was dead.

"Jae kind of made me realize I still had a heart. Guess it's his to break."

Bobby stopped hammering at the bag long enough to stare at me, and then he shrugged. "Fair enough."

I switched topics before we started hugging and sharing cookie recipes. "Hey, do you have some free time? I think I need some help with a job Scarlet gave me."

"Yeah, sure." Bobby shifted his feet, driving an uppercut into the bag. It jerked in my arms, and I had to brace myself to keep it steady. "What's she need?"

I talked about the case as he punched and weaved, going over the last time Scarlet saw her friend at Bi Mil, and the man Dae-Hoon was supposed to meet that night. He whistled when I got to the part of Dae-Hoon's former lover now being the father of the woman marrying Dae-Hoon's youngest son.

"That's too fucking weird." Bobby stopped hitting the bag. I was grateful for that. My shoulders were numb from holding it steady. "So the families kept in touch?"

"From what I can see, it's one big incestuous mess. They all know one another, marry each other. It's like a damned cabal." I shook my arms out, hoping to get blood back into my fingers. "I'm hoping you can maybe help me track down any cops who were there that night. Maybe someone saw something."

"I dunno, kid." He looked skeptical. "You've got to remember, this was after the Riots. The boys in blue were taking a beating from all sides. A lot of us did a hell of a lot of things we weren't proud of. Guys might not want to talk about a raid on some gay bathhouse. Chances are, it got ugly. LAPD wasn't known for its tolerance then."

"Like it is now?" I smirked at him.

We'd both tested the blue line's tolerance of gays in our own ways. I'd spent my time on the force as an openly gay man. Bobby came out after he'd retired and Rick died. He'd been a rock I clung to as I struggled to find some sense in what happened to me. He'd lost a few friends as word of his homosexuality spread through the ranks, but most cops were more comfortable with Bobby keeping his secrets until he got out. They weren't all that happy with me when I wore a badge, even less so when the union forced the city to cough up millions in damages, after my suicidal partner shot me and my lover up.

"Let me see who was around then," Bobby said, twisting his body to work out a kink in his shoulders. "I'll have to find out who was arrested. Does Scarlet remember the date? That'll go a long way in locating the records."

"Yeah, I can probably get you an exact date." I flexed before my arms could start cramping up. "This guy… Dae-Hoon… he worked for Scarlet's… husband? Shit, I don't even know what to call the guy."

He shrugged and stepped back from the bag, taking off his gloves and tucking them under his arm. "Stick with sir. That always works for me."

"Yeah," I agreed. We headed toward the showers, nodding at JoJo as he coached a thin young man on how to keep his elbows in when he punched.

The locker room was icy, kept cold by the gym's thick cinder block walls. I shivered when I walked in, overheated from the workout. A slender, muscular man passed us, heading for his workout. Bobby brazenly checked him out, eyes raking over the guy's legs and torso, lingering for a moment on his shoulders before making eye contact. The guy turned slightly and smiled at Bobby, who tilted his head to check out his ass. There'd be an exchange of phone numbers before we left. If he'd been alone, there'd be an exchange of bodily fluids too.

I waited for Bobby to break away from his flirting. "This Dae-Hoon guy was a bit… radical."

"Radical?"

"He got divorced. Well, he was trying to get divorced," I said. "So he could go off and be… gay. I don't know if he was expecting his lover, Kwon, to do the same, or if he just needed out."

"So he was Korean, but came out of the closet screaming show tunes?" Bobby whistled under his breath. If it was difficult for Jae to be openly homosexual now, Dae-Hoon's actions in ninety-four were unbelievable. "Seems like every Korean guy you meet is gay."

"Seems like it," I laughed. "And that Kwon guy, but I guess I'll meet him too."

"Think Kwon had something to do with his disappearance?"

"I don't know. It's an idea. I think we'll know more once we chat some people up. Kwon looks good for something. Scarlet and Dae-Hoon's kid think he's a douche."

"We'll want to circle around Kwon. See where he was first." Bobby shed his damp shirt and smacked me with it as I went by him to get to my locker. "So where do you want to start? Cops, or Seong?"

"I'm thinking cops, but let's hit up the storage unit first," I said, rubbing at the sore spot on my arm. "I've got to go back to the office and see if Scarlet had the key dropped off. Wonder if Claudia wants to help us dig through Dae-Hoon's stuff."

"Yeah, you bring that up to her." Bobby snorted. "And when she's done killing you, I'll hit on Jae at your funeral. It'll give me something to do besides drink."

"Thought Jae was too much trouble."

"Hey, he's pretty. I like pretty," Bobby said, wincing when I punched his arm. "But he's your trouble, Princess. You're welcome to him."

"WANT some coffee?" My office manager, Claudia, held up the glass pot she'd pulled from the automatic drip machine. After years of working in the school system drinking swill, the woman brewed strong, hairy-chest coffee for our office. Just the smell of the stuff kept away rats, roaches, and any other vermin within a five-mile radius.

I nodded and shrugged off my jacket, tossing it onto a hook on the coat tree we had by the door. A pile of pink message slips were stacked on my desk, and I eased into the old-fashioned leather chair I'd found at an estate sale, listening to the pleasant squeak when I leaned back. Claudia put a mug in front of me, swirls of cream still whirling through the dark brew. Tapping a spoon on her own cup, she sipped, and waited until I finally let go of the sigh I was holding in.

"Did too much, boy?" There was no sympathy in her voice. I wasn't expecting any either.

The woman raised a squillion children and grandchildren in a predominantly low income area, progressively moving them to better neighborhoods as soon as she could. She didn't entertain any excuses about her boys being poor or black. Claudia had expectations, and woe to the son who didn't rise to them. Being a member of Clan Claudia was like belonging to a lifelong survivalist camp. Her boys—and there were a herd of them—were expected to cook, clean, and repair things on the fly, and the women, or in Maurice's case, the man, they brought into the family had better do the same.

She ran her crew like a troop of Spartans: fall on the battlefield and be eaten by predators. I wasn't one of her kids, and she scared me to death.

"I needed to start stretching out the muscles. It's healed enough for some bag work." I protested the scoffing hiss Claudia threw at me. "What? Did you think I was going to let Bobby punch the shit out of me? I needed to loosen up, not take another trip to the hospital."

The loosening up part wasn't a lie. I'd debated calling Jae, after finding out he'd left before I woke up, just to see if he was okay, or pissed off about life. Rick had needed constant reassurance and interaction. Jae's wariness and fierce independence still threw me. Working out the kinks in my muscles seemed a pleasant alternative to pacing a hole in the floor.

"You end up in the hospital again, I'm going to duct tape you to the bed until I decide you're good to go." Tapping the stack of messages, she said, "Your boy called. He said for you to call him back when you come in. He should be back from Long Beach by then. I think he was down at the docks for something or other."

"What the hell is he doing in Long Beach?" I didn't expect an answer. Jae often went on excursions into no-man's lands for his artistic work. Weddings and portraits paid his bills, but they didn't scratch that creative itch he had inside of him. Shuffling through the messages, I frowned when I saw Trey's name. I held the slip up for Claudia to see. "Was he an asshole to you?"

"He said something about suing you for damage to his dick. I listened to him for a few minutes, and told him if he was stupid enough to stick it into a bottle, then he could make do without it. Dangerous enough now just having sex. If he wanted his dick chewed off, why didn't he just go have sex with a shark?"

I thought back to what I'd seen in the emergency room as the doctors were picking out the glass shards. "Yep. That's pretty much what it looked like too."

She moved easily for a large woman, probably honed from years of chasing down recalcitrant children. It took her less than a few seconds to retrieve a package from her desk and bring it over to me. "Scarlet honey sent this over for you. She called here to make sure you got it. She told me about her friend. I can't believe you're taking money from her."

"I didn't want to," I said absently. The seal on the plastic courier bag was a bitch, and I ended up using my teeth to try to tear it enough for me to pull it open. "She and Jae ganged up on me. Trust me; you don't want to get into an argument with two Asians about money. You'll lose every time. It's like going against a Sicilian when death is on the line."

"Give me that," Claudia sighed, and held her hand out for the package. "I'll cut it open. You go call him outside. I don't want to hear the smoochie noises you make when you talk to him."

I gave up on trying to chew through the plastic. Grabbing my coffee, I headed outside to the building's front veranda. I'd not checked my phone since leaving the house earlier. I had four texts, one of them from Jae asking me to call him when I could. I dialed him back, and he answered before the second ring.

"Hey, *agi*." His purr reached hot fingers into my gut and grabbed my balls. "Are you back at your office?"

"Yeah, planning on coming over?" I could entertain fantasies of my washing machine, but it was already late afternoon, and I had to catch up on the business, especially after wasting the morning sleeping.

"No, not for that." He'd paused long enough to make me smile. Jae liked sex. He didn't like getting touched in public, but close the door and things got interesting. "I have to ask you a favor."

"Sure." I took my first sip of coffee and gagged at its sweetness. The sugar cut through the bitter, but it took a moment to brace my throat for it. "Whatcha need?"

It sounded like we weren't going to talk about the morning phone call, his meltdown and anger or my inability to fix his world. I was good with that. I still didn't know how to fix his world, and even if I did, I wasn't sure he would let me.

"Andrew's sick. I need help tonight at the rehearsal dinner. Can I borrow you? It's at eight."

Andrew, Jae's sometimes assistant, was as flaky as Claudia's pie crusts. He was usually less sick, and more stoned to the gills, but he was cheap and at least knew what camera Jae asked him to fetch. I was already up to help at the reception, a risky thing for Jae since I could barely operate the point-and-shoot I used to take pictures of cheating spouses. He had to be desperate to ask me on such short notice.

"Yeah, of course." I checked my watch. "I've just got to go through some stuff Scarlet sent over and return some calls, but after that, I'm all yours."

"You were mine before I called."

Yeah, he still had a good hold of my nuts. We cooed at each other as manfully as we could, then I hung up and went inside. Claudia'd mastered the package, neatly dissecting it like it was a formaldehyde-marinated frog in a biology class. I refilled my coffee cup, leaving off any sugar, and went back to my desk to dig through Dae-Hoon's life.

A blushing, young Scarlet stared out at me from an old photograph. Beside her, an equally young Korean man with slight acne scars on his cheeks grinned as well, his arm around her. Bright honey highlights streaked their hair, thick swathes of blond through their natural black. Scarlet's brilliant pink lipstick was nearly as eye-catching as the rubber bracelets around the man's wrist, his hand dangling over Scarlet's shoulder. The date on the back told me the photo was taken only a week before Dae-Hoon disappeared. From the looks on their faces, they had not a care in the world.

Apparently, the world didn't care for them either.

Other photos captured moments of Dae-Hoon's life, small snippets of time someone thought to snatch from the stream. I stopped at one showing Dae-Hoon with two young boys, his slender arms cradling David and his face lit up with a smile for his Shin-Cho.

Hard to believe the little boy Dae-Hoon was holding would be marrying his lover's kid in a few days.

"Fucking creepy," I muttered. Separating out an envelope from the photos and a file folder, I slit it open and shook out the paper inside. For every ounce of her femininity, Scarlet's masculine side resonated in her writing. With a strong, slashing penmanship, she thanked me again, and I grimaced at the check attached to the note.

"That's a lot of zeros." Claudia peered over my shoulder. "Way too many zeros to go find a probably-dead man."

"Yeah, it's more than what we agreed to. She and I are going to have to have a talk," I grumbled. The folder rattled, and then a key ring fell out, a flat plastic card marked with a building letter and numbers. "Bobby and I are going to go digging through a storage locker tomorrow."

"She gave you a lot of money for that? I could have gotten one of my boys to do it for twenty bucks."

"It's been sitting for years. We're hoping there's something in there that can tell us if Dae-Hoon was in trouble," I said, waving the key under Claudia's nose. "Fire up the DeLorean, Claudia. Tomorrow morning, Bobby and I are going to make a trip back to the '90s."

"Huh, well... just don't come back with any of those stupid Hammer pants," Claudia said, taking another sip of her coffee. "You dress bad enough as it is."

LIVING behind my office had its advantages, mainly cutting down on commute time, so I had time to kick back after we shut down for the day. One of the biggest disadvantages was I was easy enough to find, especially when I wanted that time to relax before heading back out. Still, it was a surprise to find a sullen looking Shin-Cho standing on my front porch. Even more of a surprise was the bright red splotch starting to bruise under his left eye.

In the light of day, and admittedly after I'd had sleep, I noticed Shin-Cho was fairly attractive. Stockier than Jae-Min, his handsome face was heart-shaped but lean, probably from his stint in the military. The short-sleeved T-shirt he wore showed off his muscular arms, and his jeans were artistically torn at the knee, letting peeks of tanned skin show through. If I had to guess, I'd say Shin-Cho dressed that morning to impress someone, and by the looks of the mark on his face, that person didn't buy into it.

"Hey." I jerked my chin up. "Looks like you need some ice for that. Come on inside."

"No, no, I'm fine. Outside is okay." Shin-Cho shook his head. "I needed to… talk to you."

"If it's about your Dad's stuff, I just got the key." I held it up for him to see. "I was going to hit up the storage place tomorrow."

"It isn't about that." His shoes squeaked as he kicked at the stoop's cement slab. He fidgeted and shoved his hands into his pockets, hunching his shoulders over.

"Let me just open the door to air out the front room." Using my shoulder to hold the screen door open, I fit my key into the lock. Undoing the dead bolt, I turned the knob and swung the heavy wood door back. I let go of the screen door, letting it bounce back onto the latch so the cat couldn't get out. "Okay, what's up?"

"There's something I didn't tell you… something I don't want *nuna* to find out." Despite the cold nip in the air, Shin-Cho looked like he was sweating up a storm. "It's about Kwon Sang-Min."

"What about him?" I leaned against the porch post, kicking lightly at the door when Neko came to investigate it.

"My father isn't the only one who slept with Kwon Sang-Min," he said, swallowing. "I have too. Quite a lot."

"Fuck me," I swore. Opening the screen door, I shooed the cat away. Jerking my head toward the house, I growled at Shin-Cho and said, "Get the fuck inside. You and I are going to have a little talk."

CHAPTER FIVE

I NEEDED a beer. Badly. Problem was, Jae would be at my house in a couple of hours to pick me up, and my thirst for beer was really just my body distracting me so I didn't choke the shit out of Shin-Cho.

The same Shin-Cho that was perched on my couch and picking at the ruffled edge of a throw pillow Maddy thought I needed.

I left the beer in the fridge and came back with a couple of Cokes. Shoving one at Shin-Cho, I popped the other open and took a big gulp. He looked at me through his lashes like a little kid who'd been caught shaving the dog or eating the last chocolate chip cookie. Exhaling hard, I shook my head at the complicity of subterfuge by the men around me.

"Wait a minute. Don't you have to be at a wedding rehearsal?" I frowned at him. "The dinner's tonight, right?"

"The rehearsal was an hour ago. They're having the dinner later." Shin-Cho looked at me oddly. "I came here so I could talk to you before the party."

"Okay, start from...." I sighed. Who the hell *didn't* sleep with Kwon? "Actually, I have no damned clue where you should start from. Just start some place, and I'll catch up."

"Please don't tell *nuna*," Shin-Cho pleaded. The guy looked desperate, and from the puffy redness around his eyes that matched the welt on his face, I'd guessed he'd gotten very little sleep the night before.

"How'd you get here?" I asked.

"I drove."

That he drove himself was good. It meant there wouldn't be any sunglass-wearing, straight-faced security drones to rat out his visit to my place. Still, keeping secrets from Scarlet didn't sit right with me. The truth had a way of seeping out, usually in a frothy pile of crap aimed directly for the closest fan blade.

"Okay, we're going to talk. Then you're going to go home and tell Scarlet everything you've told me." I held up my hand when he opened his mouth to object. "Ah! Nope. Not hearing anything other than yes from you, because the next time I see her, I'm going to ask her straight up if you've told her. If you haven't, then it's your shit to deal with. Not mine. Got it?"

The yes took a long time in coming, but eventually he nodded. "Okay. Yes."

"Good, 'cause I'm not getting on her bad side," I said firmly. "She's the closest thing to real family Jae's got. I'm sure as hell not going to let you fuck that up. I screw up enough without anyone's help. How about if you start with how you hooked up with Kwon? And if that pop on your face has anything to do with him."

His hand flew up to cover up the spot on his cheek, and Shin-Cho's eyes slid away from my face.

"Yeah, okay," I hissed between my teeth. "Start talking, Shin-Cho."

Shin-Cho rolled his unopened Coke can between his hands, leeching the moisture off the aluminum. "Um... I was... nineteen? Twenty? I can't remember when. It was at Christmastime, near my birthday."

"Wait, American nineteen or Korean nineteen?" Koreans counted their ages from birth, rather than turning one after a year. It screwed me up when talking to Jae-Min and some of his friends. Some of them counted the Korean way, adding a year to their elapsed age. If I owned a bar in Koreatown, I'd have given up carding drivers' licenses after about a week.

"Ah, *man-nai*... full age. Western age, nineteen," Shin-Cho translated. "He came to our house in Gangnam. My mother was throwing a Christmas party. A lot of our family's friends were there."

It was a familiar story, an older man approaching a younger one with a bit of alcohol and a practiced song and dance. When I was younger, I'd bitten at that fish myself, but unlike Shin-Cho, I hadn't planned on making a meal of it. Their torrid love affair lasted almost two years, exploding in a spectacular confrontation when Shin-Cho discovered his then-lover making out with another man at a Seoul dance club.

"I thought he was here, in Los Angeles." Shin-Cho bit back his anger, but it fueled his words. "Sang-Min told me it was my fault, because I spent too much time at school so he needed to look elsewhere. Then I find out he'd told that man the same thing. He was doing us both. Maybe even others. I never saw him again. I didn't answer his calls. Then David tells me he's marrying Sang-Min's daughter, and I thought: God, can it get any worse?"

"Shit," I swore under my breath.

"Yes, shit." Shin-Cho slurred the word, making it last on his tongue. "Now I find out about my father? How am I supposed to feel? What am I supposed to do?"

It was getting harder to understand him as his frustration grew. Korean began to drop into his English, and after a few words, he pressed the cold can to his forehead and closed his eyes. I let him have a moment, then tapped his leg.

"Hey, if I'm going to help out, I need you to focus, okay?" He opened his eyes and stared at me without comprehension. "I need you to stick to English so I can understand you. Can you do that?"

"Yes." He struggled with the word, then swallowed. "Yes, I can."

"Good." I reassured him as best I could with a smile. "What happened today? Did Kwon hit you?"

"After the rehearsal," Shin-Cho said. "I thought I'd be fine when I saw him, but...."

"Yeah, sometimes actually seeing your ex can punch you in the gut," I sympathized. "You were at St. Brendan's, right?"

"It's pretty," he murmured. "Myung-Hee... Helena... wanted to get married there. David thought it was cool."

"So what happened between you and Kwon?"

"*Nuna* lent me her car so I could drive myself. The parking lot was full, and I came later, so I parked at the far side. I told David I would see him at the party and went to the car. Sang-Min followed me." Shin-Cho finally opened the soda can, and I half expected it to foam over, considering how he'd abused it. "He was smiling and hugged me. I told him to let me go, and he told me it didn't matter anymore, because we were going to be family. No one would think anything if he hugged me.

"He knows why the family sent me here. He said he was sorry I couldn't be more... careful, but now that I was in LA, we could go back to how things were." Shin-Cho hissed. "He told me I looked good. Better than I did before. And he touched me... like he had the right to. I pushed him away and told him I wasn't my father. I won't go crawling back to him every time he throws me away."

"Fuck," I swore. "So now he knows you know about him and your dad. Guess it was just a matter of time. I'd have to try to talk to him at some point. He might as well know that's come back up."

"He hit me with the back of his hand. He wears a ring. It's very big. It scraped me. I think that's what made the mark." He gulped at the soda, making a face at its taste. "He said my father was a whore, someone who would go to any man, and that he wasn't the only one who slept with him. That's when he told me I would be no better than my father. Because I had no wife... no family... I would be passed around from man to man until I got too old and they were tired of me. Then he walked away."

"He's full of shit." The look Shin-Cho gave me told me he thought I was crazy. "Just because you love guys doesn't mean you can't have a good life with one. Look at Scarlet and Seong."

"You... you don't understand, do you?" Shin-Cho murmured sadly. "If Uncle dies before she does, she will have nothing left of him. His family will not take her in. His sons will not take care of her. There will be nothing for her. If she dies first, she leaves nothing behind. No children, no family to remember her. No matter what happens, she'll be nothing after she dies. There's no future for her to live for. *Nuna* has nothing... will be nothing.

"I don't want that. I don't want to die alone with no one remembering me," he growled. "I want a son, someone to make sure I'm taken care of when I'm old. I want my mother to be proud enough to brag about me. I don't want to be my father. I *can't* be my father, because no one cares that he lived. Just me."

IT WAS nearly six thirty when I heard a key in the front door. I'd somehow missed Neko in my house hunt earlier that morning, and she'd greeted me when I'd come in, screaming for food and love… an interchangeable pair in her mind. A quick step around her winding body and a dubious-smelling helping of tuna and egg cat food made her happy enough to let me go shower in peace. I was out of the shower when Jae called out to me.

"Up here!" I'd gone into my walk-in closet and stared at the bank of clothes hanging there. I'd put on a pair of comfortable briefs, then was stymied by the choices I had to make. "What the hell do I wear to this thing?"

"Something clean," Jae murmured as he came in behind me. His black denim jeans did wonders for his long legs and ass, especially when he bent over to dig through my shoe boxes for a pair of loafers for me to wear. He handed me my shoes, a pair of socks, and then retrieved a pair of black pants and a matching shirt from hangers, dumping those in my arms too. "Go get dressed."

"If the cat tells you she's not been fed, she's lying." I was talking to air. He'd already headed downstairs.

The loafers squeaked slightly as I came down the stairs, and Jae grinned at me, shaking his head. "You probably need a haircut." He ran his fingers through my brown hair, tugging at the ends brushing my jaw. "But it's nice to play with."

"I got more than my hair for you to play with," I teased. "You driving?"

"My stuff's in my car." He shrugged. "But, you can drive."

I tried not to let my relief show. I'd been a passenger in Jae's car a total of three times, and after each trip, I forced myself not to kiss the ground in thanks once I got free of the Explorer. He'd learned to drive in Seoul. Apparently, no one believed in turn signals or lanes in South Korea, because Jae drove like a drunk butterfly heading to its next fermented flower.

We were three blocks away from the house when I told Jae-Min about Shin-Cho and his encounter with Kwon. The exasperated sigh he gave me back was weighted down with worry.

"Do not say anything to Sang-Min at the party," he warned me. "This isn't just a dinner for the wedding party. A lot of business people will be there. This is a big thing. Don't mess it up."

"Wouldn't dream of it," I promised. "Can I glare menacingly at him?"

"No," Jae shot back. "For once, pretend you're really Japanese, and just smile and nod. Practice having a public face. *Aish*, I don't know why I bother. It's like trying to teach a fish to drink milk."

"I promised, didn't I?" Not being totally stupid, I changed the subject. "Have you been up there before?"

We were heading to the Hills, the GPS chirping out directions as I drove. Traffic along the 101 was surprisingly light. We'd be there way before eight o'clock unless Santa Monica Boulevard was tight. The Explorer rattled a bit as I changed lanes, and I made a mental note to have the front end looked at.

"A couple of times," Jae replied. "I shot their son's college graduation party and their last anniversary dinner. They pay on time."

That was high praise from Jae. He hated chasing down money. The topic of money brought me back to our discussion that morning, and I cleared my throat, drawing Jae's attention away from the window.

"You know I'll help you—"

"No." I didn't even get to finish the sentence when he cut me off. No argument. No wavering. Just an unwavering *no*.

"Can we at least talk about it being a maybe if something big comes up?" I maneuvered around a semi, still not liking the way the Explorer was handling. Compared to my Rover, it was like steering a boat through sand. "I'm serious. If there's an emergency, it would make me feel better knowing you'd come to me. At least for a loan."

His cinnamon-honey eyes studied me, and I shifted in my seat, unnerved at the intensity I saw there. Grunting, Jae quirked his mouth in partial disgust and returned to staring out the window. After a few moments, he reluctantly said, "Only as a loan. And *only* if it's something big."

"That's all I'm asking." I'd never begged someone to take money from me. Certainly not Rick, or even Ben, who'd been happy for me to cough up cash for lunches. Even Claudia, who was reluctant about overspending, graciously accepted any bonuses I passed her way.

He responded with one of those tonal noises he and Scarlet spoke in. I didn't reply. Mostly because I didn't understand if he was consenting, or blowing me off to make me feel better.

We rode in silence the rest of the way. Traffic remained light, even when we hit the Hills, where the roads shrunk down to two lanes and were dominated by hulking Hummers and sports cars. I almost missed the driveway leading up to the house, but Jae pointed it out hiding behind a sweeping willow tree.

The word *house* could barely be used for the building we drove up to. It looked more like some place that the dog had its own suite, complete with whirlpool spa and maid quarters. The house's size and creamy stone exterior was a polite nod to a French chateau, complete with a pair of towers and a blue slate sloping roof. A valet waited for us at the top of the circular driveway, poised to whisk the Explorer off to who-knew-where. The grounds were thick with ornamental evergreens shaped like dollops of water, and the greenscapes would make a golf course envious.

It made me wonder what Kwon really did for a living, because it seemed like there was a lot of money to be made doing it.

"We can go through the house." Jae was already out of the car and unloading equipment from the back seat. Hefting a duffel bag over his shoulder, he waited until I untangled myself from the seat belt before heading up the wide front steps to the door. They opened before he could knock, and I grabbed the other bag and tripod, leaving the car for the valet to deal with. The scars on my side pulled at the weight on my shoulder, and I shifted the bag, trying to ease the ache creeping up my ribcage.

I didn't get much time to look at the interior. Jae hurried through a few rooms that left me with an impression of white and yellow walls, light furniture, and endless streams of windows. A short flight of stone steps led us down to a cobblestone patio nearly the size of an Olympic pool. An actual pool lay beyond, complete with a natural boulder façade and multiple waterfalls lit up for the evening event.

Once outside, Jae claimed a small table behind the long buffet being set up, avoiding a pair of caterers lighting Sterno cans under chafing dishes. White paper lanterns were strung up above the cobblestone patio, and a semicircle of tables were arranged opposite the food. A string quartet's tuning was nearly drowned out by a man behind a wet bar shouting toward the house that he needed limes and simple syrup. From the looks of things, there would be about fifty or so people at the rehearsal dinner.

"Shit, how many people are coming to the wedding if they've got this many coming now?" I whispered into Jae's ear.

"I think three hundred, but the reception will be bigger. More people are invited to that." Jae handed me a small handheld spotlight and a bifold holding memory cards. A white screen was set in front of the bulb to diffuse the light, and I stood still as he attached the spot's battery pack to my belt. "Don't turn this on until I tell you to. And don't take off the screen."

"Got it." I'd already done that once while fooling around with it in my living room. Took me over half an hour before people stopped looking like Jesus, and lost their halos. "No turning on the lasers. Let me know when Scarlet gets here. I need to see if Shin-Cho talked to her yet."

"She's not coming, *agi*," Jae said, looking away momentarily. He'd slipped, calling me *agi* when other people were around. I pretended not to notice. "She's... this isn't her place. This is a place for... wives, not lovers. *Hyung* will be coming by himself."

"That sucks," I muttered, but Jae'd already wandered off, his attention fixed on the quartet.

People were starting to trickle onto the patio. The crowd was mostly Korean, leaning toward spangled dresses and tailored suits. The women seemed to have a glitter and spangle fetish. Either that, or there'd been a rhinestone factory that had a going-out-of-business sale. I was half-afraid for Jae's eyes if he used the spotlight. One wrong move and his retinas would be burnt out from the back flash.

A thin-faced Korean woman wearing a gold silk sheath hurried over to Jae, touching his arm lightly as she spoke to him in whispers. She was that made-up pretty where I couldn't tell how old she was: older than her twenties, but hovering somewhere ahead of fifty. Her high heels brought her up to Jae's shoulder and looked painful, but she glided on them, as if walking on giraffe legs was something she did every day. Scarlet wore those kinds of shoes. I could never be a woman. My feet screamed in agony just looking at them. Jae cocked his head as he listened to her, and nodded, bowing slightly before she gave us both a smile and scurried away to greet people coming down the walkway.

"Mother of the bride?" I joined him, hazarding a guess at her identity. She was quickly surveying the area, smiling softly at people when she made eye contact.

"Her name is Choi Eun-hee," Jae said, steadying himself as he took a few shots of a young couple near one of the tables. The woman was touching the flower arrangement on the table, running her finger over a rose petal and conferring with the man holding her arm. "Yes, mother of the bride. She wanted to remind us to eat. I told her we will once the dancing starts."

"Did she remarry?" Jae looked up at me, frowning in confusion. "Her last name is Choi? Not Kwon?"

"Korean women don't normally take their husbands' last names, remember?" He returned to stalking the guests, and I had to stretch my legs to keep up with him. "You can call her Mrs. Kwon, but Dr. Choi would be better."

I was going to ask what she was a doctor of, but the irritated gleam in Jae's eye reminded me he was working. I was going to have to keep track of the players. These people were connected to Dae-Hoon, either through blood, sex, or in a day or so, marriage.

Shin-Cho spotted me and came over, giving Jae a small polite bow before greeting me. The mark on his cheek was barely visible, but his eyes were as troubled as they'd been when he'd left my house. As Jae messed with some of his equipment, he sidled up to me.

"My brother will be here later. I've told him about you helping with our father," Shin-Cho said quietly. "He'd like to meet you."

"Sure," I agreed. From where I stood, David seemed like one of the few sane people in the family. Although I could have been prejudiced, because he'd chosen to support his brother rather than turn his back on him.

"There, at the top of the stairs," Shin-Cho hissed. "*That* is Sang-Min."

A tall, middle-aged Korean man with a practiced smile descended the stairs and touched Dr. Choi's shoulder. I turned just enough to study his face. There was only one photo of Dae-Hoon with his then-lover, Kwon Sang-Min, and despite the passage of time, his features were easily recognizable. The good-looking, composed twentysomething young man was now a handsome, polished businessman. He scanned the crowd, waving at people mingling in the center of the patio.

Kwon spotted Shin-Cho and nodded slowly at him. The nod was arrogant and condescending, a gesture that seemed as natural to him as breathing. A faint smirk lingered at the edge of his mouth, a mocking tease at Shin-Cho's expense. Then his gaze stopped on Jae, and I saw a flare of intense interest flash across his face before dissolving behind a placid mask.

Yeah, the man was gay. A man's eyes didn't linger on another man's ass unless he wanted to plow it.

I wanted to punch Kwon in the mouth. Repeatedly. Until I wiped that plastic smile off his face.

"Cole-ah, I need a new card soon," Jae called out to me.

"I'll hook up with you later, Shin-Cho. Have to get to work before Jae kills me." I hurried over to Jae's side. The people gathered on the patio were beginning to clap, and I turned, frozen in place. Jae took the card from my fingers, ignoring my slack-jawed stare.

The bride, Helena Kwon, looked more like her father than her mother. She had his elegant features, softened with a full mouth and triangular chin. A blood-red cocktail dress hugged her slender body, and her diamond bracelets caught the light, throwing rainbows back onto the crowd. The young man with her stood a few feet behind, allowing her a moment in the spotlight as the bride. She turned, searching for her groom, and reached out one hand for him, motioning him forward.

He stepped out of the shadows, his hand closing over his wife-to-be's, and his smile was warm, much warmer than Kwon's. He waved to the crowd and gallantly swept his arm toward Helena, bowing gracefully at her sweet laughter. The lights hit his face, and my heart stopped for a beat. I snuck a look at Kwon's face. It was tight, and his smile was stretched wide, but his eyes were cold, a bitter, somber glaze shadowing them.

I could understand Kwon's reaction. He'd probably stared at David numerous times, but it would still be a shock. God knows, I was shocked down to my shoes. It was like Dae-Hoon stepped out of the photos Scarlet sent me, and came to life. David, his daughter's soon-to-be husband, was the spitting image of his missing father, Dae-Hoon, and judging by the lecherous expression on Kwon's face, Shin-Cho wasn't the only Park brother Kwon wanted to fuck.

CHAPTER SIX

"FUCK me." I whistled under my breath. Jae nudged me in the ribs with his shoulder, then gave me a look. "Sorry."

David Park's resemblance to his father was remarkable. There might have been subtle differences, but I didn't know Dae-Hoon well enough to see them. I'd only had an hour staring at Dae-Hoon's face, and seeing David gave me chills. Kwon must have freaked out when he saw his ex-lover's son. I couldn't imagine what he thought about David marrying his daughter.

"Come," Jae said. "I need to get pictures of David and Helena."

I followed him closely, flipping on the light when he asked me to. We shadowed the couple, failed stalkers with a spotlight. They smiled and waved at people they knew, the picture of a happy couple in love.

And the entire time, Kwon circled us like a bloodthirsty shark swimming by a school of minnows.

It was interesting to watch Jae work. He walked a fine line between unobtrusive and corralling people together to get a shot. We skulked around the guests: Jae, a graceful figure gliding in and out of the crowd while I followed him with a lumbering stomp.

At one point, the Park brothers stood together with their arms thrown around each other's shoulders. They both looked like their father, Shin-Cho less so than David, but their smiles were the same. I briefly wondered if Mike and I smiled that way with each other, but I doubted it. Our relationship was more a punch on the arm than a hug.

We lost Shin-Cho in the crowd a few moments later, but not before he gave me a wavering smile. Despite the crowd around us, it was clear he was being avoided by nearly everyone but a select few. My heart went out to the guy, even more so when I noticed Kwon close by, shaking hands and accepting congratulations on marrying off his daughter, all the while, his eyes on either David or Jae-Min.

Kwon was studiously ignoring Shin-Cho, his eyes sliding over the man as if he were nothing more than a shadow.

As much as it pissed me off to watch Kwon surreptitiously ogle Jae in front of his wife, watching the ping-pong match of his gaze drifting between my lover and David was pretty funny. Not funny enough for me to step aside when he finally moved in on Jae.

"Excuse me," I said, bumping his shoulder when Kwon drew close. It was a simple, petty game, one played between men interested in the same person. He eyed me up, raking over me from head to toe with a hot glare. Kwon would have set me on fire if he could. I stood still, letting a smirk curl the edge of my mouth.

From his viewpoint, he had the advantage of wealth, influence, and culture, although I was taller, and was willing to bet I had a better body. A simple word from Kwon, and Jae could lose business. It was a risk to challenge him on his own turf. I was willing to take that risk. I'd wallowed in a bitter stew about Rick and Ben before I met Jae, and while I still hadn't totally broken free of what I'd been soaking in, I wasn't going to let Kwon edge in. From where I stood, I had more to lose than he did. Much more.

Kwon said something in Korean, and I smiled, shaking my head at my lack of comprehension. He smiled back, a slithering grin that did nothing to warm me to him. He repeated what he said in English, slowly, as if I wouldn't understand him. "Have we met?"

"No, not yet," I replied softly. Holding my free hand out to him, I smiled. "I'm with Kim Jae-Min, the photographer. We're Scarlet's friends. Pity she couldn't make it today. She'd have loved to see Dae-Hoon's boy."

It was a masterful manipulation of the conversation. I was rather proud of it since it was something I rarely pulled off. My words got a range of effects, first a stiffening of Kwon's shoulders and face when I mentioned Scarlet, then curiously, what looked like a slight fear creeping into his cold eyes. He got a hold of his emotions quickly, but his limbs betrayed his uneasiness, jerking awkwardly as he turned away.

I would have liked to enjoy that moment more, and I would have, if the shooting hadn't started.

There was a clapping sound, a short reverb, and then screams, loud screams followed by terrified shouting. I caught the smell of blood and panicked, grabbing at Jae to pull him down under me. His camera tilted, falling from his hands and onto the grass. Grabbing at the edge of one of the tables, I yanked it onto its side, hoping the metal top would provide us with some sort of protection.

Like all shootings, everything happened quickly. There was no time to react with anything more than instinct.

And human instinct always seems to start off with panic.

I had the right to panic. I'd found Jae unconscious, and bleeding from a gunshot graze a few feet from his cousin's dead rent-boy. I already had a bad track record with boyfriends and guns. Panic was fully within my God-given rights, right up there with the pursuit of happiness and extra cheese on my carne asada fries.

"I'm okay," Jae murmured reassuringly. "I'm fine… I'm okay, *agi*."

I started breathing again.

My hands skimmed over his body, searching for any injury. Speckles of blood dotted his cheekbone, and my heart froze. My thumbs smeared the blood, raking the spray into uneven lines. Cradling the back of his head, I held him to my chest, waiting for my heart to start up again, willing it to catch a beat… anything to begin feeling again. My fear chilled me down to my bones, and I couldn't keep my fingers from trembling as I ran them through his hair.

Even hidden behind a patio table, I felt exposed, but he lay on the ground under me, letting my hands touch his chest. I needed to hear his heart… to feel it pumping under my fingers.

I must have looked insane, because he cupped his hands to my face, ignoring all of his rules and fears.

"*Agi*, I am okay," he said again in that husky purr that warmed my guts. "We have to help. I think Helena's hurt. I saw her bleeding, I think. Maybe David... I don't know."

There was silence around us, broken by whimpers and gasping cries. I slid off Jae and peered carefully around the upended table. Kwon was stirring nearby, his legs tangled up in one of the mission-style folding chairs set on the patio. Other party guests were hiding behind what they could, most taking cover behind tables and the potted juniper trees lining the outer edges of the patio. A few feet away from us, Helena Kwon lay in her fiancée's arms, blood turning her crimson dress nearly black. David rocked her, his hands ineffectively pressing against the wound in her side.

The diamond bracelets on her wrists were splattered with her blood, the gems now as dim as her glazed-over eyes. David's shirt was soaked through, and he shook her slightly, urging her to stay with him until someone came. There was more than blood on his hands. A pink-gray froth poured from the side of Helena's shattered head and onto the sleeve of his coat. A thin, bloody film dripped from his fingers, and David's shoulders shuddered while he tried to catch his breath. He glanced up at me for a quick moment, his eyes wild with fear and pain, then back to his lover, begging me... anyone... to help her.

There wasn't anyone coming who could put Helena Kwon back together. He just wasn't ready to hear that yet. I knew how that felt. Nothing hurts as much as your world falling apart in your hands. Nothing.

JAE and I were separated by the cops once they arrived. An ambulance crew checked over the rest of the guests. A total of five bullets were fired. Two hit Helena, two grazed other guests, and one went wide, striking one of the boulders and ricocheting back toward the patio. The detective on the scene, a stern-looking middle-aged blonde woman named Brookes, was particularly interested in my conceal license and what a private investigator was doing doubling as a photographer's assistant at a rehearsal dinner.

It was a conversation that went nowhere useful for her. I had no answers, other than I thought the gun had a silencer and the shots came from the house. The look she gave me was sour. I gave her one back, slightly less tart but disgusted all the same.

"Can I go?" I'd lost sight of Jae. He'd disappeared inside of the house along with a few of the other guests, accompanied by a few uniforms. The number of cops called onto the scene was staggering. "I need to find Jae-Min."

"I've got your contact info." Brookes didn't look pleased to let me go, but motioned me toward the house. "I don't know if he's done yet. If not, you can wait by the front door. We're closing up the rest of the house."

Spotting Shin-Cho comforting his brother, I nodded at him, hoping my expression could convey my sorrow. Sitting on one of the lawn chairs, David looked devastated, and his older brother hovered next to him. A couple of detectives stood in front of them, asking questions. I didn't need to hear Shin-Cho to know he was reaching the end of his rope. He snarled in Korean at one of the men poking at his brother. I didn't need to understand the language to know Shin-Cho was telling them to fuck off. Either they understood him, or realized they'd pushed things too far, because the detectives were making their apologies when I hit the stairs.

I found Jae in the main foyer, sitting on a spindly looking French chair and sipping at a Styrofoam cup of coffee. He'd gained a pinstriped gray suit jacket from someone, and it was tossed over his shoulders, its arms dangling down his sides. His face was clean of blood, but his shirt had a light spray of spots along his chest. It chilled me to realize how close he'd been to Helena when she'd been shot.

"You okay?" It was hard not to touch him. I had to shove my hands into my pockets to stop myself from pulling him against me. He nodded and handed me the coffee. It was hot and sweet, but not the hot and sweet taste I wanted in my mouth. "Are they done with you?"

"I think so. *Hyung*'s here somewhere. He spoke to the cops first, before they could talk to me. They weren't happy about it."

"Yeah, cops get pissed off when someone steps on their witness," I said. "That where you got the jacket?"

Jae murmured something that sounded like a yes or *hyung*. It could have been grilled cheese sandwich for all I knew. He looked tired, and I hooked my hand under his arm, gently pulling him up. He stumbled forward, catching his toes on the carpet runner. "What?"

"Let's take you home," I whispered into his ear. I didn't care who was watching us or even if the cops were done with him. I wanted to get Jae home and scrub the evening from his body and mind. He gave me a bit of a struggle, looking over his shoulder and down the hall to where I assumed Seong, Scarlet's lover, was holed up with his own gang of cops.

I gave in to my desires.

Pulling him against me, I looped my arms around his waist. He twisted a bit, looking around him, but I held him tight.

"No one's watching," I whispered into his ear. "And even if they are, I don't want you to care. Not now. Not after… this. Time for me to take care of you, Kim Jae-Min. Now shut up, and let's get the rest of your stuff so we can go home."

I RAN a hot shower, stripped Jae, and shoved him under the water. It was hard to keep my head on straight, especially with the sight of his naked body imprinted in my mind as I headed downstairs. Tossing his shirt into a bag, I knotted it up before throwing it into the bin. The cat wound between my ankles. I stepped over her, thwarting her plans for my death.

The teapot was on the stove, and there was a collection of tins Jae'd lined up on the kitchen counter. I grabbed a bottle of Jack Daniel's instead. Snagging a couple of cold Cokes from the fridge, I took the stairs up two at a time. Neko tried to trip me on the landing, and I edged the cat away from the bedroom with my foot.

She complained loudly, a pitiful wailing sound that warned of air raids and tsunamis. Dancing past me, Neko jumped up on the bed and screamed again. She wanted to be with Jae… with me… or just wanted to take up space at the end of the bed. Either way, she was throwing a shitfit about it.

I left the door open.

I'm not always stupid. Sometimes, it's easier when the cat wins.

The water was still running when I set the bottle and cans down on the nightstand. Slipping past the bathroom door, I caught Jae staring at me with hooded eyes, through the glass shower door. He was leaning with his hands against the wall and his legs spread slightly apart, letting the showerheads' flow hit him full force. His black hair was plastered down against his skull, its wet length coursing down the span of his neck.

He didn't move when I opened the door. He didn't blink when I walked into the shower fully clothed, and came up behind him to wrap my arms around his stomach. I held him, letting him shake in my arms while the water ran over both of us.

For some reason, Jae *did* it for me. There was something about him that made me ache for him. His long legs, narrow hips, and wide shoulders made my mouth water. His round, tight ass and sensual mouth made me hard. Even at the worst of times, he made me hard. My dick wasn't listening to my warnings that it didn't need to be buried deep inside of the man against my chest. It could wait. It could fucking wait forever, if that's what Jae needed.

Eventually, the heater struggled to keep up with the demands on it, and the steam from the showerheads thinned. The water was going lukewarm when Jae laid his head back onto my shoulder. Turning his face into the crook of my neck, he sighed and leaned on me, letting me hold his weight up. Reaching past him, I shut off the valves, and opened the door to grab a towel from the rack.

"I'm okay," he reassured me, trying to take the towel from me, but I pushed his hands away.

"Let me," I scolded him softly. His head was bent, and his eyes were nearly hidden by his hair, falling forward wet and long around his cheekbones. I touched my fingers to his chin and tilted his face up. "Let me do this."

I rubbed him down with the soft bath sheet, taking my time with his hands and feet. I handled his balls and cock gently, feeling their heft in my palm as I dried them, before moving up his torso and ass. His shoulders and chest were next, then his hair, which soaked through the towel. I tossed it into the laundry basket and grabbed another, wrapping it around Jae's hips.

"If you pick me up, I'll kill you," Jae grumbled.

"My shoulder hurts too much, or I would," I groused back.

The cat was warming our bed, and I pushed Jae onto the mattress to keep her company. The Cokes were still cold, and I popped them open, passing one to Jae. I reached over for the Jack Daniel's, which earned me a faint smile.

Jae sipped his soda. "Did you bring any food?"

"Whiskey's food. It's like oatmeal. Sort of," I protested as I twisted off the black plastic cap. "I'm Irish. We drink whiskey when shit happens."

"I'm Korean. We eat." He leaned against me, then held his can out. "I'll try being Irish. I don't think I can eat."

"If you really want to be Irish, you'd drink from the bottle and then pretend to sip the Coke as a chaser." I poured about half a shot of Jack into the can. "Let's start you off slow."

I drank from the bottle, leaving the other Coke on the nightstand. The whiskey burned the sides of my mouth, and I swallowed, letting the fire hit my belly. Moving up to sit against the headboard, I held Jae's soda can so he could climb over my leg and nest between my thighs, leaning his back against my chest. We sat there quietly, my left hand lying on Jae's belly while the right remained curled around the whiskey bottle. After Jae finished his drink, he took the Jack Daniel's from me and took a sip, gasping at the rawness in his mouth.

"That's…." He coughed, hard. "I drink soju, and I think *that* stuff's nasty."

"Keep drinking until it tastes good," I suggested, kissing his temple. "Then you stop. Unless you want to be really Irish, and then you keep drinking until you start telling everyone you love them."

Jae swallowed another sip and handed the bottle back to me. Leaning his head back, he stared up at my face and said, "It was shitty… what happened today. It was really shitty."

"Yeah, it was," I agreed. There was nothing else to do but agree. We left the house with no idea who did the shooting or if there'd been any reason for it.

I knew how that felt too.

Really fucking shitty.

"I feel like…." Jae murmured softly. "I feel like it's all connected to me. All these people dying. Like there's a thread or something going through me, and people I touch die. Hyun-Shik. Jin-Sang. Brian. Victoria. And now Helena. I know it sounds stupid. I didn't *do* anything. It's just… so many… so close to me."

I wasn't going to tell him it wasn't his fault. Nothing I said or did would take that feeling of dread from his chest. I would only be able to hold him when the nightmares hit.

Only fair. He did it for me.

"You know what's going through my head?" The skin on his belly was soft, and I traced his stomach muscles with my fingertips as I spoke. "Why Helena? She's what… twenty-four… twenty-five? Why go out of your way to kill her? What could she have done?"

"I don't know. She was… nice?" Jae shrugged. "I didn't spend a lot of time with her. Just about an hour, talking about what kind of photos she and David wanted. She wasn't very… complicated."

Coming from the king of complicated, I took that to mean she was a nice girl, but dim. "So David was the brain trust?"

"I suppose," he said, taking the bottle from me. His sips were getting more daring, and he swallowed the whiskey with a practiced ease. We'd be working through the rest of it if we weren't careful. "He's a lawyer. I think he's going to work for *hyung*."

"And we're back to the incest," I grumbled. "You guys kind of scare me. It's like a syndicate or cult. Very much you scratch my back, and I'll wash yours."

"How do you think I get most of my jobs?" He snorted. "And it's not like they're the yakuza. Mostly they're… *chaebol*." My look of confusion must have been epic, because he rolled his eyes at me. "*Chaebol*… they're families… rich families. What's the word for it?

Dynasties, I guess. They marry each other, have their own rules. *Hyung*'s family is powerful. So is Kwon's. Jae-Su could have worked for *hyung*'s family in San Francisco, but he's too...."

Jae's shrug was enough. His brother was useless.

Suddenly, other things made sense. Jae's living with his richer cousins, the Kims, when he was thirteen or fourteen, only to be turned out when Hyun-Shik's mother blamed him for her son's homosexuality. He'd lost more than a place to live after Hyun-Shik seduced him... he'd also lost the chance to elevate his family to those rarified circles.

I began to hate Jae's aunt even more than I had before. And in my own quaint, philosophical way, expressed my disgust by saying, "Your aunt so fucked you over. What a fucking bitch."

"You're smarter when you're drunk." Jae slurred slightly, and I grinned at him. "You've only now caught on?"

"You just explained that whole... gerbil thing. *Now* it makes sense."

"*Chaebol.*" He was patient with me, especially when I slaughtered his language. "But killing Helena still doesn't make sense."

"Someone hate the Kwon... family thing?" I suggested. "Enough to shoot... someone?"

"It would make more sense if you said someone hated *hyung*'s family, but Helena was the one who died, not David. The Kwons have a lot of money, but the Seongs have more power... they're older... have more... everything. Unless they killed her to hurt him, but he's not... David doesn't have any weight in the family yet. He's too young."

"Hold up, how does that make sense?" Either the whiskey was too strong for my brain, or I was missing something. "How does Seong count in this?"

"His family has more influence." Jae removed the bottle from my hand and drank. I'd nearly upended it on the covers, so I didn't mind when he held onto it. "Remember? David's mother is *hyung*'s sister. She's a Seong. Dae-Hoon's a Park. His family has money, but not as much as the Seongs."

"So Dae-Hoon married into the Seong... *chaebol*," I tried the word out. It couldn't have been too bad, because the eye roll he gave me was slight. I sat up, suddenly a lot more sober than I wanted to be. Jae grunted at being shoved forward, and grumbled again when I reached for my notebook to write down my thoughts. "And his sons... if Dae-Hoon had been around, they'd have been... *tainted*... by being connected to him, right?"

"Yes, but Dae-Hoon's been gone for years, and they were raised by the Seongs." He frowned. "Shin-Cho and David weren't touched by what Dae-Hoon did. Well, until Shin-Cho... what he did was stupid. Now people are talking about Dae-Hoon again, and saying his sons are like him. It might affect David too, especially since he stood by his brother."

"I'll bet you that's it," I said. "You say family's everything for you. It would be for someone like Dae-Hoon too. I don't think he died, Jae."

"Then what happened to him?"

"I think he walked away," I said, kissing the tip of my lover's nose. "They would have fucked him over, like they did you... like they did your family. I don't think he would risk that. You once told me Koreans live for the generation after them. It makes sense for Dae-Hoon to not want that for his kids. It would kill him to have his sons suffer like that. I saw photos of him with his kids. He loved them. I think he walked away so his sons could grow up without his... shame... affecting them."

I hugged him, jostling the Jack Daniel's bottle he still held to his chest. Jae protested a bit, then grumbled more when I took the bottle and set it on the nightstand with my notebook. Tumbling him onto his back, I covered Jae with my body, stretching out to capture him under me.

"I think Dae-Hoon might still be alive, *agi*." I kissed him, tasting the whiskey on his tongue. "David might have lost his fiancée, but maybe I can give them back their father. I just need to know where to look."

CHAPTER SEVEN

NAMING Los Angeles the City of Angels was a colossal joke, usually perpetrated on the stupid fool who decides to brave the midmorning rush in the special hell that is the 110, 10, and 101 triangle. It was as if Satan looked down on the city and said: *Fuck it, I was an angel. I'm going to piss right on this spot and call it mine.*

And damn, did he drink a Big Gulp or something before he took that piss.

I'd left Jae asleep with Neko curled up on my pillow. We'd finished off the bottle of Jack at some point, and lay against each other, just listening to one another breathe. Morning hit with a vengeance, especially since I'd forgotten to pull the drapes closed, and the sun punched me in the face. A few ibuprofen, a bottle of water, and a toothbrush scrubbing later, I felt more human than the throbbing, aching sponge I'd woken up as. A shower and a cup of hot, strong coffee took care of most of the rest of it, and I'd headed out to meet Bobby in the driveway, thankful for the drive-thru Starbucks a few blocks away from my house.

Yes, I had a bunch of independent coffee shops right around me, including the granola-munchers across the street, who I avoided on the principle that they wore tank tops in the summer and didn't shave their armpits. I couldn't care less if someone didn't shave their armpits. Hell, I fucked men. Armpit hair came with the territory. I just objected to it being anywhere near the open end of my cup of coffee.

"There better be fucking gold in that storage locker," Bobby complained. We'd inched forward for the last fifteen minutes, inhaling exhaust fumes and powdered sugar from the donettes Bobby brought with him. Years of sharing cars with other officers pretty much immunized Bobby against the need for a spotless interior. Anything dropped was vacuumed up or washed off the truck's leather seat. Mike, on the other hand, had issues with a stray straw wrapper left in his car.

It was sometimes hard for me to remember whose car I could accidentally spill in, and whose I couldn't. So I ate off a napkin, getting me some strange looks from Bobby.

"Want a bib, Princess?" he finally grunted. "Times like these, I miss having a siren."

"Why don't you just lean out the window and scream," I suggested. "I could even kick you in the balls so you can scream higher."

"Don't get smart with me," Bobby warned with a wide grin. "You're not too big for me to pull over to the side of the road and spank."

"I'm not your type," I reminded him. "I don't take orders well."

"True," he mused, then sobered. "How's Jae doing? Shit, that kid's had a rough few months."

I'd told Bobby about the shooting while we were in the drive-thru. The first thing he asked was if I'd gotten Jae drunk. Second thing was if I'd fucked the unhappy out of him. I reminded him that sex didn't solve everything, and sometimes what someone needed was to be held. That's when he accused me of having a vagina, because, for men, sex solved pretty much everything.

"Not as rough as Helena and David." I added Shin-Cho to that list as well. He'd have to spend a lot of time shoring his brother up. The only good thing about that was he wouldn't be obsessing about Kwon. "Fucking hell, I don't know what to say to Jae. He's carrying around this guilt about people dying around him. I don't know how to fix what he's feeling."

"Well, when you figure it out, you let the rest of us know so we can say it to you," Bobby replied softly.

I kept quiet. The past couple of months had been rough on me too. I still wrestled with my guilt over Rick's death and my growing affection for Jae-Min. I had about as many answers as David Park did right now.

"You're not sticking your head into that mess, are you?" Bobby said suddenly. "With the girl's death, I mean."

"Staying as far away from it as possible. The cops have it. What can I do about it?" I debated having another mini-donut. "Look, we're moving now."

"About fucking time." Bobby shifted the truck and consulted the GPS for the fiftieth time. "A mile. We only have a fucking mile to go. Longest damn mile of my life."

"Spoken like a man who's never been to Comic-Con."

"I've been to Southern Decadence. Now *that's* a mile I'd like to get stuck in until the end of time," he leered at me.

It took us another fifteen minutes to go the final mile to the next off ramp. It might have been the longest mile Bobby ever drove, but it was the longest fifteen minutes of my life listening to him drive it.

The storage place was only a few blocks from the freeway, and we pulled into an empty parking lot. Like most storage places in California, all that was needed to get into the lot and locker was an access code and the key to the lock the renter put on the unit's rolling metal door. The unit was an interior locker, so Bobby and I spent a few minutes in a cinderblock warren, trying to find where Scarlet put Dae-Hoon's life.

"Thank God this was inside. Imagine what a bitch it would be to open this if it'd been outside." Bobby spritzed the lock with graphite and worked the key in. Surprisingly, it released easily, and I pushed the door up, turning my head aside to avoid the dust storm falling down from its metal slats. I didn't have a lot of faith in the dangling bare bulb turning on, but a flick of the switch surprised me, and the four by four foot unit filled with light.

It was surprising to see how little of Dae-Hoon's life he'd left behind. After all the clothes were given away and the furniture sold or passed along, only a few boxes of personal items and books were left. There were about ten boxes in the unit, mostly uniform in size, and all marked with the name of a moving company that went out of business almost nine years ago. The cellophane tape holding the box flaps closed had long given up the ghost, turning yellow and brittle, despite the air conditioning pumped through the units.

"Let me go grab the duct tape I've got in the truck," Bobby said. "Start pulling things out so I can put them on the dolly. Don't lift anything heavy. That shoulder of yours is still fucked up."

I sneered at Bobby's back, but started to grab a box to drag it to the flatbed trolley we'd brought with us. My shoulder ached less than the scars along my torso did. I stretched, hoping to forestall the inevitable cramping, when one of the box's flaps fell open. I peered in and was perplexed by the stacks of notebooks I found inside. Crouching, I drew out the one on top and flipped through it.

It was all in Korean, handwritten in blue and black ink. Every so often a sandwich baggie with an old photograph inside of it was paper-clipped carefully to the page, with a passage highlighted or heavily underlined near it. Curious, I worked one bag free and pulled out the photograph.

"Damn." Bobby whistled. "Hope to hell that guy on the bottom is old enough to be doing that."

It was hard to tell how old the guy was, especially since the young man's face was hidden partially by shadows and his dark hair. I thought he could be Asian of some sort, but I couldn't be certain. The photo was black and white, their expressions caught between agony and pleasure. Limbs were wrapped into angles I knew were possible, but my hips ached with the thought of it. And the man shoving his dick into the bottom's ass definitely was Korean. Even though the photo was old, I could even name the man on top: Seong Min-Ho, Scarlet's lover.

The small mole by his right eye was the same, and so was the curve of his mouth. More lines were on his skin, but the steady gaze was the same, a piercing focus intended to intimidate and cow if he needed to. In the photo, that focus was slightly off. He was caught in midthrust, his hand curling around his lover's jaw and his thumb hooked into the corner of the other man's mouth, making it harder to recognize him.

On one hand, I wanted it to be Scarlet, just to spare her the pain of seeing her lover having sex with another man. The other part of me wanted to pretend I'd never seen it, especially if it was Scarlet. One does not need erotic images of one's friends burnt into one's memory. Or at least I sure the hell didn't.

"Shit, there's tons of these," Bobby said softly. "What the fuck was he doing?"

"Something stupid," I replied. "From what Jae told me, Dae-Hoon was running around with a pretty high-powered crowd, at least guys from influential Korean families. Shit, this blows a hole in my theory that he's still alive. If they'd known he was taking pictures of them fucking other guys, I can't see him surviving to talk about it."

"Think someone took care of him… instead of him taking a run? Yeah, it would only have to be one really pissed off guy, and that would be the end of Dae-Hoon." He was flipping through another notebook, whistling at the pictures he found there. "What was *this*? His insurance? Sex diary? Shit, I don't even want to know what this guy is doing in this one."

That was saying a lot. Bobby had very few things he wouldn't do. I was beginning to worry for Scarlet. She might have opened a can of worms there'd be no closing up. If Dae-Hoon's disappearance was linked to the notebooks, I didn't want Scarlet involved.

"I'll get Jae to help us," I mumbled, shoving the photo back into its bag. "Why the hell couldn't he write it in English? I don't want Jae reading this."

"Better than it being in Filipino, then you'd be stuck with Scarlet translating it," Bobby teased. "Jae's a big boy. If he can't handle it, he'll tell you."

I made a face. "Never mind. Korean's fine. I don't want to go to Scarlet with this. At least not until I know what *this* is."

"Tape it up, and we'll get this stuff back to your house." Bobby tossed me one of the two rolls he'd come back with. "Sooner we get done here, the sooner we can get back into that damned traffic."

The flat dolly held all ten boxes easily, and I took up the rear as Bobby pulled it behind him. He'd left the truck's tailgate down and spread out tarp and ropes so we could secure the load. I bent down and grabbed one of the smaller boxes. Bobby nudged my arm.

"Dude, it's not heavy," I protested, nearly dropping the box. "What the fuck?"

"Don't look...." I don't know why people say that. Humans' first instinct is to turn around and look. It got me slapped on the back of the head. Bobby hissed at me, "Can't you *listen* to me once in a while?"

"If I listened to you every time you told me to do something, I'd have hooked up with that het chick you thought was a guy."

"She looked like a twink. Can't blame me for that," he grumbled. "Now, I'm telling you not to look 'cause there's a car over there... the one with the blackout windows. It's right past the gate. Been sitting there since we came in, pulled in after us."

"Yeah? So they're getting a storage unit." I shrugged and shoved the box onto the truck bed, then glanced at the car. It was a black sedan with windows tinted so dark they nearly matched the paint.

"It doesn't take that long to get a unit," Bobby said. "They also were behind us on the freeway. I spotted it then. I was wondering what cop didn't notice the window film's dark enough to be illegal."

"Why would they be following us?" I asked softly. "No one's interested in what we're doing. Hell, no one even knows I'm working on Dae-Hoon's disappearance. They're just getting a unit. Quit being paranoid."

"I'm not paranoid." He hefted one of the boxes marked "books" like it was made of air. "I'm an ex-cop. So are you, if ever you remember."

Bobby was freakishly strong, with arm muscles the size of small children. I often cursed my genetics and questioned my masculinity around him, especially when we sparred. It made me want to drag Mike along with us, but my brother had fast fists. I'd take a pounding from him too, then afterward they'd bond over a beer.

We loaded up the truck quickly and tied the tarp down over the boxes and dolly. Passing through the gate, I snuck a peek at the sedan bothering Bobby. The driver and passenger were familiar, both stern-faced, sunglass wearing Asian men in suits. They watched Bobby's truck roll by, their heads nearly turning as one as we passed.

Much to Bobby's disgust, I did what any normal guy would do.

I waved at them and smiled like an idiot.

"Boy, I am disappointed in you," he sighed. "Why do I take you anywhere? Now they know we spotted them."

Needless to say, the sedan didn't follow us out of the parking lot. I sat back in the seat and helped myself to one of the last donettes, getting more sugar all over the floor mats. Motioning gallantly with my donut, I gave Bobby permission to drive on. "Home, Jeeves. We've got shit to dig through."

"You know," Bobby said through gritted teeth, "The longer I know you, the more I understand Mike beating the shit out of you when you were kids."

JAE-MIN was awake and drinking coffee when I strolled in behind Bobby and his trusty, box-laden dolly. I stole a kiss from Jae as I took the mug from his hand. He tasted slightly of my mint toothpaste. The gulp of coffee I took from his mug tasted like it could use more sugar.

"I can't believe you *waved* at them." Bobby'd grumbled nearly the entire way, and I'd kept quiet, silently gloating.

"I waved so they wouldn't pay attention to me taking a picture of their plate with my phone." I waved my cell under Bobby's nose. He mumbled something derogatory about me and snatched it from my hand. "I'm not totally stupid, you know."

"You act like it," Bobby replied. "I'll go call it in and see if someone can chase it down for us. Grab me a beer, Princess. I need one after spending the morning with you."

"He loves me," I reassured Jae, who stood in the doorway between the foyer and the living room. "Really, I complete his life."

"Huh." The look I got was a doubtful one, as if Jae didn't quite buy into Bobby's deep, abiding affection for me.

"Are you busy?" I lifted one of the smaller boxes and brought it into the living room. "I could use your help. Dae-Hoon left a bunch of notebooks behind, but they're all in Korean."

"And you want me to translate." Jae pursed his mouth and leaned against the doorway. "I'll need more coffee then. Is this how it's going to be? Every case you take is going to have something Korean that you need me to translate?"

"Just the ones with Koreans in them." I grabbed his arm before he could head into the kitchen. "Hey, I've got to warn you. There's some... stuff in these. Photos. Sex photos. I think one of the guys I saw is Scarlet's *hyung*. If you don't want to...."

"Cole-ah, I worked at Dorthi Ki Seu. I've seen... people I know do things." His shrug was nonchalant. "It won't be the first time. Since you took my coffee, I'll grab Bobby his beer while I'm in the kitchen."

He was stronger and more jaded than I ever gave him credit for. His sweet, pretty face hid some dark secrets, something I knew but kept shoving aside. Jae'd survived a hell of a lot more than I cared to admit. It was time I acknowledged that.

I still wanted to wrap him up in a blanket and keep him safe from the world. Fuck, if I had my way, I'd join him under that blanket, and we could just stay there until the end of time.

There were two boxes of notebooks. I pulled those out first and set them aside for Jae. The rest of it seemed to be books and personal papers. Thankfully, a lot of it seemed to be in English, so Bobby and I wouldn't be too useless. Bobby came back first, and he frowned, seeing me alone in the living room with the dolly full of boxes.

"Where's Jae? Do we have to get someone else?"

"Nah, he's probably grabbing us something to eat. He likes to eat when working," I said. "Well, he likes to have food around him. I haven't noticed him eating much of it while he works. Usually, Neko ends up eating the fishy bits, and then he picks at the kim chee."

"That shit's hot," Bobby muttered as he sat down on the short couch against the wall. I'd perched on the end of the longer one, standing up to help Jae with the tray of panchan and drinks he brought with him. "Speaking of hot…. Hello, Jae."

"Boyfriend," I reminded Bobby. "Mine."

"You going to let him talk about you like that?" Bobby teased Jae.

"It's the first time I've heard him call me his boyfriend," Jae replied smoothly. "I'll have to think about it."

Our eyes met. Mine were probably confused and a little bit apprehensive. His were unreadable. At least until he gave me a little smile; then they warmed up enough to make me want to drag him upstairs even with Bobby in the house.

"Focus, Princess," Bobby said, smacking me on the leg. "Happy time later. Right now, let's get this shit done."

"I'm that easy to read?" I asked.

"A blind man across the street can read you," Jae murmured, and he kissed me as he settled down on the couch beside me. "Let me see what's here."

The living room was quiet except for the sounds of us turning pages and the crunch of pickled vegetables being eaten. I'd offered Bobby a second beer, but he shook his head, telling me to bring him back a Coke. I brought back two and a refill for Jae's coffee. My lover mumbled a half thank you as he read, a frown wrinkling his eyebrows. I'd given him a small blank book to make notes in, and he wrote something down every once in a while, frowning more every time he filled a page. I peeked over his shoulder to see what he'd written, only to find it was in Korean.

"*That* does not help," I pointed out.

"I'll type it up in English later. Go back to what you were doing," he grumbled at me. "Or just go away. This is hard. Most of the slang he uses is old. I'm having trouble with some of the words."

The books were mostly useless, although one box held letters and family photos. I put those aside for Jae. A red-rope folder full of bills caught my interest, and I thumbed through them, trying to get an understanding of what Dae-Hoon's finances looked like.

"Shit, even his bank statements were in Korean," Bobby grumbled. "Yeah, I know, culturally insensitive, but damn it, this bank's on Wilshire. Would it have killed them to use English?"

"You're right. You're a dick. Some of it's in English," I said. "It's pretty easy to understand he was getting a lot more in than he was spending." The same entry appeared over several of the statements, spaced out every two weeks. "I'm guessing this is his paycheck. Jae, where does it say he worked?"

"He worked for Seong *hyung*," Jae said without looking up from his reading. "He was a liaison between the clients and the embassy. *Nuna* told us that."

"Of course he was," I said. "Wait, didn't Scarlet say he walked away from everything? Even his job? What? Six months before he disappeared?"

"Yes." Jae sounded annoyed, and he finally glanced up at me. "Why?"

"Because these deposits into his account continue up until he disappeared." I waved the pages at him. "Seong kept paying him… even after he quit. There's also other deposits, bigger ones."

"Maybe Seong felt sorry for him." Bobby peered over my shoulder and whistled at the amounts. "That's a lot of money for an unemployed guy."

"Damn, the little shit was blackmailing people. I can't find the November statement, but there was enough money in his account to set him up for a while. We'll have to find out where it went. The sons could have gotten it after he disappeared." I huffed and sat back. "I really wanted him to be a good guy. How the hell am I supposed to go back to Shin-Cho and tell him that his dad was shaking people down?"

"Gotta give it up to him for having the balls." Bobby drained his Coke and snagged the last piece of bulgolgi off the plate. "What's in the notebooks? His blackmail notes?"

"No," Jae said. "I don't know. It looks like he was writing a book... about being gay in Korea, but he uses names... real names. Maybe he was going to change them later?"

"Pretty dangerous thing to do: take money to keep quiet then spill it all in a book." I dug through the bank statements until I found the one for November. "When Dae-Hoon disappeared, he had several hundred thousand in the bank. What happened to it?"

"Easy enough to find out. Chase it down from the bank," Bobby replied. "We'll need to make a list of who donated to Dae-Hoon's little literary escapade. *Those* are the people we need to talk to."

"We will," I agreed. "Right after we talk to Scarlet. I want to find out if she knew about Dae-Hoon's extracurricular activities. She might not want us digging anymore."

"Like that's going to stop you." Jae snorted, and I lifted an eyebrow at him.

I shrugged off his disbelief. He was right. It probably wouldn't. This had gone beyond Scarlet, and I felt like I owed Shin-Cho the truth... or at least some truth about what happened to his father. Dae-Hoon could have ruined the lives of a lot of powerful men. For all I knew, someone out there knew he'd written everything down, and his sons might be the ones to pay for it, now that we'd cracked open the storage unit like it was the Ark of the Covenant.

"Can't hurt to ask," I said. "And you're right, babe. It's not going to stop me. Someone out there's got answers. We just need to find out who that is."

CHAPTER EIGHT

"HOW could he do this? We... were friends. Dae-Hoon...."

One of the constants of being a private investigator is being asked by a husband or wife to prove their spouse is cheating. In all the cases I've taken, I've never gone back to a client to say their spouse is faithful. I've had people deny the pictures I've taken are of their better halves. I've had people make excuses for their cheating lovers; hoping the person their husband is deep-throating is some long-lost, beloved cousin. I've also had people who silently take the photos and cry, their worst fears confirmed.

What it all comes down to is, people seek me out to prove something they already know. It's either a gut feeling, or red lipstick on a gay man's underwear. Either way, the brokenhearted spouse has *always* known. At least on some level.

I didn't know what to say to Scarlet. We'd put the photos and notebooks in front of her and broken her heart, fracturing the memories she had of a young Korean man she'd once loved as a dear friend. It sucked, and I had nothing to say to comfort her.

I couldn't even offer her tea.

I sucked at making tea.

"*Nuna*." Jae slid an arm around Scarlet's shoulders. "There's no way you could have known."

"But *these*?" She waved several photos under Jae's nose. "He... *took* these! Of me! And *hyung*!"

"People make mistakes, *nuna*," Jae said.

She'd hit anger, betrayal's stage two, faster than I'd expected. Like most things, Scarlet only did pissed off in the most attractive way possible. The tilt of her head and set of her mouth only showed off her elegant features and long neck. The flush of pink on her cheeks rose to a dark red, and her dark eyes flashed with fury.

Then any passing nod to beauty and grace went up in flames, as she spat out a string of Filipino so hot and complex I didn't need to speak the language to feel the hairs on my balls curling up in fear.

She was up on her feet, pacing the room to work off her anger. Still on the couch, Jae watched with some bemusement. I was glad he found it slightly funny. I was thinking of hiding the knife set in the kitchen, and possibly my hedge clippers, if I could find them.

I took refuge in my beer, sliding over to sit next to Jae. It was a calculated move on my part. She loved Jae-Min. The chances of something from my bookcase flying at his head were slim to none.

"*Nuna*, I have to ask you a few things." I caught Scarlet up short on one of her circuits. She turned, her anger only slightly abated. A lick of her tongue against her lips warned me of another spitting curse, but she held her tongue, cocking her head to stare at me with an annoyed look. "Please, sit down. Let's see if we can work some of this out."

She sat down on the couch next to the one Jae and I clung to. Scarlet was about to reach for her tea, then decided against it, snagging Jae's beer instead and taking a big gulp from the bottle. Jae and I silently exchanged looks. Then I handed him my beer since it didn't look like Scarlet was giving his back.

"Did Shin-Cho tell you about his relationship with Kwon?" I had to get that out of the way. I'd promised Shin-Cho I'd out his relationship if he didn't tell Scarlet, and I couldn't really go forward without her knowing. Especially since Kwon and his slimy, leering ways moved him up to the top of my knowing-what-happened-to-Dae-Hoon list.

Scarlet bit at her knuckles, lightly smearing her lipstick over her fingers. Blinking away tears, she nodded once. "Yes," she said, after she dropped her hand to her lap. "He told me yesterday. I wanted to talk to Sang-Min... to yell at him for everything he's done, but...." She shrugged helplessly. "After what happened last night, it didn't seem as important."

"Does *hyung* know about Kwon?" Jae asked, then sighed with relief when Scarlet shook her head. "Good. I think he'd kill Sang-Min if he did. I can't see *hyung* letting him get away with seducing his nephew."

"I'm going to be honest with you, *nuna*. It looks like Dae-Hoon was being paid to keep quiet about other gay men. We're still trying to figure out who he was extorting, but the list looks pretty extensive." I tapped the pile of notebooks. "Jae's coming up with a list of names. I'm hoping I can match them to Dae-Hoon's bank statements."

"I should tell *hyung* about Sang-Min and let him take care of it," Scarlet huffed. "We have so many secrets, Cole-ah. It's too heavy to carry. I don't tell *hyung* about Shin-Cho, and maybe he never told me about giving Dae-Hoon money to keep these... photos secret. How long do we do this? How much more can we carry?"

"*Nuna*, we don't know anything yet," Jae said. Neko padded in, jumping up onto the couch to see if there was anything she could filch from the coffee table. "Not about Dae-Hoon, anyway. Kwon Sang-Min—we know enough about him to make Shin-Cho stay away from him."

"To be honest, I'd hoped Dae-Hoon was still alive," I explained. "It made sense that he walked away from everything to spare his sons from... all of the crap that he'd have to take for being gay. Now, I don't know. Could someone have killed him over this? And I don't just mean Seong or Kwon. I mean anyone you might think could have done it."

"*Hyung* would never kill anyone," Scarlet whispered. "I would swear my life on it. Someone else? I don't know."

"Grace killed Hyun-Shik because he was gay," Jae murmured. Bringing up his cousin's murder wasn't helping matters. If anything, it fed into Scarlet's fear and anger. "I'd think what Dae-Hoon was doing would make someone want to kill him. Look at what happened to Shin-Cho. Dae-Hoon could have destroyed a lot of families if this had gotten out."

"We're going to have a list of suspects a mile long." The bank statements would take us some time to match up with the journals, but Jae was willing to dig through the papers to help. "*Nuna*, can you think of anyone that Dae-Hoon was afraid of?"

"If he is still alive, then that would be me," Scarlet growled. Jae murmured a small reproachful sound, and she sighed. "It could be anyone, Cole-ah. Most of the men here... in Los Angeles... chose to be here, but others are... in exile from their families... from their *chaebol* because they are gay or odd. *Hyung*... he wants to be here. There are fewer eyes on him in America, but at the same time, he will never rise very high in the family because of it."

"Then... why stay here? If he wants to...." I still wasn't quite sure how a *chaebol* functioned. It sounded like a bunch of families where the gene pool was shallow, and no one was allowed to swim in it. "His family owns a bunch of businesses, right?"

"Yes, and other interests," Scarlet replied. "If he were in Seoul, he would be expected to work for the family's companies, either as a department head, or even a chairman of one of the smaller businesses. Instead, he is here. The Los Angeles business is his, although it is connected to his family's. His influence is limited in Seoul, but here, with other Koreans, it is strong."

"And that's a bad thing?" I was still confused.

"Compared to what his family owns, his business here is... small," Jae explained. "He has sons. *Hyung*'s staying here so his sons can be a part of the *chaebol*'s influence, not just his business. It's better for them there. They have more opportunities."

"By staying here, away from Seoul, he protects his sons from scandal... any scandal," Scarlet said softly. "He protects his sons from me."

"You're someone he should be proud of." I reached over and touched Scarlet's hand. It was hard not to be angry, at least a little bit. I let it fill me for a moment before I took a deep breath. "I thought everyone knew about you... and him."

"Everyone close to him knows, but we do not... cross certain lines," she said. "And thank you. You're a sweet boy, Cole-ah."

"The party." I exhaled. "Jae said something about the party and the wedding being a place for... wives."

"It was... for *chaebol*," Scarlet replied. "His wife is in Seoul. If she were here, she would have gone. Society will only allow so much being shoved in its face. It's something *hyung* and I both know... both agree on. His sons have benefited from *hyung*'s older brother's guidance. Their uncle is seen as their main influence. In that way, any scandal that falls on *hyung* doesn't touch them."

"I kind of guessed that for Dae-Hoon," I said. "That's why I thought he was still alive. Now, I'm not so sure."

"We all have secrets." Scarlet sounded tentative. "But I still can't imagine anyone I know doing that."

"Doesn't mean they did it themselves. There's lots of people a guy can call up to take care of a problem. Murder isn't a new thing," I reminded them. "People have been doing it probably before there was fire."

"How about if I look through the list of men, and *nuna* can see if anyone jumps out at her?" Jae suggested. "Maybe that is someplace to start?"

"I have a couple of someones to start with," I said. "For one, Kwon. He had the most to lose. Secondly, and I hate to say this, but Seong is someone we have to look at. There was no reason for him to keep paying Dae-Hoon after he quit the firm."

"Unless *hyung* was doing it for his nephews." Jae cleared his throat.

"Probably someone else to add to the list." I began to write down a list of people to talk to. "Where is Ryeowon staying?"

"Near us. On Van Ness," Scarlet said. "Ryeowon didn't want to stay with us. Well, she won't stay with *hyung* if I am there. And he refuses for me to be anywhere else."

"Good for him. What about her husband? She remarried, right?" My handwriting suffered when I wrote quickly. At the rate I was going, I'd have to pay Jae to translate my own notes too. "Is the husband here?"

"Yes, he's here," Scarlet replied. "His name is Han Suk-kyu. He's a department head for the Seongs' media business. The boys went with her, but they came to visit *hyung* every once in a while. I don't think they're close to Suk-kyu. They're closer to *hyung*'s older brother, Min-Wu. I don't know about now... since what happened with Shin-Cho."

"Did David do his military service?" Jae asked. "Or are they going to try to avoid it?"

"Service?" I tried to remember what Jae told me about the Koreans and their military. "They have to enlist before they're what... thirty?"

"Yes, for almost two years." Scarlet drained the rest of Jae's beer and set the bottle down a bit too hard. The glass clinked against the storage chest I used for a coffee table. "David was in a skiing accident when he was younger. They won't take him." She shrugged and smiled sheepishly. "He has a rod in his ankle, I think. The alarms go off in the airport when he goes through. It's very embarrassing for him."

"Did *hyung* go?" Jae asked. His voice was soft, and there was something in his tone that I didn't understand. Scarlet didn't seem to have that problem, shaking her head emphatically.

"No, he didn't. The family... got an exclusion for him." Her hands needed something to do, and she picked up a bottle cap to play with. "Now, everyone is more likely to go. Before, for the *chaebol*, not so much."

Jae gave me an *I'll explain later* look, and I nodded. We had a lot of those kinds of looks, usually given to me when talking to Scarlet or his other friends. It seemed like a lot of my conversations with people Jae knew happened after they left.

"Do you want to talk to Seong *hyung* before Cole does, *nuna*?" Jae asked.

"Does he have to?" Scarlet blinked, and her eyes watered, threatening to ruin her makeup. She reached for a napkin and dabbed at her lashes. "No, no... I know he does. Yes, I'll talk to him first. I should talk to him first. At least... so I know... what he knew... what he did."

"Do you want me to stop?" I hated asking that, mostly because I'd hate stopping. "There are men who should... know about these books. Or maybe one who knew and didn't want it to get out."

A man was more than likely dead, and he'd left an array of victims behind, victims that should at least know their secrets were safe. But, in doing so, I was running the same risk as Dae-Hoon and opening myself up as a target. Someone in Dae-Hoon's many notebooks might have decided to permanently rid himself of his financial drain. Opening up old wounds and murder tended to bring out the worst in people.

"No, I don't want you to stop." Scarlet dropped the bottle cap and squeezed my fingers. "Someone should pay for Dae-Hoon's death if he is dead. I don't think the police would look into it."

"That's something else we still haven't looked into," I said. "If the cops were there at Bi Mil that night, someone might have seen something, or know about Dae-Hoon. Bobby's looking into that end of it."

"What happened to all the money? The money he got from the other men?" Jae mused. "Did his sons get it?"

"I don't know," Scarlet admitted. "Things were complicated then. It was easier to let the family deal with him being gone. I took care of his apartment, but I paid movers to pack everything. His wife... she'd already left for Korea. I don't know if there is anything in there his sons might want. If there is, please set it aside. It might help them now that... Helena is gone."

"We'll look, *nuna*," Jae reassured her. "Let Cole do this for you. He'll figure it out. I know he will."

IT WAS late by the time we bundled Scarlet up and headed home. My stomach was dead empty except for a couple of beers sitting there, and Jae's belly grumbled as Scarlet's car pulled away from the curb.

"Why didn't you tell her about the men in the parking lot?" Jae asked. "She should know someone was following you."

"Not until Bobby comes back with some info on their license plate," I replied. "Honestly, I don't know what to think about the car. It could be innocent, or maybe even some guys Kwon sent after me. Shin-Cho really fucked us over by telling Kwon."

"Huh." It was a neutral noise, one that said he wasn't ready to commit one way or another. I was very used to that noise.

His hands were shoved into his jeans' pockets. We were outside. Touching wasn't something we did when we were outside. The thing at the Kwons' was an anomaly, a step or five away from Jae's normal. It didn't mean I didn't want to touch him. He'd told me once he wished he felt safe enough to be touched. When he leaned against me as the car turned the corner, my heart sang like we were in an old black and white film's dance number.

It was stupid, but I grinned anyway.

The best part about my neighborhood was its mix of residential properties and small businesses. Old Laundromats were now restaurants, and some of the smaller homes were converted to shops, as in the case next door, a florist. A particularly enticing offering on my street was a tiny Italian café. It specialized in a Chicago-style pizza with enough cheese to choke a cow. The smell of tomato sauce, basil, and garlic tempted me.

"Want to get a pizza?" I knew what to say to seduce my lover. I was romantic that way. "Extra cheese and lots of mushrooms…."

"No pepperoni." He tangoed back, flirting with the offer. "Sausage."

I succumbed with a nod, then froze when Jae slipped his hand into mine. He took a step, but I was rooted in place, nearly jerking him back. He cocked his head, and I felt his fingers beginning to slip free, but I tightened my grip, stepping forward. "Don't let go, Jae. Okay? Just don't."

"I want to try to… be in your world right now," he murmured. "Just for a little bit. Okay?"

"Okay," I said as casually as I could. Mike left me a message while we were with Scarlet. He needed an answer about Jae or Maddy was going to kick his ass, because she needed to know how many people were going to be at her dinner table. "Mike texted me earlier. His parents...."

"Your parents," Jae interrupted me, sneaking a scolding look at me under his long lashes. "They are your parents too. Even when you're mad at them."

"Our parents," I corrected. "They'll be here tomorrow. He wanted to remind me about having dinner there. Guess he thought I'd skip town or something."

"You would," Jae replied. "It's a reasonable thing to assume."

"Because you know me so well," I snorted. We stepped around someone's plants they'd set out by their porch to water, avoiding the puddles as much as we could. "You'd also know I don't want to go."

"But, your sisters will be there, yes?" He quirked a grin at my sigh. "You should go. When is it?"

"Monday night." Sighing did not win me any sympathy, but it did get a chuckle out of him. "Do you want to come with me?"

That brought him to a standstill. His eyes narrowed, and another one of his noncommittal, semidisgusted noises escaped him.

"Why?" he finally asked.

"Why?" It seemed like an odd question. Why else would I want my lover to come with me? To share my pain and suffering. I was also more likely to keep my teeth gritted shut if Jae was there. I knew my limitations. "Why what?"

"Why do you want me to come with you? Do you want me there to support you?" Jae tugged on my hand when I tried to keep walking. "Or do you want me there to rub me in your father's face? Will he be nicer to you if I'm there? Or will it not matter?"

"Oh, trust me, he won't give a shit if the Queen of England was sitting down at the dinner table with us," I quipped. "He'd ask her if I could borrow her tiara, so I could put it on my faggy head."

"Then why go? Because of your sisters?" He'd begun chewing on his lower lip, a sure sign he was anxious. I wanted to kiss away the marks he was leaving, but we'd just graduated to holding hands in front of my house. If I kissed him, he'd run off screaming in terror.

"Because I promised Mike and Maddy I would go. Just like I promised Mike I'd see if you wanted to come too. I haven't seen Tasha since I left, and I've only seen the other two in pictures. Pictures Barbara sent to Mike, by the way." My eyes stung, and I blinked, biting the inside of my lip. Taking a breath, I continued. "I just wanted you there because... fuck, I need you there. Yeah, it's kind of to rub my dad's nose in shit. Mostly because I want to show him I've got this really great guy, and he can just fucking go to hell."

"You're asking me to sit there and listen to him hurt you then?" Jae asked quietly. "To sit at a dinner like that, and listen to him say things to you? I'm not family. I can't speak against your father. It's not... right, but it will be hard to just sit there. I don't know if I can."

"I'm also asking you to come to dinner to meet Maddy and my sisters," I pointed out. "But mostly, it's because I need you."

He stared at me. Jae stood there and stared at me, weighing me and judging me until I thought I'd go crazy in the silence between us. A car passed by us, and the man driving rolled down his window, slowing down. Jae flinched, and I held onto his hand tighter, refusing to let go. His face flushed, either with shame or anger. I couldn't tell which, but his fingers were still in mine when the car stopped by us. He was scared. The fear of being seen as a gay man rolled off him in waves.

I'd be damned if I was going to let go of him. If I had my way, I'd hold onto him until we starved to death.

"Hey, can you tell me how to get to the 10 from here?" The man frantically waved a piece of paper with a list of directions on it. "The damned directions say stay on Venice, but I got turned around."

"No, you're good." I nodded down the street. "Keep going straight until you hit La Brea, then turn. That's the easiest."

Jae's arm went slack while I finished giving the guy directions. He was quiet when I turned back to him, his teeth chewing on his lower lip again.

"Look," I said, stepping in close. I kept his hand in mine, holding it against my chest. His pulse raced under my fingertips, his heart pounding a mile a minute. "I know… this… being who we are… being *what* we are isn't easy for you. And I know I'm the first guy you're trying to be like this with—"

"Not the first," Jae murmured, shaking his head. "Hyun-Shik…."

His dead, somehow remotely related cousin. The same cousin who seduced him when he was fourteen, tossed him to the wolves to become a dancer at Dorthi Ki Seu, a private club that catered to closeted gay Korean men. The same cousin that entertained himself with male prostitutes working at the club, and was subsequently shot to death by his own sister for being one of those closeted gay men.

I *was* not standing in good company.

"Yeah, let's not bring him up right now." I sighed. "Jae—"

"Let me think about it, okay? About the dinner. About…." He clenched my hand tightly, then relaxed. "About this."

It was a fair thing to ask. I was being selfish. I knew I was being selfish, but when I read Mike's text all I could think about was Jae, and how much easier it would be to have him sitting next to me.

I didn't think about how it would be for him.

"Okay," I agreed. "We're still good for the pizza, right?"

"Yeah, I don't want to cook." He smiled at me, the same shy, almost goofy smile that tugged at me the first time I met him. "Too much reading. Not enough lazy time. I need more lazy time today."

"How about if we get the pizza to go, then?" I leaned over and lightly bit his neck, making him laugh. "I can give you a really good lazy time."

"That's never really lazy." The smile turned erotic, and he pulled slightly away, tugging me along.

"Sure it will be," I said, following. "You just lie there. I'll do all the work."

CHAPTER NINE

THE pizza ended up on the floor.

Or maybe the stairs. I had high hopes that it landed right side up on the side table in the foyer. With my luck, the box toppled over and hit the cat, who now was plotting her revenge while covered with stringy cheese and spicy tomato sauce.

We'd made it as far as the front hall before Jae slid his hands up the back of my shirt. They were cold against my warm skin, and I yelped, hunching my shoulders forward to get away. He retaliated by shoving his fingers down the front of my waistband and yanking me toward him.

Surprisingly, my open mouth made an easy target for his hot tongue.

Jae was a sleek, long pleasure under my hands. The buttons on his 501s popped free with a simple push and tug of my fingers, and we both lost our shirts someplace on the stairs. I didn't have to worry about shoes anymore. Having a Korean lover meant falling into the habit of leaving them by the front door. I was determined to do some research to see if I could convince Jae his culture actually demanded *all* clothes be left at the door.

Then again, if that happened, I'd never leave the house.

Somehow we made it to the bedroom without falling down the stairs and breaking our necks. I shut the door, leaving the cat outside to either continue with her world domination or feast on upside down pizza until she puked.

Pushing Jae back onto the bed, I grabbed at the ankles of his jeans and tugged, yanking them off quickly. A few seconds later, I was staring down at one of the most beautiful men I'd ever seen, sprawled out on my bed linens wearing nothing but a pair of black briefs and a wistful smile.

The briefs came off faster than the jeans did.

"*Agi.*" He reached for me, but I shook my head, pushing his hands away.

"No, let me look at you," I murmured. "Let me… taste you."

Jae's pale skin shone under the soft light. He was a contrast of cream and pearl against the dark-green sheets, with splashes of darker rose on his chest, his nipples hardening as I watched. His slender cock glistened at its wet slit, already damp from need. I was torn between smearing his seed over the bulb and watching him writhe, or licking him clean so I could have him in my mouth as I kissed his body.

I licked him.

And held an explosion of stars on my tongue.

I didn't want to swallow. Ever. But I did, knowing there'd be more. If I had my way, I'd die with Jae's taste in my mouth. It was scary, how fast I was falling… how quickly I'd fallen.

Fuck, it was going to hurt when I hit the ground. And fuck me if I didn't care.

I started at his thighs, hooking my thumbs under his knees so I could pull his legs apart. He resisted briefly, then let me in, with his shyness turning his face nearly as pink as his lips. There were times when he couldn't watch me love him; then there were moments when he was bold and needy. Tonight, he looked away, closing his eyes so his dark lashes shadowed his cheekbones.

I knew this side of Jae. Vulnerable, a little scared to trust, and trembling under my questing mouth and fingers. Stroking his thighs as they parted, I laid a gentle kiss on the tender skin above both his knees. He squirmed, and I nipped him, growling softly to keep him still.

Then he giggled.

It was definitely a giggle. Hardly a manly chuckle or a hearty guffaw. No, it was a bubbling pop of laughter he cut off by biting his lip and staring down at me with a barely repressed smirk. The honey gold in his eyes flashed, and Jae dropped his head back onto the pillows, his body shaking with mirth.

My tongue on his balls ended that quickly.

"Yeah, laugh while you can, monkey boy." I played with them, rolling one to the side with the tip of my tongue. My hands remained on his thighs, stilling his quivering with a firm touch. I teased him, never touching his cock until I crawled up to his belly. Then I only brushed my fingertips along his shaft before grabbing at his hips. Biting at the skin around his belly button, I murmured, "Stay still, damn it."

The rough and soft of a man's body was an erotic thing. I loved the heady scent of Jae's warm skin, and the rasp of his sparse body hair on my hands and mouth. Plum-colored nipples were a delectable treat, hardened to tight tips with a flick of my fingers. The muscles of his stomach jumped with every kiss I ghosted over his ribs, and the dark hollow of his navel was a thing of beauty, flat with a slight dip to it and a lip of skin begging to be gnawed on.

He was also slightly ticklish, so my mouth on his belly button made him squirm, even more so when I cupped him and squeezed lightly. I nibbled, taking my time with the taste of him, fondling him slowly. His hands drifted down to my shoulders, and I bit harder, loving the feel of his fingers digging into the meat of my arms.

"*Agi....*" he moaned, drawing out the word until it purred with a guttural growl. His teeth were making short work of his lower lip, and his knees were spread apart, his hips undulating to meet my fingers around his shaft. "*Now.*"

Some men enjoy teasing their lovers by drawing out foreplay and sensual torment. It was one way to go. Jae, however, was old enough to know when he wanted me deep inside of him. Since he also made most of my dinners and possessed sharp teeth he liked to bite with, I usually gave in.

Also, I'd be a fool not to want to be buried in my lover. The world tightened to a place where only he and I existed when I was inside of him, my arms wrapped around his body. There's only so much stupid I'll admit to, and teasing Jae when I could be loving him was a line I wasn't going to cross.

"Turn over," I said, rising up to kiss his nipples. "Hold onto the headboard."

He slithered up the sheets, getting on his knees and reaching his arms out to wrap his fingers around the top of the wooden headboard. Jae's movements were deliberate, graceful, and economical in motion. I'd reached for the handle on the nightstand drawer when the sight of him spread out and waiting for me made me pause. I was already hard enough that my cock was painfully aware when it brushed against the sheets. I didn't need to see Jae's head drop so his hair fell forward, or the slight pink tip of his tongue run over his chewed-on lower lip.

"Shut up," I told my dick. "We're getting there."

Sliding up the back of Jae's body, I reveled in the feel of his skin on my stomach and chest. The weight of him pressed back against my crotch made my blood sing. I bent forward when he tilted his head up, capturing his mouth with a fierce kiss. He tasted of citrus soda and cloves, a fragrant reminder of the Djarum Black he smoked while waiting for me to grab the pizza from the pickup window.

"I fucking love your mouth." I couldn't get enough of the taste of him. Even with Jae's tongue lapping at mine, I needed more.

"You can love it more," he teased, pulling at my lower lip with a playful nip. "Or you could love me more with yours."

Kissing down his neck, I skimmed my teeth over his shoulder and bit down enough to have his skin on my tongue. I swallowed, enjoying the flavor of his skin, and worried at the flesh I had in my grip. It would bruise, a light plum mark he'd wear hidden under his shirt, but I liked knowing he walked around marbled from my teeth.

"You like that?" I asked when he moaned in pleasure. "I know I do. I like tasting you. I love having you in my mouth."

I bit him again, harder, so he would feel it for days after we'd left our bed. Cupping my fingers, I pressed the furrow between his cheeks.

The skin gave beneath my touch, and I teased him, circling his entrance with a slow, wide arc meant to drive him crazy.

I must have succeeded, because Jae gripped the headboard tight enough to turn his knuckles white, and swore at me in a mingle of English, Korean, and what I suspected was Filipino.

Arching his back, Jae rubbed his ass against my hand, then pushed until it was trapped between us. "*Agi*, now. *Please.*"

I blindly searched for the bottle of lube I'd lost somewhere in the sheets. Of course, I found the condom first. I put it to the side, not wanting to lose it, then thought better of it.

I was a quick study on how to open and roll protection on with my teeth, and one hand. The foil packet went one direction, and the latex sleeve slicked over my hard cock before I'd taken a few breaths. I'd left off searching for the lube as I sleeved up, running my free hand up over Jae's shoulders and back to keep him hot and wanting. He twisted slightly when I touched him with my fingertips, his hips weaving away from me as I traced the bones of his spine.

"Taking too long." His words were rounding with his arousal, hollowing out his vowels and slurring at the ends. I loved making him so hot his English suffered. "*Aish....*"

The bottle was nearly under Jae's knee, sunk slightly into the soft mattress foam. I nudged him aside and pulled it free, kissing the small of his back to apologize for the delay. He made an impatient noise when I finally got the bottle open, the top loudly clicking when I pressed it down. The slick lubricant poured out onto my hand, and I spread it liberally over Jae to ease my way in. He shifted again, bending his knees slightly and angling his legs so he opened up wider to let me get him ready for me. I bit his right cheek when he growled at me again to hurry up.

"I don't want to hurt you," I said, licking the spot. I stared up the length of his stretched out body to his hands gripping the rail. "Well, not like that."

It was the most exquisite torture to feel Jae's body resist mine. His entrance pushed at me, like he pushed at me nearly every other minute of the day. Then suddenly the way was open, and I plunged into the hot depths of his core. I fought to go slowly, reveling in each pleasured hiss and strangled moan coming from Jae's parted lips. He'd dropped his head again, so all I could see was his hair and the curve of his neck, his shoulders tense with taut muscles while I worked in deeper.

I covered him with my body, needing to feel all of him on me. Beneath me, his ass flexed, taking me further in with each slow thrust I gave. It was an agonizingly sweet minute before my thighs met the backs of his legs, his tightness drawing all the moisture from my mouth and bringing my balls up to rest in the curve under my cock.

The laughter in his murmurs was gone, burnt away from the fiery need bubbling up inside of him. His shoulders hunched, and I met him when he thrust up, driving my length into his center. I fought to find purchase, first on his hips, digging my fingers into the sparse, lean muscles there, then edging up so my hands covered his, our fingers intertwined on the headboard.

"Want you," Jae hissed. Leaning his head back, he turned his face slightly so his cheek was against mine. Damp with a faint sheen of sweat, his skin slid over mine, the friction warming the spot where we touched. His breath was hot on my neck, filling the hollow of my throat. Every pant felt like a butterfly kiss on my skin, licking between my collarbone and jaw. "More, *agi*. More."

He said other things, but his English fell away under his rushing, guttural Korean. I didn't need to understand the words. I knew what he wanted. He needed to feel me stretching him apart, his body straining to take my width. I drove in hard, reaching past his entrance and into the depths where I knew his pleasure lay. Lifting my head and squaring my shoulders, I thrust up, searching for that singular place inside of him that would set him on fire.

I found it, and with a long, sizzling stroke, found it again. The sound Jae made tickled every nerve in my body. It was a low, sensual plea, reaching into my belly with its thundering need. I liked that sound. I wanted him to make it some more.

Jae, very thoughtfully and wordlessly, agreed.

His pitch changed when my pace picked up, and his fingers tightened around mine. So did his hold on my cock. Jae felt like velvet around me, and we soon found our rhythm, rising and falling together. The sound of our bodies meeting filled the room, a driving beat underscored by Jae's soft cries and the creak of the bed frame.

A bead of sweat dropped from my forehead and hit the stretch between Jae's shoulder blades. Bending my head down, I licked at it, rolling the mingled salt of our bodies on the roof of my mouth. The tiny shudders rocking Jae's body told me he was close, and the hot, mangled string of Korean he gasped out reassured me he was ready for my touch.

As I slid one hand free of the headboard, he hissed and grabbed a tighter hold of the other, keeping me stretched across the length of his spine. Undulating under me, he urged me to go faster... move in deeper... to do anything to ease the yearning tension building up in him. My captured fingers ached from his hold on them, but I refused to shake loose, wanting that simple touch when I drove him over the edge.

The head of his cock was slick with his need, and I took my time covering it with my palm. Wrapping my fingers around his shaft, I slowed my thrusts to tease his erection with every stroke of my hips. His cries turned raw, and Jae grunted when my fingertips found the thick vein running under his sex. He pulsed in my hand as his heart pounded blood through his excited body. I hooked the flat of my thumb on the ridge of his glans, pulling him off in a quickening stroke.

"Come on, baby," I whispered hoarsely. "Give it to me."

I felt him go over and followed him as closely as I could.

The world bled away, leaving me floating and only aware of the man who held me inside of him. His cock twitched in my hand; then my fingers were wet with his seed. I inhaled the pungent Jae-ness in the room. It blended with the musk of our sweat, and the citrus scent of the soap we'd both used. He clenched around me and murmured something sweet and cloying under his breath... something I didn't understand, but I felt it punch me in the gut with the fervor and passion he put into it.

I spilled into him, gasping when my own heat poured around me. Closing my eyes, I rode the shockwave rolling through me. My hips thrust again, driven by need and instinct more than anything else. Under me, Jae shuddered, and his sex crested again, filling my palm.

Letting go of his cock, I wrapped my arm around his chest and held him against me, my balls rolling up tight between my legs. Jae rocked still, milking the last few currents of pleasure from my sex. Panting hard, I continued to meet his thrusts, slowly bringing us back down from the clouds.

The sound of wood cracking was the only warning we had; then the rail gave way under our joined hands. Startled, I regretfully slid free of Jae's body and pulled him back onto me to keep him safe. The bed lurched forward, then tilted violently to the side. Another shattering crack punctured through our heavy breathing, and the headboard gave way, sending the mattress and box spring to the floor.

The jolt of the bed falling startled us, and Jae clung to my arm for the short, wild ride. Dust bunnies flew out from under the box spring, fleeing the carnage. I inhaled a mote or five, and coughed, jerking Jae with every convulsion. Lying on my side, I caught my breath and surveyed the damage.

"I think we broke the bed," I declared resolutely. The rest of the headboard chose that moment to finally give in to gravity, and its posts crashed to the floor. The footboard, resigned to its destruction, gracefully toppled down to the carpet, making a small thump when it hit. "Yep, pretty sure about it now."

"You'll have to get a new one," Jae said from inside my embrace. His breathing was still hard, gradually returning to normal, and his hair was damp, clinging to his forehead and cheeks. "I think we also have to change the sheets. Maybe even the pillowcases."

I shifted, and the moistness of the bed linens confirmed Jae's assessment. Murmuring my agreement, I lay with him in my arms, coughing again to get the grit out from the back of my throat.

"We could just leave it on the floor," Jae suggested, then looked at my face. "No, eh?"

"No. Where would I lose my socks then?" Our hearts were finally slowing down, and I grinned to hear our pulses catching the same beat. I didn't want to let him go. Especially not after having him open up under me. I kissed his forehead and sighed. "You hungry?"

"Yes, but food can wait," he purred, and shoved me over. I flailed and grabbed at the edge of the mattress. We were sticky and sweaty, so Jae slid over my thighs with a graceful ease. My cock protested a bit when he tugged it free of its latex prison, but recovered to stir feebly as his tongue licked around the sensitive head.

"Well...." I was going to play it cool, but my dick had other thoughts, stiffening when Jae's lips ghosted a kiss over my shaft. "Since we already broke the bed...."

Spreading his hands over my scarred chest, Jae smirked up at me and said, "Let's see if we can break the floor too."

CHAPTER TEN

MONDAY veiled the city in a chilly early morning fog, cloaking the neighborhood with a fine, opaque mist. The threat of rain hung in the air, a heavy water taint with a hint of asphalt rising up from the roads. I tossed one of my leather jackets at Jae before he headed out the front door. He caught it and quirked an eyebrow at me.

"I'm not a little kid," he said, tossing the motorcycle jacket back at me.

"It's cold," I replied, opening the door enough to let in a whip of wind. "'Sides, I like knowing you're out there with something of mine wrapped around you."

That earned me a skeptical look and a derisive snort. Some people get a good-bye kiss from their lovers before they go off to work. I get disdain, and if I'm lucky, a wet hairball in my shoe.

"Humor me." I held the jacket up, and after a moment, Jae slid his arms into the sleeves. Despite his broad shoulders, I was still bigger than he was, so the black leather hung loose on him. He looked young, a delectable study in black, ivory, and glittering brown eyes. I kissed him, bringing color to his full lips, and he let me fix the collar around his neck.

"You're silly." He leaned over to grab his camera case from the table by the front door. "I've got to go. I want this light."

We'd spent Sunday buying a bed, and then testing it out, finally admitting defeat at staying in bed all day in favor of Thai food. After the stress of Helena's death and being indoors for hours, Jae was ready to prowl through some abandoned buildings with nothing but his camera to keep him company. Checking his pack one last time, he snagged his keys from the hook on the wall and said good-bye to his cat lazing on the landing of the stairs. I followed him out, locking the door behind me, and spent a few moments admiring his ass as he loaded up his Explorer with his gear.

"Cole-ah, about tonight." Jae stopped and grabbed my T-shirt to pull me close. "At your brother's...."

"I'll tell him you can't come," I said, letting him off the hook. "You've had a crap weekend."

"No," He said, shaking his head. "Tell Mike I'll be there. I want to come to dinner."

"Babe, the last thing you need in your life is my father," I replied. "Really, it's going to be fucking shitty. He's going to be shitty. Fuck, I can't even promise he won't be shitty to *you*."

He looked at me with that odd look he sometimes got on his face. It was a look that made me doubt my age, because it was like staring down into a stone's soul.

"I'm not going for him," he murmured, tugging on my shirt. "I'm going because you want me to. I'm going because you need me. If you're going to stand in front of your father, I should be there next to you. It's only right. It's what you'd do for me. Call Mike. Tell him I'm coming."

The kiss he gave me guaranteed my coffee wouldn't need to be sweetened, and I stood there, numb and more than a little bit giddy, as he climbed into his SUV and backed out of the driveway. I got a wave. Then Jae was lost in the creeping fog, his car's rear lights disappearing in a slow red fade.

It was early, too early for Claudia to be in the office, so I spent a few minutes making coffee and checking the thermostat. The short walk from my front door to the office chilled me down to the bone, and the scars along my belly twisted and ached. I waited for the coffee machine to spit out its love for me, then filled a mug to take back to my desk.

I shot off a quick text to Mike's cell phone, telling him Jae would be at Maddy's dinner, and shoved aside my misgivings of taking Jae with me into the lion's den. I didn't pray. My connection with God mostly had to do with thanking Him for letting me find a cold beer in my fridge, or a parking space near the door during Christmas time, so I wasn't on any formal standing by any means. Still, I sent a heartfelt *Dude, don't let my Dad fuck this up* plea, and got to work.

Spreading Dae-Hoon's family pictures out on the desk, I compared the images of a smiling Korean man with his children against the lascivious images he'd taken of gay men having sex. Jae and I debated on whether to give Scarlet the pictures of Seong, eventually deciding to bury them as deep as we could. The youth in the picture appeared to be a young Scarlet, and despite Jae's assurances he could handle what he saw, his cheeks turned pink at the sight of his beloved *nuna* engaged in blurry carnal relations with her lover.

Still, even without knowing the men in the photos, I felt dirty looking through them. I was looking at someone's deepest fears and secrets. Even after all these years, the men in the photos still probably lived dual existences, jumping from one shadowed moment to the next to scratch an itch inside of them they hated.

I reached for the baseball I kept on my desk. It wasn't a remarkable ball, unsigned and insignificant. Rick, in some strange quirk of his nature, adored baseball. More importantly, he loved the Dodgers. He wasn't even from Los Angeles, or further back in the team's history, Brooklyn, but ever since he'd been a little boy living in Boonfuck Somewhere Else, he'd loved the Dodgers.

Couldn't tell you anything about the players, and sometimes got the rules wrong, but he loved that fucking team.

I'd sprung a few bucks, hard-earned bucks at the time, to get third base line tickets. As luck would have it, a foul ball popped up and straight into Rick's hands. His green eyes widened, a perfect match for his open mouth, and he held the ball up for me to see. Then complained loudly about how his hands stung from the ball hitting his palms.

It was one of the few things I had of Rick's life with me. His conservative family stripped our place of anything that remotely resembled him, including his dust-mop dog. Still, after all of that, I could say we'd lived our lives out in the open. Something neither Dae-Hoon nor his blackmail victims were able to do.

I still missed Rick. Some part of me would always miss him. I still absently bought Sweet'n Low when I went to the grocery store, even though no one I knew used it. I had four boxes of the stuff before I finally came to my senses and threw them out. I hadn't yet gotten out of the habit of buying creamy peanut butter, because Rick hated the type with nuts, and I still skimmed the airfare prices to Bora Bora for a fantasy vacation to a place I'd never had a desire to visit but was always somewhere he'd dreamed of going.

"Definitely not how I wanted us to end up, but we were okay, weren't we?" I said to the baseball in my hand. "With Jae, I've got to make some compromises. It's different from being with you. Not... you two are different. Wherever the heck you are, honey, I hope to God it's someplace you're happy."

Claudia came in while I was working on my second cup of coffee and a stack of Dae-Hoon's finances. It was a confusing mess of numbers, and one I was about to toss out the window. I'm sure the look of disgust on my face was comical, but not as funny as Claudia's double take when she saw me sitting at my desk.

"You look like you've been a busy boy this weekend. Is that your bed lying broken against the dumpster?" Her outfit that morning was a nod to the fifties housewife, a smartly pressed chartreuse number with large white buttons running up her generous bosom. If it was anyone else, I'd have said it was a great retro find. Knowing Claudia, she'd bought it new from Kress stores, or sewed it herself while fighting off zombie alligators with a butter knife.

"That color's nice on you," I said instead, and she smiled at the compliment. "And yes, that's my bed. We had... an accident."

"Last time I had that kind of accident," she remarked over her shoulder as she filled her own coffee cup. "I wound up pregnant with Malcolm."

"Yeah, as hard as I try, I don't think I'll be able to get Jae pregnant." I leered at her when she rolled her eyes at me. "Not like I'm not willing to try."

"You are a nasty thing this early in the morning." Sitting down at her desk, she fired up her computer and brought her cup up to her bright red lips. "Why are you here already? Got into a fight with your boy?"

"Nah, Jae got squirrelly. It's been a rough weekend." I told her about the shooting at the rehearsal celebration, and then discovering Dae-Hoon's blackmail empire. "So he woke up needing to go take pictures of old buildings. The fog made him happy. Something about the light."

"That poor kid." Claudia tsked. "Not Jae. Well, poor Jae for being there, but that David boy."

"Yeah, he looked shattered. Going to be rough for a bit. He'll do okay once he gives it some time." She gave me a sidelong look, and I raised my eyebrows at her. "What?"

"It's good to see you coming out of your funk," she told me over the rim of her cup. "Just saying, Jae's been good for you. First time I met you, I thought you were just waiting for Death to come for you."

"And still you decided to work for me," I replied dryly.

"You paid, and I was bored," Claudia pointed out. "You're better now. You even wake up before noon, and here you are in the office, and coffee made before I hit the porch."

"Don't get too used to it," I warned. "I'm lazy. I like sleeping in."

"I never denied you're lazy," she sniped back with a satisfied smile. "You just do more living now when you're awake."

I was spared the humiliating task of coming up with something snappy to say by my cell phone ringing for my attention. Scarlet's number flashed on the screen, and panic hit me. If anyone hated to get up before noon, it was Jae's *nuna*. Her calling me before the morning hit double digits would make a stone crack with worry.

"Morning, Scarlet," I said. "Whatcha doing up so early? Or haven't you been to bed?"

"It's not *nuna*." Jae's voice hit me harder than I expected. I must have made a noise, something shocked or panicked, because he quickly cut me off before I could form words. "She's fine. I'm calling on hers because I forgot to charge mine. It died right after I got here."

"What's wrong?" I swallowed the lump in my throat and waved away Claudia's offer for a refill. She frowned at me when she heard me speak, caught halfway between desks with the steaming coffee pot. "Are *you* okay? Where are you?"

"I'm fine," Jae said. A loudspeaker echoed near him, and the sound crackled over the phone line. "I'm at Cedars."

"What are you doing there?" I stopped to take a breath. He probably could get more out if I shut up and let him talk.

"Hold on, I'm outside." The chatter around him subsided, and I could hear his deep sigh. "Shin-Cho went out… looking for company last night."

"Did someone get a hold of him?" It was still dangerous for single gay men to be out on the streets at night. All it took was one or two assholes to scream obscenities, and the cops would be called to pick up the pieces of some unlucky guy who'd only gone out to get his rocks off.

"Yeah, kind of. He's been shot," Jae murmured. "What was he thinking? Helena *died* the day before, and he goes and does this."

"Everyone deals with stress differently, babe," I reminded him. "We were kind of doing the same thing ourselves."

"We didn't go out looking for it at a bar." Jae was more of a street kid than I liked to admit. He had no patience for people putting themselves into dangerous situations they couldn't handle.

Of course, he generally put me squarely in the no-street-smarts and stupid-situation category, but where Shin-Cho was concerned, I wasn't going to argue the point.

"What happened? How is he?" My stomach sank. "Is he okay?"

"He's still in surgery." It sounded like he was exhaling from a cigarette drag. "From what the cops said, he and some guy were behind the bar, and someone shot them. No one knows if it was a drive-by, or if the guy walked by. One of the guys working there found them when he went to take out the trash."

"Fuck. How's the other guy?" I was trying not to think of the night Ben shot us, but it was creeping in on me. The smell of blood clung to my memories, edging away the safe little life I'd built up since then.

"He was dead when the cops got there. I think *hyung*'s going to see if he can help his family." Jae's voice thickened with anger. "Why would Shin-Cho do something so stupid?"

"Because...." How did I explain desperation and emptiness to someone who'd been willing to go through life alone rather than be ostracized by his family? Jae liked sex. He seemed to love it with me, but we'd had to strike a balance with our time together and the feral independence he needed. "Because sometimes when you hurt, you don't want to be alone. Even if it's something as stupid as a back alley blow job. It's something."

"Could have gotten him into Dorthi Ki Seu," Jae grumbled.

"Sure, hook him up with a guy he's going to have to pay at a place where *nuna* works," I said. Sometimes, Jae's thinking jumped the rail, and I couldn't make sense of where it went.

"No one would have said anything," he shot back. "It's private, and they wouldn't be picking bullets out of him right now. And that other guy would still be alive."

"When did this happen?" I asked, changing the subject. "It's kind of late for a hookup."

"This morning. Early," Jae replied. "Like, three? I don't know. What time do normal bars close? I don't even know where it was."

"What do you need me to do? Does *nuna* need anything?"

"She's upset. *Hyung*'s here too." A siren popped loudly near Jae, and he waited a moment for it to die down. "Shin-Cho's mother is here. She came as soon as *hyung* called her."

"How's he holding up? David," I clarified. "First Helena, and now his brother."

"He's why I called you," Jae said. "He wants to talk to you. I guess Shin-Cho told him about their dad. Can you come up?"

"Now? Sure."

"David *really* wants to talk to you." I could imagine him giving one of his helpless people-are-crazy shrugs. "I think he needs to be able to… control something? Right now, everything is bad, so he needs to do something. Maybe he wants to tell you to stop looking for Dae-Hoon."

"Can't do that," I replied. "Scarlet and Shin-Cho hired me."

"I don't know, then," Jae admitted. "All I know is he's pacing back and forth. *Nuna*'s upset because Shin-Cho went out and got himself shot, and *hyung*'s grumbling because his sister's… well, it's hard being around them."

"And you're outside smoking," I added.

"Yes, it was either that or drink coffee," he grumbled. "They have shitty coffee. And the tea is black or bad herbal."

"Do you want me to stop at Starbucks?"

"Maybe stop at a liquor store instead." He took another drag, one hard enough for me to hear over the phone. "I might be ready to try being Irish again."

IT WENT without saying I hated hospitals. That being said anyway, I needed a few moments before I went past those sliding glass doors. It was times like these when I wish I smoked. If I'd been smart, I'd have taken Jae's advice and stopped for whiskey.

Still, it surprised me to find Scarlet lurking at the smokers' corner, wearing a beleaguered expression and a pair of six-inch black stilettos most women would think twice about wearing. Even in the bright light of day and dressed in a man's shirt and black capris, Scarlet looked like a torch singer. Her long black hair was up, with a few tendrils down around her face, and her blood-red lipstick left a promise on the cigarette filter, a promise a lot of men passing by were more than willing to take her up on.

"They'd be surprised at what they found, no?" she growled under her breath when I drew near. Taking one last drag on her cigarette, she snuffed it out in a sand-filled canister. "Do you think any of them would even look twice if they knew what was between my legs?"

The look on her face was ugly, a soured curl she wore to hold back the tears turning her eyes red. I didn't have a handkerchief to gallantly whip out to offer her, so I did the next best thing. I wrapped my arms around her and held her tight to my chest.

"Why?" She gripped my shirt, probably more to stop herself from hitting me than for support. I didn't have an answer for her. Mostly because I didn't really know what she was asking. "They hate me. They don't even know me, and they hate me."

"Seong's sister?" I guessed, and she nodded, sniffing into a piece of tissue she'd hidden someplace on her. I couldn't imagine where. Her capris looked like they were poured onto her tight body, and left to dry. Probably the shirt. "Fuck her. Baby, you're so much of a woman, you turn me off when I hold you."

Her laughter was good to hear, especially when it washed away the tears in her eyes. I got a fierce hug and a slap on the ass as a thank you. All in all, it was a good trade off.

"You are a good boy," she said, hooking her arm around my waist. "Your Jae is lucky to have you."

"Yeah, let's see if he says that when he finds out I didn't bring any whiskey with me." I used her for support to walk through the doors. My stomach clenched around itself, and my guts ached, threatening to disgorge my coffee on the lobby's marble entrance.

"He'll forgive you," Scarlet promised. "You make him happy. I forget sometimes. That's all a man really needs."

The happy man in question was waiting for me in a room crowded by Koreans. There was a clear divide among those gathered. One side of the room bristled mostly with the ubiquitous black-suited security and Scarlet's lover, Seong. Kwon was there, lurking near a brittle-faced older woman whose expression soured when she spotted Scarlet coming in with me. A man I could only assume was Shin-Cho's stepfather stepped up behind the woman and placed his hand on her shoulder.

If Seong had a hand in Dae-Hoon's disappearance, I was willing to forgive him, because he stood up from where he was sitting and held a hand out to Scarlet. She took it, and he pulled her into a passionate hug.

Jae stepped out from the cloud of black suits, his eyes narrowed with a slight anger. He was too controlled and distant to be hugged, not like his fiery *nuna*, but the desire was there. Our fingers brushed as he handed me a cup of the swill he'd disparaged earlier, and I let my touch linger on his skin. I didn't exactly grin when his cheeks went slightly pink.

Not exactly a grin. But close.

"Shin-Cho's out of surgery," Jae murmured. "He's going to be okay. The doctors are waiting for him to be settled before they let anyone visit him."

"By the looks of some of these people," I whispered into his ear. "I hope that's a very long time."

I spotted David sitting to the side, away from the fray, but still its poisonous tendrils crept over and consumed around him. He looked rough. That was the only word I could use. From the looks of things, he'd not slept since the rehearsal dinner, and knowing how he felt, I imagined he'd kill for a moment of peace.

David looked up when I approached, the wariness in his face fading away when he saw it was me. The poised, happy young man I saw at the wedding was gone, replaced by a grief-stricken man worrying if he was going to lose his brother as well. He glanced at the slightly crumpled paper cup he held in his hand. I wasn't surprised to see it was half-full.

"You're the man my brother hired, yes? Cole McGinnis?" David stood up and held his hand out to me. I shook it and nodded. "Thank you for coming. Kim Jae-Min said you would. You're a good friend."

"Yeah, I try to be. Hey, there's a coffee shop across the street," I said. "Since Shin-Cho's not going to be up for company for a bit, we can head over and get something decent to drink."

"I'd like that." He sighed and threw the cup away. "And while we're there, you can tell me why my brother is digging up dead men, and why Helena had to die for it."

CHAPTER ELEVEN

DOT'S COFFEE SHOP was a no-nonsense kind of place. The décor ran to white walls and worn Formica countertops, the gold-flecked kind, with a dented, thick stainless steel ring around it. The booths and spinning counter stools were red vinyl, cracked in places, and the larger of the rips were patched with duct tape.

Black-and-white tiles covered the floor, and a faded sign taped to the swinging glass front door announced an egg, bacon, and toast breakfast could be had 24/7 for just under four bucks. Its clientele ran to the tired and worn hospital staff running across the street in stained scrubs looking for something quick to eat while the booths were sporadically filled with sad-faced families or couples, their long vigils staining their face with fatigue.

David fit right in.

He ordered a large tomato juice with no ice and checked the level of the Tabasco sauce on the table. I went with the coffee and some sourdough toast. The waitress was an older woman with clearly no expectations of a large tip. From the looks of things, people who sat down at Dot's were doing so only to have somewhere else to wait. We weren't much different.

"Thank you again for coming. It's been… crazy," David said when his juice arrived in front of him. My coffee was quick on its heels, and we went through the motions of doctoring our drinks to our liking. I used cream and sugar. He loaded up on salt, pepper sauce, and a squirt of the lemon slice that came with the juice.

"I'm sorry about Helena. I wish there were more I could do for you there," I apologized. He shook his head, not wanting to touch on the subject. "I'm not sure what I can tell you. I was hired by your brother. Anything I've found out is confidential."

"I probably know more than you think. Shin-Cho told me he'd hired you, and you found out... things about our father. Very unpleasant things. I'm talking about the blackmail. Not the gay part. I've known about the last one for a long time, even though the family tried to hide it from me."

"Couldn't have been easy." It sounded to me like David was much more attuned to the family secrets than his brother. "From what Shin-Cho told me, he'd only recently found out."

"Let me tell you about my brother, Mr. McGinnis." He stirred his juice, more interested in swirling the salt crystals down into its depths than drinking it. "Shin-Cho might be my *hyung*, but he's always been... what the family calls fragile. They've taken greater care about talking in front of him. He does things without thinking them through. I've spent most of my life cleaning up after him."

David might have been his father's spitting image, but the cool, collected exterior he was showing me was pure Seong. It wasn't hard to see the thread of ruthlessness the family seemed to breed through their men. David finally took a sip of his juice, and set it down carefully before meeting my eyes.

"I already knew about the money. My stepfather told me before the... party," David announced. "*Hyung* talked to me about it last night. That's when I told him I already knew about it, but how my father got it... that wasn't something I knew."

"So you knew, and you didn't tell your brother? Kind of a big secret to be keeping from a guy who theoretically is entitled to half of what your father left behind."

"The only thing my father left behind was his two sons," he said firmly. "When I found out how he got the money, I knew it wasn't ours. It belongs to the men he preyed on. My father wasn't the victim here, not where the money is concerned."

"I'll give you that," I conceded. "But his disappearance does make him a victim if one of those men killed him."

"It would be best if my father stayed *disappeared*." The fatigue and anguish of the past two days were hitting him, and David fought to keep his words from running together. I pushed my plate of toast toward him, and he picked up a piece slathered with butter, biting into it with disinterest.

"Because he was gay?" I asked softly.

The look David gave me was nearly comical. It was a perfect blend of disgust and astonishment, before resolving to a scoffing dismissal. "No, for me, it's because he used those men. For the family, yes, because he was gay. For me, I don't know if I can forgive what he did to those other men. I just don't know."

Waving the toast point, he continued, "My brother has always idolized my father. They were close. Too close for the family to like. There are some people who worry that my father... that our uncle... influenced my brother to be the way he is. Some whisper behind our backs that my father touched Shin-Cho when he was younger, and that's why my brother has a hard time finding his way in life."

"Is that what you think?" I asked cautiously. Hearing David repeat the accusations that his father molested his older brother didn't jibe with the image of Dae-Hoon Shin-Cho gave us. Still, stranger things have happened than a son worshipping the man who betrayed his trust.

"No," David practically spat. "My brother is who he is because he's Shin-Cho. My father, my uncle, or even *hyung*'s lover has nothing to do with Shin-Cho loving men. But I can't protect him from the rest of the family. I made the family angry by asking him to be my best man, but he's my brother. Who else would I ask? He's my *brother*."

"He wanted to find out what happened to your father." My coffee was refilled by the same waitress, a ninja with a glass pot moving about the booths on crepe-soled shoes. "It doesn't bother you that Dae-Hoon walked away from his life?"

"Bother me?" David appeared to be thinking on it, then shrugged. "No, not now. Maybe when I was younger. Now, no. It was a long time ago. My uncles, the Seongs, raised me. I know it bothers Shin-Cho. He misses our father, but he's chasing a ghost. He's spent his life chasing ghosts. It's why I didn't tell him about the money as soon as I found out. I'd already angered the family. For once in his life, I needed him with me. I was getting married."

"How did your stepfather find out about the money?" I added more sugar to my coffee. "Did the bank contact him?"

"Han Suk-Kyu said the bank here contacted my mother a month ago, but since the money is my father's, it's really his sons'. Mine and Shin-Cho's. They were doing an audit of some kind and needed to update the account information. I don't have all the details. I found out about it before we… before the rehearsal."

I gave David some time to compose himself. He looked away and took a deep breath, blinking rapidly until his eyes cleared. Shifting in his seat, he began to play with one of the forks on the table.

"It's a lot of money." The vinyl on the booth seats squeaked as I leaned back. Even at minimal interest, after so many years, Dae-Hoon's account could be in the millions. "Why'd he wait so long to tell you?"

"Shin-Cho… he'd just left the military. Things were difficult. Han Suk-Kyu thought it would be a nice surprise, like a wedding present from my father, and something for Shin-Cho to use to get on his feet. He wasn't very happy last night when I told him I wanted to give the money back."

"How is the money yours?" I asked. "Your parents were still married when he disappeared."

"It's complicated," David said. "My mother remarried. In Korea, she doesn't have any claim to my father's estate any more. That includes anything he might have overseas."

"Did you talk to your brother about this? About giving the money back?"

"Yes. He told me about what our father did. I spoke to Suk-Kyu-ah after that." He sighed heavily. "My brother isn't… he doesn't make good decisions about his life. Look at last night. With everything going on, he left Uncle's house and went looking for… sex. Why? And why did Scarlet lend *hyung* his car to go out there?"

"Her," I corrected.

"What?" David cocked his head in confusion.

"Scarlet. Her," I repeated. "She prefers to be called her. We call her *nuna*."

We stared at each other for a long second. I hoped I'd improved my unreadable expression, but I wasn't going to bet on it. My own brother said I was the worst poker player in the world. More specifically, he said a kid hyped up on cotton candy had more control than I did.

David made a small sound and nodded thoughtfully. "Sorry, I think of her as a man. I'm not… used to all of this."

"No worries," I said, shrugging it off. "Takes a while. She was your dad's best friend. What he did came as a shock to her too, and I think she's sorry she didn't get to see you guys grow up."

"It sounds like a lot of people have regrets from that time," he admitted. "I can't take that money. It's got my father's blood on it. And I have to wonder if it has Helena's blood on it too. None of it made sense to me. Why would someone kill her? Then Shin-Cho told me about how my father got the money. Maybe someone he stole from was trying to get back at him through us."

"You think someone shot her to get back at your family for this?" I contemplated the possibility. "Unless they weren't aiming for her. She wasn't the only one hit."

The timeline of events lined up a little bit. Someone in Dae-Hoon's pictures could have known Han Suk-Kyu was going to tell his stepsons about the money, but if revenge was a dish best served cold, shooting Helena would be like a frostbitten TV dinner from the back of the fridge. It was a very roundabout way of getting back at someone, especially if that someone was Dae-Hoon, and not Kwon.

He could have fried me on the spot with the anger that flared up in his eyes.

"I know it's probably not something you want to hear." I leaned closer. "I'd like to agree with you that it's connected to the money, because it would make some sense of things. Hell, it could still be connected, but I have to toss it out there that she might not have been who they were aiming for. They could have been trying for you, or even Shin-Cho, and just missed. Hell, the shooting in the alleyway could be connected. It might not have anything to do with two gay guys making out behind a bar."

David looked away, turning the thought over in his head. His features were still, and his eyes grew distant. Finally, he licked at his lips and calmly nodded. "That makes sense. Especially if it was someone who lives here. Not everyone goes back and forth to Seoul like Uncle does. They can get to us now. Not like before."

"I'd suggest you take precautions," I said. "Even if we don't know for sure, it'll be a smart thing to do. Your uncle's got guys he uses. I can talk to him about getting some protection if you want."

"No, I'll be fine." David smiled. "It's funny. The family distances itself from Uncle because of... Scarlet, but he's the first one who offered to help after... Helena. And now, here with Shin-Cho, he's the one I can count on. No matter what happens between him and the others, I'm still his family. There's nothing more important to him than that."

"Yeah, I get that." I did understand what he meant. Maybe not to the depth that he and Jae meant it, but if I hadn't had Mike, my life would have been beyond shitty after my father kicked me out, and it would have been pure hell after Rick died.

His cell phone sang out a little tune, and David grimaced. Checking the message, he sighed heavily, and gulped down the rest of his tomato juice like it was a shot of moonshine.

"Shin-Cho's been moved. I want to head back over in case he wakes up." Putting down the glass, he dug out his wallet and put a twenty down on the table. "If Shin-Cho agrees, I'd like to know what you find out. Especially if... all of this is because of my father."

"I can't make any promises." I stood up to follow him back over. "It's up to Shin-Cho."

"That's fine," he said softly, and gave me a slow, assessing look. "I can't promise you what I'll do if you find out who did this. So we'll be even."

I DIDN'T stay at the hospital much longer after that. After checking in with Jae, I'd wanted to see about talking to Seong about Dae-Hoon, but Scarlet was against it.

"He didn't do anything," she insisted as I was getting into the Rover. "He told me he kept paying Dae-Hoon because *hyung* felt they were still family, so he was responsible for him. He didn't know about the blackmail. I swear to you."

Jae leaned over into my open window. We were close enough to kiss, so close I could feel his warm breath on my mouth. I parted my lips, taking what he felt he could give me, inhaling the kiss he couldn't give me. His lips quirked to the side, and he looked away, eyes shining with amusement. His fingers closed over my forearm, and he gave me a quick squeeze.

"I agree with *nuna*," he murmured under his breath. David's stepfather had followed us out, heading straight for the smokers' area to light up. He watched us from his spot under the canopy, the smoke from his cigarette flying away from his face as the wind picked up. "*Hyung* wouldn't hurt Dae-Hoon. Besides, everyone already knew he was gay. That's why he was sent to Los Angeles."

I nodded, but my attention was still on Han Suk-Kyu. When I'd come back from the diner, he seemed very cozy with Kwon. It could be my back was up where Kwon was concerned. He was a predator, and I didn't like him around Jae, but Jae could take care of himself. If anything, I pitied Kwon if he made a move on him. What Jae left behind, Scarlet would take care of. Still, Han Suk-Kyu's beady eyes followed everything Jae and I did as we talked.

"Watch yourself, okay?" I wanted to kiss Jae, so Han could see he was mine. It was childish and unnecessary, not to mention it would embarrass the hell out of Jae-Min. Once again, I reminded myself Jae was the source of cuddles and food. Not someone to piss off without just cause. "I'll see you at home?"

"Later," he promised. "Now that Shin-Cho's going to be okay, I'm going to head out to the old zoo at Griffith Park. The light's shot for the buildings I wanted to hit up this morning, but it'll be good there."

"Be careful," I said. He rolled his eyes at me and stepped back from the Rover. "Well, at least call me if you get arrested for trespassing. I'll bail you out."

In the end, I agreed with them about Seong. He wasn't at the top of my list of people who'd want Dae-Hoon dead. If anything, he seemed to be the one person whose life most closely resembled Dae-Hoon's. Except on all accounts, Seong's turned out much better.

Bobby's truck was parked in front of my building when I got back. I found him sitting in Claudia's chair with his feet up on her desk. I smacked his boots when I passed him, knocking them off. He swung an open hand at my ass, but I quick-stepped out of the way.

"You should shuffle that quick in the ring," he snorted. "It would save that pretty face of yours from getting banged up."

I debated another cup of coffee, but the pot was empty and the machine was off. Snagging a bottle of iced sweet tea from the fridge, I slid into my own chair and rocked back, popping open my drink. It was noon, and my office manager was nowhere to be seen. "Where's Claudia?"

"She went down the street to the farmer's market." He saluted me with a water bottle. "Said something about kale and strawberries. I'm holding down the fort. Not that there's a lot to hold down. Do you have *any* clients?"

"I'm picky," I sniffed when he snorted at me. "And fuck you. I did you a favor with Trey, and look at how that turned out."

"True," he conceded. "Trey's an asshole. Don't know what I was thinking. Kind of like when I do favors for you. Like finding an ex-cop who was there the night Bi Mil got raided."

"No shit." I nearly choked on my tea. "Is he willing to talk to us?"

"Yeah," Bobby said. "But it gets even better."

"Dae-Hoon's living in his basement?" I guessed.

"Not that good," he sighed, and shook his head. "He's gay, and would you believe, he hooked up with some Korean guy he met at the bathhouse. They've been together for years. He can meet with us tomorrow morning around ten. I promised him I'd bring doughnuts."

"Fuck me." I whistled. "I could kiss you."

"I'd take the fuck, but it would ruin our tragic and unrequited romance," Bobby drawled. "I've also seen Jae cut an onion. I'd worry he'd do the same to your balls."

"What makes you think it's going to be my balls he cuts?" I couldn't stop smiling. If the cop could remember anything from that night other than a big black car, it would mean a welcome break.

"Because I know your boy." Bobby rocked back and forth, making Claudia's chair squeak loudly. "If he got mad, he'd take revenge on you. Me? I'd be like the glass bottle on Trey's dick. Once it's broken off, it's just trash."

CHAPTER TWELVE

"HEY." I met Jae's gaze in the reflection of the bathroom mirror. Dots of shaving cream speckled my jaw, and I pursed my lips into an air kiss for him, only to get some of the cream in my mouth for my efforts. I made a face at the taste and spit out what I'd gotten on my tongue into the sink.

I'd spent the day successfully avoiding thinking about the dinner with my family, only to have it come rushing up to hit me as I stepped out of the shower. If there was one place I *didn't* want to be that night, it would have been Mike's house. I'd never been a coward, and running away from my problems, while attractive, never really solved anything, but pulling Jae into bed and staying there for a week sounded awfully good.

"Let me take a shower first. Then we can get going," Jae said, stepping past me. The towel around my waist grew uncomfortable when he began stripping off his clothes. It got worse when he slid his T-shirt off, and I could see the trail of bite marks I'd left on his shoulder and spine.

"Hmmm." I did my best purr and wrapped my arms around his waist, moving in close so he could feel my cock pressing up against his ass. "You know…."

"Out." His hands worked my arms free, and Jae turned around, pushing against my chest. "Go get dressed. I pulled some clothes out for you. They're on the bed."

The door shut in my face before I could protest my rough treatment, and I gave in to a small sulk. Luckily, Neko was in the same mood, and she mewed at me from her place on the bed, clearly disgusted by the presence of my pants and shirt on her lounging area.

I got dressed in the charcoal-gray slacks and dark-red button-up shirt he'd laid out for me. It would have been more comfortable going over in jeans and a T-shirt, but from the looks of things, Jae had other plans. I left off the tie. There was only so much dressing up I was going to do for my own execution.

Jae's keen gaze skimmed over the open collar of my shirt when he came out of the bathroom, but he didn't say anything about my lack of tie. He dressed quickly, much quicker than I would have liked, but I had no complaints at seeing him in black dress pants and shirt. To be a pain in the ass, I offered him the ebony silk tie he'd put out for me, but he slapped my hand away to go look for a pair of socks.

We were quiet leaving. I wanted to ask him about his day, the parts I hadn't been involved in, but Jae didn't seem in the mood to talk. Turning the CD player on, a whispering, sensual Korean song seeped out of the Rover's speakers. He smiled at the music, and his hand reached over to grasp mine. Talking was no longer important after that.

An unfamiliar sedan was parked on the circular driveway of Mike and Maddy's Hollywood Hills home. I pulled the Rover up behind it and turned off the headlights, leaving enough room to turn around if I wanted to make a quick escape. The garage doors were closed, effectively cutting off my sneaking in through the back door that connected the carport to the rest of the house. The sleek contemporary house was private, overlooking the canyons, and its large square windows were lit up bright enough to cast shadows on the front walk. I could see people moving around behind the sheer curtains on the lower floor, and I swallowed, bracing myself for the inevitable.

"It'll be okay," Jae promised me, brushing his hand across mine. "I'll protect you."

I laughed, imagining my slender, muscular lover standing up to a man who'd carried fifty-pound packs through jungles for a living. Still, it was easy to slide my fingers into Jae's grip, gathering strength by touching him. I rang the bell, and its cheerful toll chimed through the house. A few seconds later, Maddy opened the door, and I was lost in her tight hug, nearly dropping the bottle of expensive wine I'd bought to look civilized.

They'd just gotten together when Rick'd been killed, so to say Maddy had seen me at my worst would be an understatement. She gently bullied me through physical therapy, pointing out she'd done it as well, and kicked its ass. When a tall Nordic woman with a gap-toothed smile, and missing the lower half of her legs challenges you to beat her doing curls, no man with his balls in the right place would let her down.

I had my ass handed to me. Wrapped up in a pretty bow, and all.

Her short blond bob tickled my nose when I leaned in close. I thought I heard my ribs crack when she tightened her embrace; then she let me go with a hard slap on my ass. Maddy had Jae in a bear hug before I could warn her off, and he gracefully didn't growl or bite her. Her enthusiasm surprised him before his prickly nature could kick in, and she stepped back just as quickly as she'd snagged him, clasping him on the shoulders to get a good look at him.

"Oh, he's so beautiful, Cole," she crooned at me over her shoulder. Winking at Jae, she said, "It's good to finally meet you. Mike's told me *nothing* about you, and Cole's just as close-mouthed."

"Jae, this is Maddy McGinnis, scourge of fellow architects and runners," I said, waving my hand between the two of them. "Maddy, this is Jae-Min Kim, photographer extraordinaire, and a man with the poor sense to get involved with me. Don't scare him off. I haven't had him long, and I'd kind of like to keep him around."

"It's good to meet you." She finally let go of Jae, and he gave her a slight bow, tucking his shoulders in. "I'm glad you could drag Cole to dinner."

"He asked me," Jae murmured politely. "I only had to drag a little."

"I actually told him I needed him. He promised to hold the door open so I could bolt," I said. A pair of slim gray curves rested near the bench in their foyer. "Hey, are those new legs?"

"Yeah, they're made for running. Aren't they cool?" She grinned at me and tugged up her trousers so I could see her left foot. It curved naturally into a two-inch open-toe heel, ending with delicate crimson-painted toenails. "These are new too. They're adjustable, so I can wear flats or heels. I'm trying them out, but so far, I like them."

"And they fit into your legs?" I picked up the flexible curve by the bench. Its bottom was wider than her other running legs, made to slide into a knee socket rather than fitting into her leg connection. The foot attachment resembled a tank tread, and I tested its spring back on my hand. "I kind of liked the other ones."

"Those are for sprinting." She laughed. "These are for long distance."

"The other ones are these cool metal blades," I informed Jae. "I kept telling her to sharpen the edges so they were like knives, so when she ran, she could kick out and take people down like a ninja. She didn't seem to like that idea."

"People would tend to notice if I left legless people behind me when I ran," Maddy laughed. "They'd think I was contagious."

"Think of the terror you'd strike in the hearts of your competitors," I suggested, putting the foot down. "Mad Dog McGinnis, pestilence incarnate."

"You're silly," she said, taking the wine from where I'd put it down. "I'm guessing this is mine?"

"You think I'd drink something as girly as wine?" I fell into step behind her. Jae hovered by the door, and Maddy turned to look at him questioningly. I glanced back, and he looked down at his shoes, finally deciding to slide them off his feet.

"I feel odd walking into a house with shoes on," he explained to Maddy.

She laughed and nodded. "Hey, you're talking to the person who leaves her feet by the door. I understand. Come on in to the kitchen, and grab something to drink. Then we can go outside together."

The house was a canvas of crisp lines and retro furniture. Maddy's taste ran to an updated British Mod vibe. I asked Mike how he felt living in a set from *Velvet Goldmine*. He gave me a blank look, and said he didn't care what the house looked like, so long as Maddy lived there. That being said, I was shocked when he told me he'd replaced the kitchen floor. Neither the house nor Maddy were Spanish tile friendly.

So it was no surprise to see tatami mats covering the tile.

Maddy spotted me glancing down at the floor and shook her head. "We're not talking about it. I'm going to San Francisco in a week. It'll be gone when I get back."

I opened my mouth to speak, and she shot me a dangerous look. Holding up my hands, I begged off the scolding. "I was just going to ask where everyone was."

"Outside on the patio. Mike thought it might be better if we ate out there. The girls are using the pool," she said, softening her voice. "You ready for this?"

"Yeah." I helped myself to a beer from the fridge, offering one to Jae. Twisting open my bottle, I took a big gulp. "Let's go do this."

HE'D changed.

My boogeyman was slightly older, a little more wrinkled, and the brown hair I'd inherited from him was now shot heavily with silver. There was a slight slump to his shoulders, but they were as thick as I'd remembered. His Irish complexion ran to a ruddy bronze from the time he spent out in the sun, and the hair on his exposed forearms was nearly blond. I must have grown a bit since I'd left home, because I topped him by an inch or so, but from the belligerent jut of his jaw, I'd say he took it as a personal insult he had to look up a little bit to meet my gaze.

Oddly, as I stared at my father for the first time in over a decade, I couldn't pinpoint what I felt. The anger and confusion in my head seemed distant, an echoing refrain of a fight I could barely remember having. Behind me, I heard Jae asking Maddy about the succulents she'd planted on the hill behind the house, and the squealing laughter of the three young girls playing in the yard's brightly lit, black-bottomed pool.

His hard green eyes followed me as I walked across the patio, narrowing when I stopped to slap Mike on the back to say hello. They became slits when a slender, coltish teenage girl splashed out of the pool and slammed her soaking wet body into mine.

"Cocoa!" I didn't care that Tasha was dripping wet and my shirt would probably suffer from the chlorine in the pool water. Her arms came up around my neck, and I hugged her tight, lifting her off the ground easily. The tiny toddler who followed me like my own babbling shadow somehow had become a beautiful young woman.

"Hey, Tazzie." My heart seized up, and I found the air in my lungs too scarce to keep me alive. I closed my eyes and cradled her head, refusing to let her go until I'd gotten my fill of holding her.

It was Mike who broke us up, rapping me on the shoulder. "You need to meet the girls, Cole. Have Tasha introduce you."

Strange couldn't begin to describe how I felt being introduced to my own little sisters. They looked like echoes of Tasha, snapshots of ages I'd missed. The middle one, Bianca, was about twelve, and a bit owlish in round black-rimmed glasses, but her shy smile was welcoming. Unlike Tasha's waist length locks, she wore her hair in a bob similar to Maddy's, and judging by the hero worship in her blue eyes when my sister-in-law came out with a tray of food, she'd chosen her hairstyle to purposely emulate her idol.

"And this is Mellie," Tasha said, waving her hand in an elaborate flourish at the littlest one. Leaning in, she whispered into my ear. "I told them all about you, Cocoa. So don't try to pull any of your nose-stealing tricks."

"Hey there, Mellie." I crouched, so we were at eye level. She studied me with a serious intent only a five-year-old could give.

"My real name is Melissa," she finally announced, lisping through her missing front teeth. "Daddy says you're a fucking frigate."

I'd never actually been in a moment where the world stopped, and I could have heard a pin drop if there'd been one to toss on the floor. I definitely was in one now. It was kind of funny to see the reactions of everyone around me as they figured out the real word my little sister meant to say. There was a moment of comprehension, then a look of abject horror.

"Tasha, why don't you take your sisters and clean up so we can eat dinner?" Barbara limped carefully through the french doors off the living room. "Shower the chlorine off. You'll be itchy if you don't."

Tasha shot me a sympathetic look as she hustled our younger sisters into the house. Mellie went easily enough, but Bianca was a bit more reluctant, casting a soulful look back at the pool. I finally stood up, wincing at the twinge in my side as my scars feigned abuse.

Where my father wore the decade hard on his face and body, Barbara looked as if barely a day had passed since I'd last seen her. Her hair was different, a brighter blond and curling down to her shoulders, but her face was smooth, and with only a whisper of makeup to enhance her eyes. Leaning on a purple metal cane and dressed in a pink sweater set, she was a fine representation of the Junior League chapter she belonged to.

Seeing Barbara brought back memories of hot chocolate chip cookies and glasses of cold milk waiting for me after school, campouts in our backyard in a shoddily erected tent, and the first kiss I got from another guy, which happened, oddly enough, in the front seat of her Toyota.

Unlike my father, seeing her hurt, and I had to turn away, my eyes burning, because, just like the last time, she did nothing to defend me.

I needed air. Strange, since I was outside, but I needed space. Keeping my pace steady, I strode past Jae and back into the kitchen. He reached out for me as I went by, our hands brushing briefly. He cocked his head questioningly, then followed me, a lithe, fearless shadow I'd knowingly tossed into my own personal hell.

"Don't go after him, Barb," I heard my father say. "That faggot always ran from a fight. Why should now be different?"

Jae closed the door behind us before any more pearls of wisdom dropped at our feet. I leaned on the kitchen counter, pressing my palms on the cold granite top in the hopes it would cool me down. He placed his hands on my back, running them up my sides until they rested on my shoulder blades. Sighing, he leaned against me, pressing his entire body to my back and legs. We were still like that a second later when the back door opened, and I heard the distinct click and shuffle of someone walking with a cane.

"I'd like some time with Cole, please," Barbara drawled. "If you don't mind waiting outside, Mister...."

I turned around, hooking my arm around Jae's waist to keep him near. He quirked a sardonic smile at me and jerked his head toward the door, silently asking me if I wanted him to leave. Cupping his face with both of my hands, I brushed a gentle kiss on his full lips and murmured into his mouth, "Go on. I'll be okay."

She waited until Jae left before turning to me with a revolted look on her face. It soured the prettiness she cultivated, curling her upper lip in an ugliness I'd not seen before. "Did you have to put on that disgusting display? Or was that just for my benefit?"

"Actually, that was for my benefit." I was surprised at how calm I sounded. I didn't feel calm. I hurt. Deep inside of me, the anguish bubbled and simmered, finally coming to a boil to burn my throat and mouth. Staring at her, everything I thought I would feel for my father suddenly struck me full in the face, and I nearly reeled back, surprised at the bleeding cuts in my soul.

"Fucking hell," I laughed.

"Language, Cole," Barbara snapped. "I won't have you swearing in front of me."

"Oh no, but you won't correct my father when he says I'm a fucking faggot in front of my little sister? We all know what she heard. She's just too young to know the word." I cocked my head at her. She started to open her mouth, but I cut her off before she could say anything. "You know something, Barbara? I came here expecting a fight with Dad, and then I realized something when I heard Mellie. He *always* sounded like that. I wasn't really shocked. I shouldn't have been surprised when he kicked me out, but you... you were a huge fucking surprise."

"What would you have me do?" She leaned the cane against the back door and crossed her arms. I knew that gesture. I'd seen it often enough growing up to know she wasn't in a mood to discuss anything other than what I had to do to get out of trouble. "Did you want me to break up the family over your sickening habit? Would that have made you happy? Destroying the rest of us?"

"I'm gay, Barb," I snorted. "Not an addict."

"Did you think I wanted your sister growing up around that?" she pressed, tapping the counter with her long fingernails. "I needed to protect her from...."

"From what? Me?" I stepped toward her, and she jerked back, squaring her shoulders. The pearl buttons on her sweater trembled as she fiddled with her collar. "What were you protecting her from? Seeing me happy?"

"Is that what you are? Because from what Mike tells me, happy is not how he described you," she spat back. Her voice rose slightly, a trembling warble that promised angry tears were on the way. "You were gunned down by your own partner. You nearly died. You don't think that he did it because you're a homo?"

"And where were you?" I shot back. "Huh, *Mom*? Where the fuck were you when they were taking my dead lover away from me and leaving me nothing but shreds? I'll tell you where. Standing on that same fucking porch you stood on when Dad spat in my face and told me to get the fuck out."

"I will not stand here...." Barbara made to grab her cane, but I put my hand on its handle before she could reach it.

"And be spoken to this way?" I completed for her. "You know what hurts the most?"

She trembled next to me. A part of me cried at the thought of the woman who nursed me when I was sick being afraid of me, but the clarity of what Jae'd been telling me over the past few months finally hit me. His biggest fear was his family turning their backs on him, and some part of me denied it would ever happen. Probably because I'd denied it had happened to me.

"Fuck me," I swore softly. "I keep telling him I understood how he felt, and I had no fucking clue. Not until right now."

"Let me get past you, Cole. I'm going outside now," Barbara said tightly, reaching again for her cane.

"You were the *only* mother I ever knew," I whispered. "I don't remember my other mom. I never met her. I don't remember a time when you weren't my *mom.* I expected you to stand up for me. Because you're my *mom.* But see, you threw me away, Barbara. You threw me away like a piece of dog shit you found on your lawn. Like I was nothing to you. Like I *never* meant anything to you."

"You were never *nothing* to me," she replied softly. "I just can't... I can't have you be... that way."

"It's who I always was. Who I am," I said, letting go of her cane. "You were my mom. The person who was supposed to love me no matter what. I counted on you for that. I counted on you loving me, and you left me with nothing. If Mike hadn't... stayed with me, what the fuck do you think would have happened to me, after Rick died? I probably would have eaten my gun. I was that messed up. I fucking needed you then. If there was any time in my life when I needed you, it was then, but you never came. How am I supposed to come back from that?"

"It would have been easier if you'd died." She leaned over, and delicately hooked the cane's handle with her fingertips. Adjusting her cardigan, Barbara tilted her head up and stared me down. "I won't lie to you, Cole. It would have been so much easier, because now I have to deal with Tasha wanting to see you, and she's headstrong enough to be trouble if she doesn't get her way."

If she'd kneed me in the balls, I couldn't have been more surprised. I didn't have any strength left in me to breathe, and my lungs were growing tight.

"Your father is the one who agreed to her seeing you, not me," Barbara sniffed. "So be sure to thank him. I would hope you kept your perversions hidden when the girls are around, but I have a feeling it would be useless to ask you for that one small favor. So when you're done, please know I'm going to be the one who's going to be left cleaning up after you."

She was out the door before I could catch enough air to respond. Leaning against the wall, I stared at the googly eyed black cat clock Maddy hung in her kitchen until I was steady enough to walk. When I no longer felt the sting of razors in my gut, I headed back outside, smiling when Tasha wrapped her arms around me and called me Cocoa.

Jae's hand came up to touch the small of my back, and I felt him tremble through the contact. I didn't need to look at him to know his mouth was thin with anger. I reached for him, pulled him into a one-armed hug. I whispered that it was all right... that he didn't need to defend me against my father even as I understood he was torn by an ingrained filial duty. Leaning over, I kissed him to take in the unspoken words lingering on his tongue.

The spiced caramel taste of him was enough to wash away the bitterness of Barbara's words.

My father's snort of disgust only sweetened the taste of Jae in my mouth. I would spit in the face of gods to hold onto my lover. Spitting in my father's face wasn't even on the short list of things I would do for Jae.

Tasha bolted to find a bathroom free of younger sisters, and then Maddy turned, tilting her chin up in a stubborn display of defiance. As gay as I was, I could see why my brother fell in love with her. All she needed was a fat pony, blonde braids, and a horned helmet, and I'd have fallen to my knees and sung *Die Walküre*.

I'd fear for my dick if she ever gave me the filthy look she gifted Barbara. My balls whimpered just being in the collateral damage range.

Maddy's legs murmured tiny clicks as she approached me. Hugging me tightly, she gave me more of the incredible strength I'd already taken so much of after Ben shot me. I didn't need the whispering affirmations she gave me, but they were nice to have.

Nearly as nice as the raging fury banked in Mike's eyes. His face was flat, without any expression when he faced our father and said, "This is the last time either of you are coming to this house. The girls... they'll always have a place here, but from this moment on, my front door is closed to you."

"You're going to throw away your family over a faggot?" My father's words weren't a shock. If anything, they were a balm over the raw wounds Barbara left on me in the kitchen.

"That faggot *is* my family," Mike snarled. "You, sir, are not."

I MADE it about half a mile before I had to pull over. I'd held it together through the dinner, knitting my mouth into a smile, but it was a brittle, ashy thing plastered onto my numb face. Rounding the corner, Mike's house finally disappeared behind us, and I lost it. Tucking the car into a lookout offering a view of downtown Los Angeles, I left the Rover running and finally broke down. I hunched over the steering wheel and let the fragile wall I'd hidden behind all evening fall.

My tears hit hard and fast, pinpricks of pain stinging me with each drop I tried to blink away. My heart felt like it was throwing up glass, bleeding out from a thousand tiny cuts sharpened by Barbara's coldness. Jae-Min reached over and gathered me close, murmuring something I couldn't understand, but his warmth reached down into the iciness she'd left behind. I let myself be tugged over, rocking in his arms as he cradled me through the worst of it.

I don't know how long we stayed there, the engine running and the lights on, but the windows were fogged over when I finally was able to look up. His face was as wet as mine, and I touched his cheek, hating that I'd brought him so much pain.

The smile he gave me chased away the last of the demons stabbing my guts, and I hugged him, not wanting to let him go. He kissed my face and wiped my tears away with his shirt sleeve. Pulling me over to the passenger seat, Jae got out and went around to the other side of the car to get in.

"Let's go home, *agi*," Jae whispered, patting my leg before putting the Rover into drive. "I'm here, Cole. I promise, okay? I'm here."

CHAPTER THIRTEEN

"RISE and shine, Princess." A gruff voice broke through the comfortable darkness around me. "Time's a'wasting, and we've got places to go."

I mumbled someplace tight and filthy Bobby could shove himself into, but he didn't take my advice to heart. Instead, he yanked the sheets off my naked body, and his broad hand struck my right cheek. The burn hit quick, and I sat up, trying to keep the weight off my sore rear.

"What the fuck?" I bared my teeth and hissed, rubbing at the massive palm print welting up on my ass. "What the hell do you think you're doing?"

"Waking you up, so we can go visit William Grey in Pasadena." Bobby grinned mischievously and eyed my naked body. "You know, kid, I've never really taken a good look at you. You're pretty hot. Even when your eyes are swollen shut."

I resorted to the classics and told Bobby to fuck off before sliding off the bed. Stumbling to the bathroom, I recoiled like a B movie vampire when I hit the light switch. Dragging myself under the full glare, I stared at the wreck of my face reflected back at me in the mirror.

Bobby wasn't far off in saying my eyes were swollen shut. I looked like a badly made-up version of Charlie Chan's mother. My hair was wild, sticking up around my head as if trying to run away from my brain. Considering the night I'd spent, I didn't blame it for wanting to check out of the Cole motel.

I'd woken up sporadically throughout the night, startled awake by my own thoughts. Every time I emerged from the terrors stalking my dreams, Jae was there, his arms wrapped around my chest and one leg draped over mine. Feeling his heartbeat against my ribs calmed me, and I soon drifted back under, only to wake up an hour or so later. It was a lather, rinse, and repeat cycle, but eventually my brain kicked in to the fact that Jae wasn't going anywhere, and I fell off into a deep sleep.

Until Bobby's hand met my ass, and now I wondered if I was even going to be able to sit on that side of my butt for the next few days.

The shower took care of most of my aches, including a blast of cold water to bring down the sting on my ass. Best part about sharing a shower with Jae-Min was smelling like him the entire day. Down side, my dick reacted to Jae's scent on my skin, and I spent most of my time telling my little head to get a hold of its craziness until we saw Jae again.

My little head mocked me, listening about as well as my big head did.

A beaten-to-hell vintage Dr Pepper T-shirt hung from the hook on the closet door. It would have been easy to miss except for the bright neon-pink Post-it Note safety-pinned to it. Even though Jae's sharp black writing took up most of the paper, the square's color burned my eyes more than the bathroom lights did. Grinning, I undid the pin and set the note free.

Wear this. I wore it last night to sleep, Jae wrote. *That way, you'll have me around you today. See you later for dinner.*

"Our Jae-Min," I told an uncaring Neko sprawled on the bed I'd vacated. "He is silly."

"Do you want coffee now, or drive through?" Bobby shouted from downstairs. "Never mind. Fuck it. Drive through. I'm not waiting for the coffee to brew. Hurry your ass up, Princess. I need some joe."

"Yeah, he says that when he's picking up guys at the bar too," I muttered at the back of Neko's head. "Except he's screaming for Dick instead of Joe."

Bobby waited until we'd gotten coffee and were on the 10 before his patience wore off. Glancing quickly at me, he set his paper cup into the truck's cup holder and said, "You wanna talk about it? The dinner?"

Who the hell in their right mind ever wants to relive the fight where they get their teeth kicked in and they choked on their own blood? I slurped a sip of latte from my cup and shook my head. "Nope."

I'd spent enough time talking. Lying in the dark with Jae's hand on my chest, I'd spilled out everything poisonous I held inside of me. My throat closed up from choking back tears, and in the quiet between my confessions, Jae held me as my body fought to get rid of the toxins injected into me by my ex-mother. When I'd finally exhausted myself, he'd offered no platitudes or there-there babies. Instead, he'd come back from the bathroom with a damp, cold washcloth and wiped my face clean of the salt crackling my lashes and cheeks.

The silence comforted me more than words. His warmth became the light to keep the monsters away, and now as I sat in Bobby's truck, I felt the slither of his hands on my skin as the T-shirt I wore moved against me.

"Not... now," I offered Bobby. A true friend knew when to push and when to back away. Bobby was a true friend. He only grunted and nodded as he drove.

"Just let me know," he said finally. "I'll get some whiskey, and we can go drive to the beach to scream at the ocean."

"Deal," I agreed.

By some benevolent fluke, the 10 was relatively clear of assholes and traffic. The construction was still there, metaphorical logs damming the stream of cars as if placed there by psychotic beavers. This being Los Angeles, freeway construction was an ongoing evil. It was a giant game of Russian roulette, played with a Californian's drive time and the gunpowder bursts of rain to delay progress.

We hit the 110 in no time at all, and meandered through the winding, haphazard freeway's curves with ease. Bobby sang along with George Thorogood as he drove. My coffee was still hot when the 110 ended abruptly at Pasadena's South Arroyo Parkway, beginning the whispers of its love-hate affair with Los Angeles.

I'd long since come to the conclusion that Los Angeles wishes it could wipe Pasadena off the map. They bicker and fight like wild dogs or, rather, in Los Angeles' case, a pack of wild dogs against an old, white-muzzled Chihuahua. When people think of Los Angeles, a certain idea comes to mind: a myth of fast-moving cars, bouncy women, and ritzy lifestyle LA works hard to maintain. The city itself consumes the smaller cities around it, slowly absorbing communities' identities until they start referencing themselves by their proximity to Los Angeles itself.

Pasadena, through sheer stubbornness, refused to give in to Los Angeles' greed.

And man, that pissed Los Angeles off.

Rather than allow its smaller sibling its own identity, Los Angeles spent over a century choking Pasadena's lifelines. Until recently, getting in and out of Pasadena was a bitch, and even now, connected to other freeways besides the clogged, two-lane 110, the sleepy city under the mountains was treated like it would take a mule train and five months' rations of food to get to. Tell the average Angeleno you were heading to Pasadena, and they'd kiss you on both cheeks and tell you to suck on a lime to avoid scurvy—once they were done trying to cover their look of horror and asking you if you had to visit a dying aunt.

Personally, I think Los Angeles is pissed off about Pasadena's Rose Bowl, and looks for ways to stomp on the smaller city's toes as often as it can get away with.

Bobby turned right onto Green and swore loudly, hooking the truck over to the left lane. I tried not to laugh, but a chuckle worked free, and he glared at me as we sat at the red light.

"Hey, I make that mistake all the time," I apologized. "Easy mistake to make. Colorado. Green. Not like Colorado's a big wide street that everyone uses."

"How'd you like to catch the Metro back to your house?" Bobby threatened. "Better yet, I can drop you off over by Mount Wilson, and we'll see how you laugh your way from there."

Bobby's grumbling only made me laugh harder, and he blew out his cheeks like a puffer fish. Pointing at the light tree dangling above us, I nudged him. "It's green, dude. Kind of like the street name."

"Fuck you, Princess." There wasn't any heat in his swearing, just enough of a bluster to tease, and I settled back into the seat, watching Pasadena crawl past us.

The Boulevard was a sparkling testimony to Pasadena's mildly eclectic, semi-granola culture, a mingle of coffee shops, high-end department stores, and posh restaurants. Hints of old money and conservatism reared up in the flocks of smartly dressed men and women lounging about with nothing to do but sip tea and gossip. A life of leisure was something to aspire to, and Pasadena was more than willing to offer it to those who could afford it.

Hardly anything remained of the tragic face the city wore during years of encroaching gang violence. Hardly anyone now spoke of the Halloween Massacre, but the heavy police presence along the main strip told everyone Pasadena didn't forget, and would gladly rise up again to smack down anyone who threatened its idyllic existence.

Much like its crotch-grabbing and raspberries at its bigger, grumpier sister-city, Pasadena had no tolerance for anything eating its way out from the inside. I liked that in a city. The weather still was too hot in the summer and sucked frozen donkey balls in the winter, but it was a nice place as cities went, and not without its attractions.

I spied the Cloak and Dagger bookstore before we hit our next turn. Bobby followed my gaze and murmured, "Ever go in there?"

"Yeah, it's a nice place. Mostly mysteries, I think," I said, remembering the last time I'd made it out to Pasadena. "Guy who runs it is fucking hot."

"*That* makes me almost want to take up reading as a hobby." He laughed, and the traffic in front of us thinned enough for us to make a right turn. Checking the directions on his GPS, Bobby turned left again, and found a spot to park on a wide, tree-lined residential stretch.

The houses ran to large Craftsman-style bungalows with dark-green lawns. Colorful flowerbeds edged the walks and wound up toward side-yard gates like rainbows after a storm. One house had a toddler's three-wheeler next to the front door, but that was the only sign of a kid on the block. Bobby's mud-splattered truck seemed slightly out of place in a neighborhood of BMWs, but it was tough and held up its massive head as best it could.

We walked up to a tidy-looking triple-peaked house with a covered porch that ran along the entire front of the building. The door opened at the first knock, and a veritable god stood in front of us.

He was older than Bobby by a few years, but from the muscles moving under his fitted T, there was no evidence he was slowing down. If anything, William Grey looked like he could still go out and kick ass if ever there was a zombie invasion in his neighborhood. Movie-star handsome, his silver hair was thick and cut into a boyish tousle that fell over his forehead. His bright blue eyes lit up when he saw us, and he stepped back, his bare feet squeaking slightly on the polished wood floor.

"You must be Bobby Dawson," he said, holding his hand out for Bobby to shake. I introduced myself, and his hand covered mine in a firm grip "Come in."

The interior of the house matched the outside, soft furnishings that whispered of a soft, comfortable life. Something familiar filled the air, and I sniffed, catching a whiff of the spicy red sauce Jae liked to cook with. William motioned for us to sit down, and offered a round of iced tea or coffee.

"Tea would be great. Thanks," I replied. Bobby murmured his agreement and sat down. I wandered.

A baby grand piano took up one side of the long room, and I drifted over, examining the photos set up on its glossy black top. They seemed fairly recent, showing William with an Asian man near his age, smiling and hugging at various locations. Sometimes other people joined them, but predominantly, they depicted either William or the Asian man.

"I don't add sugar, so I brought some so you can add your own," William said, coming back into the room with a tray. He spotted me by the piano, and for a brief second, his smile softened wistfully. He nodded his chin toward the large black and white photograph I held in my hand. It was a sweet picture of him and the other man kissing in the rain. "That's one of my favorites. Charles hates it. He said all he could think about was he was going to drown from the water running up his nose."

"Get your ass over here, Cole, so we can let Grey get back to what he was doing," Bobby growled at me.

"It's okay. It's a slow day for me. Charles is at work. I'm just cooking dinner, and it's in a crock pot." He shrugged and sprawled back into a wide chair. "If anything, I was curious about what you were doing. When Mark called and asked if I would talk to you, I was surprised to hear someone was looking for Park Dae-Hoon."

"You knew Dae-Hoon?" I picked up a tumbler of tea and sipped at it before adding some brown sugar. I tried not to get excited about the prospect of another person who might help us track down what happened. That pipe dream was quickly shattered when William shook his head.

"I knew of him," William said carefully. "I'd forgotten about him until yesterday. He went missing at a club, or something. The shields were floating a theory that he'd been killed, but no one turned up anything at the time."

"The trail must have gone cold quick," Bobby said. "Especially since he wasn't American."

"We had other things to worry about then," the man admitted. "LA was a shit hole to work in. I transferred out here to Pasadena. At least the city out here was doing something about the crime rate. And honestly, it was easier on me and Charles. People out here tend to mind their own business. I did the rest of my time and got out. Charles found a teaching spot at CIT, so life's pretty good."

He told us everything he remembered about that night, which wasn't much. The most notable thing he remembered was the arrival of several long black cars. "It was like the Secret Service arrived."

"Were you inside?" I knew what Bobby was saying. So did William.

"You're asking if I went in and cracked heads like the rest of them? No, not that night," he admitted. "But, I had before. I'm not proud of it but... what was I supposed to do? You couldn't run the risk of someone finding out you were gay back then. I know some guys who got it much worse than some panties in their locker. There were a lot of cases of blue on blue back then that the brass ignored, because as far as they were concerned, some faggot got what he deserved. The thing with me and Charles was new. I wasn't going to fuck it up."

"Yeah, we know about that kind of shit." Bobby shot me a glance.

I shrugged. Hell, if Ben shot me because I was gay that would at least have made some sense, but he'd known since we'd first met. Why wait years to put holes in me? Killing Rick was as stupid. They'd spent hours together watching some game on the tube and drinking my beer. As conspiracy theories went, it was weak to think Ben was luring us into a false sense of security only to ventilate us in front of a restaurant.

"Charles is from LA too?" I asked.

"No, he's from some place in South Korea. Um, Gangnam-gu in Seoul." William took a lemon slice and squeezed it into his tea, rattling the ice around with a spoon. "He came over after his family found out he was gay. His brother... um, Dae-Su... pretty much smuggled him out before they could do anything drastic to him. It's not... good to be a homosexual in Korea. He hasn't been back since."

"He's Korean?" I glanced back at the pictures. "He didn't like his Korean name?"

"No, nothing like that." He smiled. "He just wanted to put it all behind him. He thought it would be easier to do that if he took a more American sounding name, so he chose Charles. After a few years, he got his citizenship papers and changed his name officially to Grey. Well, now he's Doctor Grey, so he's slumming it by sticking with me."

Curious, I asked, "What was his name before?"

"Bhak Chi-Soo." William laughed at Bobby's grimace. "Yeah, I like Charles too. Do you know a lot about Koreans?"

"His boyfriend's Korean," Bobby replied. "With a better name, though. How about if we focus on what we came here for, kid?"

"Sorry," I apologized. "It was a long day yesterday. My brain's not all here."

I took notes as William talked, but my mind kept wandering off. After scribbling down the names of other cops that were there that night, I looked up. "Did you see Dae-Hoon at all? Or just the cars?"

"I might have seen him." He looked slightly surprised to come back to that point. "I did see several young men getting in the cars. Um, one was alone. There were men in suits around that car. It was gone before we started taking down details."

"There weren't any records of Dae-Hoon's arrest?" I asked, flipping through the notebook. "The report said there were what, twenty men taken in that night. Seven went to the hospital for injuries sustained during their arrest. Dae-Hoon doesn't appear on either list. We know he was there that night. We have a witness placing him there, but no one saw him get out. Could someone else have snuck him out without the cops knowing?"

"I don't know," William said. "It was pretty crazy, and I was outside. He could have gotten away in the confusion."

"The problem we're having with that is he never surfaced again," I said. "No note. Nothing. Either someone killed him, or he walked away."

"It *was* easier to disappear back then," Bobby pointed out. "Not a lot of the people-tracking we have in place now."

"He wasn't a citizen. He was like Charles, coming over from Korea on a visa. He'd need help to drop off the face of the Earth." I frowned at my notes. Everything we chased seemed to come to a dead end. Even the money trail left us nowhere. Dae-Hoon took nothing from his accounts, leaving a small fortune to his sons. "He left a lot of money behind, and didn't make arrangements for it to get to his family. Why would he stockpile the account and not make sure his kids got it?"

William frowned. "Dae-Hoon left money behind? Wouldn't his bank have contacted his wife?"

"She was gone from the country almost right after he went missing," I said. "The bank didn't even know he was missing. They kept rolling over his accounts until recently. I guess if I were a bank guy, and I had a multimillion dollar account no one touched, I'd keep my mouth shut too. Looks good on the books to have that in the assets column."

"Bobby said he had kids... sons," William said, leaning forward. "They must be pretty old by now."

"Yeah, one of them was going to get married this past Saturday," Bobby murmured. "Some fucking asshole shot up the dinner. His fiancée died."

"Damn." William inhaled sharply. "I read about that. Fuck, it was one of his kids' girlfriend?"

"Yeah." I nodded. "A day later, the older brother was shot outside a gay bar. He's pulling through, but kind of going through the same shit Dae-Hoon did. The family doesn't want his gayness touching them. Those kids have some fucked up life right now."

"Are they doing okay? The sons?" He placed his tea down, missing the coaster he'd pulled out to protect the coffee table from moisture.

"As well as can be expected." I explained the situation about their mother and stepfather boycotting the wedding, but coming to Shin-Cho's side following the shooting. It hurt more than I'd imagined, talking about it. I kept thinking back to the days I'd spent lying flat on my ass in the hospital hoping the next person who opened the door to my room would be my father or Barbara. "He'll have some scars, but he's doing good. His brother's strong. David's got a good head on his shoulders. He'll take care of his older brother."

We talked briefly about anything else William remembered, but my notes were lean of anything worthwhile. He saw us out with a promise to Bobby to hook up for some fishing at some later point. Bobby unlocked the truck, and I climbed in, sliding the seat belt over my chest.

"That was a waste of time," I grumbled. "Unless there's something he's not telling us."

"I think Dae-Hoon had help getting out of there," Bobby remarked. Turning the truck around, we headed back to Colorado. "There's no way he'd have been missed by the cops that night. From everything I've read, it sounded like they were shooting fish in a barrel."

"So someone there that night knows what happened to Dae-Hoon." I mulled it over. "Another cop?"

"Or maybe even someone he was blackmailing," he said. "Dae-Hoon might have thought he was safe because they knew each other, but the guy might have had other plans. Think about it. The guy shaking you down is there, and cops are bashing people's heads in. How hard would it be to convince some scared young man that he was safe?"

"*Just follow me, and we can get out of here?*" It sounded plausible. "You know what we haven't done? Run the list of Dae-Hoon's victims against who was arrested that night. Betcha there'd be someone there who might have seen something. He'd know Dae-Hoon. Shit, I'd want to keep an eye on the bastard blackmailing me. He'd be the first person I noticed when I walked into the room."

"That's what I love about you, Princess." Bobby grinned. "You've got some brains to go with that pretty face. Not a lot, but enough to make me not want to drown you. Let's head back, and find out who was there and dancing to Dae-Hoon's tune."

CHAPTER FOURTEEN

THE worst part about being a private investigator is holding your pee while waiting for a guy to crawl out of some other guy's wife's bed. The suckiest thing after that is digging through mounds of paperwork for the one tiny item that will prove you've got something to chase down. With arrest reports of nearly thirty men, Jae's notes from Dae-Hoon's journals, and the names of men off the bank statements, we were definitely in a previously unknown second circle of Hell.

"Can I be racist?" Bobby asked wearily. I didn't know how he'd gotten the arrest records, but I wasn't going to argue about privacy laws or any other nonsense. I needed to find out what happened to Dae-Hoon. Screw anything else.

"Sure, go ahead." I stretched, rocking back in my chair.

"So long as you don't cut up any of my good sheets to put over your head, I don't care," Claudia interjected, staring at him over the rims of her cats-eye glasses.

Bobby grunted at her in agreement and waved the report he'd been going over in the air. "Why the fuck don't these people have more than seven last names? And all the first names are the same, just jumbled around. It's like trying to figure out who's who at a fucking twins' picnic."

"I don't know if that counts as racist," I replied. "I think it was kind of set up that way. I'll ask Jae, but I think some emperor did it. Or I might be confusing that with the writing system. I don't remember."

It seemed like hours before we hit the last pile, but it was worth the effort. In the end, we had five names that matched either the journal or the bank statement to an arrest report. We'd gone through five pots of coffee and a few orders of Thai spring rolls, but those five names were like finding gold.

"Okay, I've got a date." Bobby stood and stretched. His spine crackled when he twisted from side to side, and I teased him about getting old. "Still got enough in me to see you in the ring tomorrow."

"Nope," Claudia announced. "He's not going to get beat on until the doctor says he can. I'm not spending my days in here smelling that ointment he uses when he's hurt."

"Nice, now you've got a woman protecting you, Princess," Bobby teased, dancing out of Claudia's reach when she leaned over to slap his legs. "Hey now, watch the goods. I've got plans for that later."

"I'll watch your goods," she grumbled at him. "Go wash your cup out. I'm not your maid. I didn't pick up after any of my boys. Don't think I'm going to wipe *your* ass."

"Yes, ma'am." Bobby saluted her.

I gathered up the trash to take out to the dumpster while Bobby washed up. I turned off the lights and held the door open for Claudia to go ahead of me. She stopped to grab her purse and was nearly on the front porch when I heard someone coming up the steps.

"McGinnis!" I knew the skinny guy now standing on my porch. I would probably never get the memory of Trey's masticated dick out of my head, but it was better than ever having it in my mouth, even before the glass bottle chewed through it. If anything, he looked rougher and more strung out than he did when I'd left him in Urgent Care. He waddled a bit, bouncing around on the balls of his sneakers. A sour smell rolled off him, and his pupils were large, swallowing up his irises.

"Go home, Trey," Bobby said, pushing lightly at the kid's shoulder. "You're tweaking."

"I want to talk to Cole here about my dick," Trey slurred, spitting as he spoke. A speck got on Claudia's bare arm, and she looked down at the drop in disgust. "What are you looking at, bit—"

My hand was around his throat before he could finish what he was saying. Squeezing until he choked on his own tongue, I leaned in until we were nose to nose. "You *ever* talk to her like that around me, I'll tear off what's left of that fucking dick of yours and feed it to the cat. Got it, *bitch?*"

Trey gurgled, and I shook him, waiting for his face to turn beet red before I pushed him away. Putting his fingers to his throat, he bent over, gasping for air. If he could, he'd have boiled me alive with his eyes. "What are you going to do about my dick?"

"Probably nothing," I drawled. "I didn't put your dick in that bottle. You did. Shit, you weren't even paying me to be there. If anything, I should sue you for mental trauma, but any judge who met you would tell me I should have known better."

It was late afternoon, and people were coming back from work. The occasional car drove by, some slowing down to park at one of the restaurants to grab dinner or coffee before heading home. It was something Claudia and I didn't pay attention to. It was a natural part of the day, kind of like the morning screaming of I love yous from the couple across the street as they drove off to work.

I didn't notice the small two-door coupe slowing down in front of my building. My focus was more on Trey, and dislodging his barnacle ass from my front porch. If push came to shove, hopefully one of Claudia's mountainous boys would be by soon, and the three of us could hold him until the cops came. My first choice for his jailer was Bobby, since he'd gotten me into this mess to begin with.

Trey was hit first. One moment I was looking down at him, and the next I was eating pieces of his hair and bone. The shots were loud, echoing, and bouncing back against the buildings around us. Bullets tore through the thick wood posts holding up the porch roof, and I felt the sting of something crease my back.

I stood there, waiting for more bullets to hit me. I was back at that damned restaurant, wondering why Rick stopped talking… horrified when his body started to come apart in my hands. Any moment now, I'd go under, submerged in my own darkness and pain.

"Get down!" Bobby screamed.

His shout broke me from my memories, and I dove to the ground. Claudia'd gone down awkwardly, and she moaned, curled over onto her side. Bobby's hands were under her arms, and he yanked hard, trying to get her to cover. His shoulder was bleeding, but from the looks of things, it wasn't bad, just a graze.

Things were happening too quickly to do anything more than react. I grabbed Claudia around the waist, careful to keep my head down, and heaved, dragging her behind the hip-high broad stone wall I'd opted to close in the porch sides. Trey's body twitched and flailed on the steps, his limbs refusing to believe his head'd been blown clear off his shoulders.

My ears were ringing, and it took me a moment to realize the shooting had stopped. A siren was circling in the distance, and I heard a babble of screams coming from the street. One high-pitched screech was making my head hurt as the woman kept keening and yelling about going after the car.

The scars along my side were protesting the rough treatment, and they seized when I tried to sit up. My shoulder barely whispered a complaint, and I sent it a silent thanks. My back was sticky when I drew my hand across where it stung, but the blood was only a smear, not a gushing wound I had to worry about.

Claudia was a different story.

There's a point when fear is actually painful. It starts with the tightening of gums, as if my teeth were trying to escape the emotional horror that was coming. Following that, my stomach tries to flee, turning inside out like a ravenous starfish. Bile filled my mouth, and I swallowed wrong, taking the acid into my lungs and searing what air I had left inside of me.

I couldn't move. Even as I watched Bobby work on Claudia's chest and stomach, I was frozen in place. Her rosy complexion was ashen, and her hand was freezing cold when I squeezed her fingers. I was like a little kid again. Jostling her shoulder, I begged for her to wake up, promising anything I could just to see her open her eyes.

"Hold it together, Cole." Bobby's gruffness snapped me back into focus. "Fucking don't fall apart on me, man. I don't need that shit right now. Put your hands on her chest and push in. We need to keep the bleeding down."

She was soft, a pillowy woman whose core was harder than steel. Other than Bobby and Mike, she'd been the first one I'd opened up to, after the shooting. Even Maddy'd taken a bit of time before I warmed up to her, but Claudia'd strolled into my heart, and threw open the windows I'd hammered shut to keep the light out like I was something that just needed a good spring cleaning. It wasn't the first time I'd touched her, but it was the only time when she hadn't hugged me back.

That's how Claudia's son Marcel found us, our hands clasped over his mother's lifeless body, trying to hold her together. He'd come to pick up his mother, something the brood divided among themselves, so everyone could have that half-hour drive alone with the woman who was the center of their family.

His scream was a horrible thing, anguished and tearing, drowning out the ambulance's sirens rounding the corner. His howls lasted seemingly forever, and we fought to have him give us space to hold her together, but he wouldn't let go.

It took both of us to pull him off her, and even then, it was a mean struggle. The EMTs were brisk, a crack triage team who had her hooked up to strings of plastic tubing with blood and fluids before I could find my voice. A gurney whisked her into the back of the ambulance, and Marcel stumbled around, mutely holding onto Bobby for support. Our hands were covered in Claudia's blood, and the cops were beginning to tape off the front walk, keeping the onlookers from strolling up the cement path to take a closer look at the dead body on my steps.

I sat down on the hard ground, hitting the dirt and grass with my clenched fists. The tears I'd been too scared to let go finally came, and I bit my lip, sobbing in hitched breaths as uniforms began corralling people who'd seen the car flee. My fingers trembled when I dug out my cell phone, and I swallowed, unsure if I could even speak as I dialed. A soft voice answered on the second ring, amused and affectionate in my ear.

Shaking, I struggled with what to say, then finally gave in to my fear and pain. "I need you, baby. Please... just come. Claudia's been shot, and... I need you. Bad."

THE hospital waiting area looked much like it did when we visited Shin-Cho, except for the sheer bulk and noise of the people gathered there. Unlike the nearly wake-like atmosphere around Shin-Cho, Claudia's clan gathered as a wall of strength. A few were standing together, praying with their heads down and hands clasped around each other's waists. A man I didn't know stood with them, clutching a bible in one hand as he led them with a sonorous, flowing voice. In a corner, a couple of toddlers played on the carpet, watched over by a teenage boy who'd not yet grown into his feet.

I did a fast headcount, then lost track of the final number just as quickly. Most of Claudia's sons were there, as well as wives and grandchildren. I recognized some of them, but others were strangers, including a small Asian woman sitting beside a large, grieving dark-skinned man. She ran her hand over his bald head and gave me a tiny smile when I walked into the fray.

I made it three steps in before someone who looked like Malcolm came up to me and put his hand on my chest. I had to look up to meet his angry eyes. Most of Claudia's brood and sub-brood were taller than me by five inches or more, a mean feat since I topped over six feet in my socks.

"Get the fuck out of here." He chewed his words, spitting them out at me in a rapid fire burst. "You're the reason Nana's here."

"Sit down, Gareth, and that's your one warning about swearing." A petite black woman in a sleeveless dress scolded the young man. "You're making a fool of yourself. Your grandmother would want him here. Don't make me slap some sense in you."

He glowered at me for another moment, then shuffled off to stand against the wall with other members of his herd. They gathered around him, either offering support for his speaking up or chastising him for being an ass. It was hard to tell with the worried looks everyone had on their faces.

"Hey. Good to see you, man." Martin, Claudia's oldest, approached me. Drawing me into a bear hug, he squeezed what little life I had left in me, after seeing his mother shot. I felt like a child standing next to him, and if he'd wanted to, I was pretty sure he could pop my eyes out of my skull just by slapping the back of my head. "Momma's doing okay. The doctors say she was lucky. The bullets didn't hit anything they have to worry about. They're taking them out now."

"Thank fucking God." I reeled back with relief. Just as quickly as I spoke, I deflected the sharp looks I got from most of the adults with an apology for my language. "I'm sorry about this, Marty. I really am. I'll take care of all of this. Promise."

"I know, dude." He grinned down at me. "You're a good guy. Hell, Momma says you're the kid she had with the ice cream man. "Come on. Sit down. We're just waiting for the doc to come back and tell us where they're going to put her."

Next to me, Jae was eyeing the massive collection of Claudia's legacy. He edged closer. I didn't blame him. Emotions were running high, and there was no guarantee that we'd make it out the doors before some pissed off Claudia-kid tried to rip our heads off. He hovered, finally perching on the arm of the chair one of the grandkids had been told to give up custody of so I could sit down.

There was too much noise around, and it was too hot. Every few seconds, someone brushed against my leg or arm. With each passing second, my skin grew tighter around me until I felt like I couldn't breathe. Something horrible was working out from deep inside my chest, and I rubbed at the scars on my side, willing them to stop rippling spasms through my torso.

I didn't realize Jae'd stood up until he tapped me on the shoulder and crooked his finger for me to follow. I looked around, not wanting to leave the room in case someone came with answers to questions I couldn't even voice. He silently insisted, sliding his hand under my upper arm and pulling me to my feet.

"Come on," he murmured into my ear. "Let's go outside for some air. I asked Martin to call me if they find something out."

It was a shock to see the night sky. I don't know what I was expecting. Maybe some part of my brain was willing time to stop, but the world didn't care that one of the women in my life was bleeding out on a table somewhere. Around us, people were shuffling into the hospital, intent on their own business. An older couple passed by us, carrying flowers and a bunch of balloons shouting "Congratulations" across their Mylar skins.

"I should get some for Claudia, flowers or balloons," I mumbled, looking down. I was still wearing the Dr Pepper shirt, its hem soaked up with dried blood. My jeans were speckled in places, and while I didn't remember falling to the lawn, I must have, judging from the ground-in grass stains on my knees.

"Maybe without 'Congratulations' on them, though," Jae said softly. "Unless getting shot is something like a McGinnis skills test. I can't see you getting a lot of employees if they have to be shot at least once in order to work for you."

I couldn't hold back a laugh. It sounded rusty and painful, but it was still a laugh. "Sometimes I forget you've got a sick sense of humor."

"I use it sparingly," he said, nodding. "It makes it more special."

"Oh, it's special all right," I agreed. "Hey, did you talk to Bobby?"

"Yeah, he's coming by in a bit." Jae shuffled his feet and jerked his head toward the smokers' circle. "Come on, keep me company."

We kept to the far side of the area, straddling a bench so we could face each other. He drew out a *kretek* and lit it, pulling a mouthful of fragrant clove smoke into his lungs. I stared at him until he shifted uncomfortably under my gaze, but still he said nothing, shooting me an odd glance once in a while.

He was still the exotic creature I'd first seen at his relatives' house. A quiet, conflicted young man who, I'd since learned, laughed softly and cuddled a miniature furry tornado to his chest as he worked on his computer. Looking at Jae still took my breath away, but now I could see the man beneath the beautiful exterior. He didn't use words to tell me what he thought, usually letting small things speak for him, like a morning cup of coffee waiting for me when I stumbled into the bathroom before heading to work. I understood the wildness inside of him, that driving, passionate need to prowl through dark and abandoned places, to capture pieces of art only he could see.

It was that deep passion he drew on when he took me inside of him, sometimes riding my hips and bruising my shoulders with his clenching fingers. It ran in him, unseen by most, and I was humbled to be included in the tiny circle of people he let in.

"Don't ever change," I murmured, leaning forward to kiss him before he could take another drag on his clove. "Just be you."

"I have to change," he said, returning my kiss with a fierceness that made my heart beat faster. "But it'll be for the better. For us both."

"Thought I'd find the two of you out here." Bobby broke the moment, and Jae ducked his head, suddenly aware we'd kissed out in the open where people could see him.

Bobby put a hand on my shoulder and squeezed. He'd grabbed spare clothes from someplace, probably the back of his truck, because the bright blue shirt had JoJo's gym logo emblazoned across the front of his chest. Tossing a plastic grocery bag at me, he said, "I brought you something to change into."

"Huh." I held up a gray shirt bearing the same logo. "We'll be twins."

"It was all I had." Bobby shrugged. "Wear it with pride."

I pulled the bloodstained shirt off and shoved it into the bag. The small bandage across my back where the bullet grazed me pulled as I moved, but for the most part, it was the least annoying of my past wounds. I used a few of the baby wipes Bobby tossed into the bag to clean off any smears left on my belly, smiling reassuringly at Jae when he frowned at my bare torso.

"Just that line on my back. Promise." I shook out the shirt. "The rest isn't mine."

"Didn't I tell you not to get shot?" he said, pursing his lips in disapproval. "I think I distinctly said, *do not get shot*."

"It was a crease," I protested. "That doesn't count. You got creased. Remember?"

He grunted at me, unconvinced by my argument. Taking one last drag, he exhaled a plume of smoke, then extinguished the rest of his *kretek*. "Do you want something to drink? The vending machines have iced green tea."

"That'll be great." I snagged his hand before he could leave. "Thanks, babe. For being here."

"Of course I'm here," he said, giving me a look that told me he thought I'd gone mad. "Claudia is your *nuna*. Where else would I be?"

"Can I get a coffee? You know, me? The person who saved his life?" Bobby shouted after him. Jae waved the air without looking back, and I chuckled at Bobby's sigh of exasperation. "It's like I don't even exist."

"I'm fine with that." I grumbled when he hit my shoulder. "Dude, not there. Bullet, last month. Remember? Fuck."

"Yeah, sorry," he apologized, but it didn't look like he meant it. "You're so much of a mess, I don't even remember where I can slap you. How are you doing?"

"It's a fucking shock. I'm going to kill the person who did this." We were the only ones out in the cancer zone, but the air was still thick with the musty smell of cigarettes. "I'm glad you came. Thanks."

"Not a problem." He shook off my gratitude with a smile. "I spoke to the hospital admin lady. They'll put Claudia in a private room. I told her you'd pay for it."

"Fuck, I didn't even think about that. Thanks. It'll be better for the family. They'll want to hover."

"Again, not a problem. You've had other shit on your brain," Bobby replied. "The cops want to talk to you again."

"Yeah? Why?" I couldn't imagine what else I could tell them. We'd spent more than a couple of hours going over my involvement with Trey and hadn't come up with a single reason someone would want me dead.

"They found the car. Someone on your street wrote down the license plate number," he said softly. "It's a rental."

"Okaaaaay." I drew the word out. "I still don't know anything else."

"They're wondering if maybe you've got a Korean lover, or something," he said, his eyes shifting to the hospital entrance where Jae was just coming out, carrying a bag and a paper coffee cup. "The gun was in there, along with a bunch of papers in Korean. There's also photos, Cole. Of Shin-Cho coming out of your house. They asked if you were cheating on someone. I told them about Jae...."

"This was not Jae," I spat at my best friend. "There's no fucking way this is Jae."

"I don't think it is, kid," he said, holding his hands up in surrender. "But I do think it's connected to what you're working on. Someone wants you dead, Cole. Someone who knows you're poking around in Dae-Hoon's shit. We have to find out who was driving that fucking car before they finish what they started. No matter how much you piss me off sometimes, the last thing I want is to see you dead, Princess. The last fucking thing I want."

CHAPTER FIFTEEN

THE place shouldn't have looked the same. Not by any means. But with the exception of police tape flapping in the late night breeze and the dark gouges in the white paint of the porch pillars, the building pretty much acted like nothing happened.

There were a bunch of beeping machines in a nearby hospital that would tell a different story, but the building couldn't give a shit.

I was tired and emotionally worn out. Claudia'd been moved to ICU with a tentative relocation to a private room in the morning. The family chased me out, promising to tell me if anything went south, but the doctors reassured us she was fine, and her vitals were strong. The only thing I was scheduling was waking up in the afternoon, and maybe crawling downstairs to get something to eat. Depending on the hospital, I'd hit up Claudia for a visit once they let people in to see her.

There was a message from a Detective Wong on the machine when we got home. I listened to it for a few seconds, then walked away, letting the soft-voiced cop drone on while I hunted for a beer in the fridge. Behind me, Jae made himself a cup of hot tea, leaning against the counter to watch me shuffle around the kitchen.

"Are you okay?" he finally asked. I turned to face him, the beer bottle touching my lips.

"I think I'm too tired to think," I admitted, taking a swig of Tsingtao. "My hair is yawning."

"You should eat something," Jae reproached. "All you've had is tea and that beer."

"Beer's a grain. Like whiskey's oatmeal." He snorted, and I downed half the beer, then dumped it down the sink. My stomach was gurgling, and the back of my eyelids felt sticky with sand. "Babe, I'm not hungry. Really. I think I just want to fall over."

Neko took offense to us lying down on the bed, and took off for parts unknown in the house. I doused myself long enough in the shower to soap up and rinse the hospital smell off me, then crawled under the covers. The lights were still on, and Jae was in the bathroom, brushing his teeth.

That was the last thing I remembered before I woke up screaming.

As nightmares went, it was a good one, very well directed and starring a well-rounded cast of nearly everyone I loved, past and present. An odd inclusion was my actual mother, something I'd never experienced before. I'd barely thought of my mother, Ryoko, much less dreamed about her being featured in my own private Valentine's Day Massacre.

I couldn't wake up from what I was seeing. No matter how hard I tried. Carefully walking through the dead and dying, I went from body to body, looking at the remains of faces I had in my heart. Finally stumbling upon Jae-Min, I bent over to cradle his head. His dark eyes opened and looked up at me, trusting and vulnerable in pain.

That's when I brought my Glock up to his temple and blew his head away.

Screaming probably wasn't a strong enough word for what I was doing when I jerked up out of the nightmare, but I wasn't being particular. I just needed to audibly expel the horror and hatred I had inside of me when I came out of the darkness.

"*Agi*! Cole-ah." Jae was frantic, running his hands through my hair, then cupping my face. "I'm here. It's okay. Just a dream, *de*?"

It took a long minute before I could speak, and my heart pounded, trying to break free of my body. Jae left for a second and came back with a bottle of cold green tea. Urging me to sip at it, he kneeled by my side until the shakes were gone and I could look at him without closing my eyes.

"Fuck." I needed to learn another language. Something stronger than Korean or English because, from what I could tell, neither had good enough curse words. I needed something that sounded foul and spitting with some guts to it.

"Do you want to talk?" he asked softly, as if speaking too loudly would send me off the deep end again.

I shook my head and reached up to touch his face. He'd turned on the sconces framing the window above the headboard, and their soft light cast his face into golden planes and deep blue shadows. His lashes brushed my thumbs when he blinked, tickling my skin.

"You are one of the best things that has ever happened to me," I whispered.

"Better than pizza and beer?" Jae teased.

"Better than whiskey and bacon," I reassured him with a gentle kiss.

Jae's smile was half-shy and mostly erotic. The black-winged angel who'd first enticed me shone through the worried young man who'd held me until my world righted itself. Now, Kim Jae-Min had other plans for me besides comfort.

His fingers were warm on my belly, roaming along my rib cage and feathering the scars he found there. He touched other places, other things, and any thought of sleep crept away. My cock thickened when his palm grazed over my hip bone, and I reached for him, wanting to pull Jae closer in.

He wasn't having any of it just yet. Stretching his arms out over his head, Jae worked his shoulders from one side to the next, that sensual, secretive quirk still on his lips. Naked, he was a thing of beauty. Lean, hard muscles moved under his pale, flawless skin with the barest shadow of hair under his arms and between his legs. I knew the landscape well enough, a silken dream to touch with hidden spots of musky velvet I liked to lick, because he squirmed under my tongue.

"Sit up. With your back against the headboard," Jae whispered. I must have looked at him like he was more than a little bit crazy, because he kissed me on the corner of my mouth. "Move."

The sheets were hot, and damp from my sweaty thrashing, so they stuck to me as I slid up. The sound of a familiar drawer opening made my mouth water, and despite the aches along nearly every inch of my body, I found I needed Jae around me.

Good to know he was thinking the same thing.

Jae wasn't one for preambles. Foreplay was a few rough kisses and maybe some fondling. He played dangerous games sometimes, trusting me not to overpower him and just take what I wanted. It was what he was used to. Our gentle lovemaking confused him, but he found himself liking it. And then there were times when he needed to take, and be taken. For Jae, it seemed to connect us on some level only he understood. It'd taken him only a few weeks to learn it was okay to go slowly sometimes.

Apparently, this wasn't one of those times.

He straddled my thighs, leaning in to place his mouth on mine. I had to work for the kiss, drawing out his encouraging moans with supple licks of my tongue. The faint light from the sconces made his body gleam, and I stretched my arms out to touch his shoulders, skimming my palms over his tender skin. My calluses caught on his smoothness, roughing his ivory skin to rosy patches. Nuzzling his throat, the scruff on my chin left behind a thicker burn, marking him as mine.

Stroking my dick, Jae made short work of any reluctance my flesh might have had about waking up. My cock throbbed, a milky drop already creeping from my slit. He dipped the pad of his thumb into the crevice and came up with my seed, his eyes on mine while he sucked himself clean.

He gripped me and laid the condom cap on the head of my cock, careening his thumb around the glans. Bending over in such a way that made my spine ache, he kissed one side of my dick's velvety head and then the other, running his tongue under the flange. Sitting back up, he rolled the latex down over me, its fit tugging down on my skin and catching on a stray hair at my shaft's root.

Even through the condom, the lube was cold, and I chuckled, twitching when a dribble of it rolled down my dick and headed for my balls. His fingers caught it before it hit the sheets, and Jae smeared it around my sac, rolling me in his palm.

"Keep doing that, and I'm not going to make a very good plaything for you," I said.

"Then why do I have you around?" he teased, winking at me as he lifted his hips up to settle down in front of my cock.

Leaning over until our chests nearly touched, he reached behind and fit me against the crease of his body. His gaze never left me, his eyes only narrowing when the head of my cock began its ascent into his heat. The resistance was exquisite, and I clasped my hands on his hips, slowing him down to a near crawl, so I could fully feel the penetration.

His body resisted me, coyly playing at seduction while Jae pushed down. The slide of his entrance took an eternity of nearly painful pleasure, then I was submerged, filling him as he plunged down on me. Buried up to the hilt, I cupped his left cheek, rubbing my thumb against his lips as he turned into my touch, nuzzling my palm. A cant of his hips brought me nearly to tears, especially when he stopped, poised at the zenith of his motion.

"You are going to fucking kill me," I gritted out through my clenched teeth. Only about an inch or two of me was outside of his heat, but the cold air on my exposed shaft was a shocking contrast to the suckling warmth of his body.

"I like doing this," Jae murmured, rocking back until I was engulfed once again. "I like having you like this."

Sitting back, he spread his hands over my belly, running them down my sides, and up over my hips. His legs were folded, shin down, next to mine, pushing my thighs together. Squeezing his legs together, I felt the pressure on my trapped balls, and I arched, trying to ease the ache boiling there, but his weight kept me trapped against the mattress.

A few more tilts of his hips, and I was gasping, my cock riding a wave of pleasure with my balls twisting in a vise made of my own inner thighs. He rolled as slowly as he could, surging up a few inches on my shaft before coming back down and holding me in place. I clenched the sheets, not trusting myself to keep my fingers from digging holes into his legs. New drops of sweat beaded my forehead and cheeks, a rivulet following the line of my jaw then the curve of my neck.

This time, it was his tongue that caught up the drip, and he lapped away the salt water coming from my skin, taking it into his mouth with a delicate furl.

"I need... you." His eyes were dark now, nearly black with want. Lying under him, crucified by his flesh and the sheets wrapped around my hands, I couldn't think of any better way to die. "I want us... together. Without anything between us. I've never...."

"We can, baby," I whispered, letting go of the bed linens to capture his wrists. He refused my touch, shaking his head emphatically. "We can do it now. I've been tested, especially since...."

Gripping my chin so I couldn't look away, he said, "You can't trust me. Not with what I've done. Not with who I've done. It's not safe for you. I won't... lose you to that."

"We'll check, okay?" I bent my head down and kissed his thumb, the one that took my seed into his mouth. "I'd do that for you. I trust you."

I almost crossed the line of no return. He heard it in my voice and jerked back, as if I'd slapped him, but he didn't slide free of me and stalk out. I took that as a good thing.

What he said next, I took as the greatest thing I'd ever known.

"Okay," he murmured. "I want that from you, *agi*. I want to feel you... give to me. I want to feel you come inside of me. I don't know why... I don't know why you...."

I thrust up, burying as much of myself into him as possible. Pulling my legs up, I cradled him closer until our shoulders touched, and I could wrap my arms around his waist. When I moved my hands over his back, his spine tensed and became hard pearl bones under my fingertips. Between us, his cock rubbed against our hot skin, leaving a trail of moisture between us in a sensual, wet kiss.

I let Jae set the pace. He chose a punishing run, needing to feel the rawness of my cock against his tender skin. It was rough, nearly violent, and so hard I was afraid he would tear himself open. Curled up against one another, I held back as much as I could, prolonging our climax by slowing him down when it felt like my balls were about to rip free of my body and come all over the bedroom. Any language Jae knew was lost to him, replaced by guttural, soft sounds. I didn't need anyone to tell me what they meant.

Fuck me. Use me. Make me feel *something*, Cole. Then, in the crying torrent of desire and naked want, I heard a gentle, crying sound escape from his bitten lips.

Love me... that sound whispered.

As much as he hated being what and who he was, I trusted at least one of the things hidden in my tough guttersnipe lover... the young man who saw the world as an oddly beautiful creation only he could capture on film. He saw love amid the weeds and broken cement. He saw the beauty in the aging skin of a man who lived his life as a woman. Even if he couldn't see happiness for himself, he exposed it for others.

I held him, gripping his shoulders to drive him down onto me. Slick with sweat, he slid over me, anchored by his legs and my hands. His ass clenched, refusing to give me any slack. If I wanted to leave him, I would have to fight for it. I would have gladly surrendered, except I needed the friction and liked the gasping, erotic hitch in Jae's moans when I found the sweet spot inside of him.

There wasn't enough leverage for me to fully reach the depths, and I growled, the only warning he had before I flipped us over. Now on his back, Jae grabbed at my upper arms, and I slid my hands under his shins, keeping his legs bent double so I could spread them apart and keep him from moving.

That's when I did my damnedest to pierce the emptiness he held deep inside of him.

Picking up the pace, I slammed my cock until I felt Jae fold in around me. Angling up, I found the curl I'd been looking for and drew my length against it. With every stroke I took, I made sure he rode me, rasping the head of my dick across his center until his own sex wept with anticipation. Only then did I let go of one of his legs and grip his cock in my hand. It pearled, giving into my touch before my fingers were fully wrapped around the engorged head. A few strokes was all he needed, but I refused to give them to him, choosing instead to lightly skim over the silken skin at the base.

"*Cole-ah.*" The soft kitten moans were gone, replaced by a demanding roar and the scrape of his nails on my arms. The raking scratches stung, and I laughed at the fierceness in his face.

We fell into a rhythm, the slap of our bodies a thundering beat for the sounds we made. My thigh muscles ached, but I kept my pace steady, drawing Jae's pleasure out, then returning back into his warmth. He mewled and tried to jerk his hips up so his cock would fill my hand, but I pressed his hips back, snapping forward to fill him once, then twice again.

"Want me, baby?" I whispered, nuzzling his ear. I was close. Too close, really, to make demands, and if he'd been in his right mind, he'd have known it. Instead he merely leaned in and took a bite out of me.

Already on the brink of losing myself, Jae's teeth working into my skin wiped out my control. I came when he did, falling when he gave me his release. The smell of Jae's seed inflamed me, and I captured his mouth, needing the taste of him on my tongue. I milked him, working slowly up from the root of his cock until I reached the head. He arched into my chest, his hot come splashing up onto our bellies. When my own climax hit me, I couldn't breathe, caught between the beautiful expression I'd brought to his face and the electricity pouring out of my dick and into the latex that kept me from filling him.

We collapsed in on ourselves. Jae slithered off me, languidly reaching for the washcloth he'd used to wipe my face of the night sweats I'd woken up from. I took the cloth from him, rolling him gently over onto his back, and cleaned up the drying stickiness on his skin and between his thighs. Stumbling to the bathroom, I flushed the condom and ran cold water over the end of a towel, reluctantly wiping away Jae's climax.

He was lying on his side facing the bathroom when I came out, his hooded eyes drowsy and satiated. Jae reached for me, hooking his fingers into mine as I turned off the lights. I held his hand as I crawled over him, spooning up against his back. He stretched his legs back, wrapping them through mine so we were joined from the waist down. Slinging one arm around his waist, I bent forward and kissed the back of his neck, blowing on the sweat-drenched hair at his nape.

"Don't say it, *agi*." His voice was soft, a pleading entanglement I'd resigned myself to.

"I'm going to one day," I responded. This time I kissed the rise of his upper arm, lightly scraping my teeth over the tender skin there. "I might not wait until you're ready to hear it."

"It'll... break me, Cole," Jae whispered. "This... is so much. I am so scared...."

"I'm scared too, babe." It was easy to admit, especially to the man I'd fought so hard to have. We each bore scars from the battle that brought us together, both on our skin and in our souls. "Shit, you wiped up my nightmares tonight. You don't think I'm scared?"

"It's different for you." He shimmied back into my embrace until there was no room between us. "When you're scared, you push forward. No matter what your dad said, you never run away. All I do is run away."

"You can always run to me, you know," I suggested, resting my chin on his shoulder.

"I think that's what I'm most afraid of, *agi*." The quiet between us was ripe with emotion. "Suppose I run to you, and you're not there?"

"I'll be there, babe," I promised. "You have to have faith in someone. I know it's fucking hard. And if I let you down, then you have my express permission to kick my damned ass, because it would be the stupidest thing I've ever done in my life. Hell, it's probably the biggest scary thing in the whole damned world after someone's kicked in your teeth, but have faith in me. Let me... love you. Please, just let me love you."

CHAPTER SIXTEEN

BOBBY found me on my hands and knees scrubbing the porch steps. Elbow deep in fake-pine smelling foam, I nodded a hello at him and told him there was coffee on in the office.

Before I'd even brushed my teeth, Detective Wong called me to talk about the case and give me the go-ahead to go back into the front of the building. Jae offered to postpone a family portrait shoot and help me clean up, but I let him go with a kiss. Wong'd told me the lab had someone do it for me, a favor for an ex-cop. I thanked him for it. I was being sincere. I'd left the force in a hail of bullets, shot by my own partner. That led to a bunch of scars, an enormous cash payout, and the collective hatred of nearly every cop I'd ever known. Wong was a big fricking surprise.

There wasn't a drop of blood on the slats, and the grass was soaked to the roots. Still, I'd put down the Pine-Sol and bristle brush I'd brought out, and unrolled the garden hose. The damage to the posts had been mostly cosmetic, but I wanted someone in to look at the window frame that'd been hit. The glass rattled when I'd touched it, but it seemed to hold. That's when I started scrubbing the porch down.

I needed to wash yesterday off my porch. Hell, I wanted to wash yesterday right out of existence, but the porch was at least something I could do about it.

The screen door creaked behind me as Bobby joined me out on the porch. I'd poured so much of the cleaner down onto the porch floor I couldn't even smell the coffee in Bobby's cup. He settled down in one of the Adirondack chairs I'd bought so Claudia and I could sit out front and people watch when we were really bored. She scolded me for being silly, then arrived the next day with long, thick pillows, because the hard wooden seat would make her butt hurt.

"Hey, Lady Macbeth," Bobby grumbled, and nudged my ass with the toe of his sneaker. "Give it a rest. You didn't cause this shit."

"I know." I splashed the rest of the bucket over the area and rinsed off the froth with the hose. After winding the hose on the rack, I went inside to wash my hands and get a cup of coffee. By the time I returned, Bobby'd already set himself up to watch a gaggle of young hipster students settling into an outdoor table at the café across the street.

"They're like some mutant love child of a beat poet and an unwashed grunge rocker," Bobby snorted. "How is that a good look?"

"I don't know. Claudia wants to tie them all down, hose them off, and shave the nuked hamsters they've got growing on their faces."

The café's granola-munching owners did one thing right; they hired a guy named Joe who could make a mean sandwich. On lazy days... and some not so lazy days... I would pop over to grab a pastrami on toasted sourdough and curl myself up in a feral ball to eat it in peace. I'd more than once walked the gauntlet of pretension and theatrical ennui. It was more annoying than the pseudo-intellectuals who gathered there on Saturday nights to discuss the age-old contest of Batman versus Superman.

It was a life filled with senseless noise. Especially since neither of them had anything on Namor.

"Good, when she gets back to work, I'll help her." He nudged me again, this time with his elbow since I was sitting in the chair next to him. "Plates came back on that car at the storage place."

"Shit, I forgot all about that." I had. It was on my master note list to follow up, but after yesterday, it'd jumped way down in priority. "Anyone we know?"

"Yep, registered to one Crisanto Songcuya Seong. And man, I probably just fucked that name up."

"Who the fuck is...." I stopped myself. "Seong? As in Scarlet's Seong."

"Actually, even closer." Bobby grinned. "That *is* Scarlet. The car's registered to her. I think it's the car Seong's boys use to drive her around. Hard to tell. There's a fleet of them."

"Why the hell would she have someone following us?" My brain already hurt from lack of sleep, no food, and too much coffee. "And not tell us about it?"

"Funny you should ask that, Princess," Bobby answered. "Because that's what I said when I called her this morning. Seems she told two of Seong's boys to follow us out there to help with the excavation. You were hurt, and she didn't want you to reinjure your precious little snowflake body. Maybe they decided to blow her off, or thought we were big and strong enough not to need their help, but that's why they were sitting in the car. Avoiding work. She was pissed off when I told her they only followed us out there and sat."

"She'll tear them new assholes through their noses." I was in awe of Scarlet's temper. I'd been on the soft end of it once, and it wasn't pleasant. Then something else hit me. "Shit, you don't think Seong's going to dump her, do you?"

"How the fuck did you get there?" Bobby nearly choked on his coffee. "The dude moved to fucking Los Angeles and gave up his family for her. You've seen them. They're like Jessica and Roger Rabbit."

"I know. It's stupid," I admitted. "Sometimes the people who work for those kinds of guys know about shit before anyone else does. I just wondered if they thought Scarlet's on the way out, so *fuck her, we don't have to do what she wants. The boss'll protect me.*"

"Plausible." He smacked the back of my head. "If it were anyone but Scarlet and Seong. Hell, I think Mary'd sooner divorce God than those two breaking it off. Don't think stupid shit. Or better yet, don't think at all. All you seem to come up with after crap happens is stupid shit. Give your head a break."

"Stop hitting," I mumbled, rubbing at the spot. It was like I was five and he wanted my lunch money. "Or I won't tell you what the cops said."

"So someone finally called you?"

"Yeah, Detective Dexter Wong." I gave him a brief rundown about Wong dismissing Jae as a suspect. "He got with Brookes, who was there at the Kwons. They think Shin-Cho's shooting and the one here are related to Helena's murder. Bullets are the same type. He's hoping ballistics can match them to the same gun."

"Kind of hope it does." Bobby nodded. "That explains the gouging in that post there. Did the lab do that? Looks like beavers got at it."

"Yeah, I'm debating replacing it or using wood putty. Haven't decided yet." I straddled the chair's sloping leg rest. "Hey, did someone get a hold of Rocket? I mean, about Trey? I realized this morning I've been so fucking focused on Claudia, I haven't even thought about Trey's family or someone telling Rocket."

"Dude, Trey's family *is* Rocket. They're first cousins." Bobby noticed my shudder. "Totally legal in California. And yeah, I called him after the cops did. Kid's a tweak, but even they have feelings."

"He doing okay?"

"Yeah, sounded like it," he said. "He's Trey's only living relative. Looks like he'll inherit everything, including the sex shop. He didn't seem too broken up about Trey. Mumbled something about living by the dick, and dying by the dick. I think he thought Trey was shot by the cops."

"I'd say that's cold, but I've met Rocket." I whistled. "That's probably the deepest thought he's ever had."

No one could blame us for flinching when a black sedan pulled up and parked in front of the building. Bobby and I both glanced at each other, slightly shamefaced, but there was a silent code of forgiveness for our jumpiness. The shame factor for Bobby went up when a short Korean man in a suit got out to open the door for the delicate older woman sitting in the back.

Dressed in a high-end pencil skirt and blouse, Seong Ryeowon looked like she'd been born with pearls pouring from her mouth. Even under the bright California sun, her skin shone flawlessly and was as smooth as porcelain. Her driver, standard Seong-issue, remained by the car, and her mile-high stilettos made tick-tick noises on the cement.

I'd been on the wrong end of little old ladies before. As far as I was concerned, the most dangerous fucking thing in the neighborhood right now was the elegant, thin-faced woman heading up my walk.

"That's Shin-Cho's mom. We saw her at the hospital, remember?" I muttered to Bobby. Standing up, I brushed what I could off my jeans and met her at the steps. The biggest problem with Korean names was I didn't know how to address a married woman. I went with what I hoped was right. "Madam Seong."

"Mr. McGinnis." There was no mistaking her for anyone other than Seong's sister. She carried herself with her chin up, a firm mouth, and an expression on her face that said she expected me to curtsey. She glanced over at Bobby and dismissed him with an icy smile. Her accent was much stronger than her brother's or Jae's, but Seong Ryeowon spoke confidently and clearly. "May I speak with you in private?"

I held the door to the office open for her and wiggled my eyebrows at Bobby. He snorted and went back to sipping his coffee and silently disparaging the young men across the street. Leading Ryeowon to my little-used meeting room, I offered her tea or coffee, but she shook her head and made herself comfortable in one of the large leather chairs.

The room was originally a formal dining room, but when I converted the house, I instead set it up for private meetings. With only a loose collection of brass-tacked leather chairs and a large rectangular coffee table in the room, I'd hoped to convey a more intimate environment. Bobby said it looked like a Victorian gentleman's club, and all it was missing was an old English explorer with an enormous white mustache and pith helmet snoring in the corner.

"Thank you for seeing me," she said, squaring her shoulders.

Up close, I could see Shin-Cho in her features. He had a more fine-boned look than his brother, and Ryeowon definitely played that up. I wanted to condemn her for how she treated her eldest son, but the truth was, she'd been there when he went down. As angry as she was at her brother's choices and lover, she was there for her sons.

"Are you sure I can't get you anything? Water, perhaps?" Jae must have been rubbing off on me, because I was uncomfortable not bringing her anything.

She studied me with a tilt of her head, then said, "No, no. I'm fine. Thank you."

"What can I do for you?" I'd left my coffee outside with Bobby, and I felt naked with nothing for my hands to do. Clasping them in front of me, I leaned forward in my chair. "If it's about Park Dae-Hoon, I'm afraid that information is confidential unless your son gives me permission to share it with you."

From how I spoke, someone would think I had tons of information and was moments away from pulling the mask off some geezer and proclaiming him the villain. Truth was, we still had to track down a couple of men on the list of Dae-Hoon's victims in the hopes they were still in America.

"That is fine. I am not here about Park Dae-Hoon," Ryeowon said. Her hands were busy, a nervous busy as she adjusted her watch then tugged at the cuff of her sleeve. "My son, David, told me to come talk to you about something that happened before we left Seoul. He thinks it is important, because it might involve Shin-Cho."

I'd brought a notebook and pen with me in case I needed to take notes. Flipping the tablet open, I nodded. "Okay, what would you like to tell me?"

Ryeowon cocked her head and peered at me down her nose. "How much do you know of the *chaebol* families?"

"My... Korean friends have told me a bit," I replied cautiously. There was a very thick line I couldn't cross: sharing my relationship with Jae. "Your brother, Seong *hyung*, is from a *chaebol* family, and a lot of South Korean companies are run by them."

"We *are* South Korea," Ryeowon stated. "What our families produce, how we behave, any scandals that we are involved in... all of these things are scrutinized and gone over. The *chaebol* are held to a higher standard, because we are the face of South Korea. Every day for us means a delicate balance of behavior. We cannot allow ourselves to be seen as...."

"Less than perfect?" I supplied.

"Yes. We are the perfect South Koreans, yes." She started to shift in her seat, then corrected herself. The nervousness was gone, replaced by an imperious reserve. I murmured some sound she took for assent, and she continued. "My son Shin-Cho has always had difficulties meeting the demands of the family. He was always close to his father, and when Dae-Hoon chose to... leave us, Shin-Cho was devastated. David was younger, and not as under the influence of Park Dae-Hoon. It was easier for him to adjust to having another man as his *hyung*. My older brothers provided that for him, but Shin-Cho... rebelled."

"Rebelled how?" From what she was describing, it sounded like a boot camp more than a childhood.

"He had difficulties making friends with other boys from *chaebol* families. Instead, Shin-Cho would go out of his way to avoid playmates, even at school. It was not because he was being selective. That at least would be a saving grace," she murmured. "Instead, he would not come home after his studies, and he roamed areas he shouldn't have been in. I cannot tell you how many times we had to send security out to find him. When he graduated, it became even worse. Sometimes he would not come home for days, and he refused to attend the university we arranged for him."

"I'm not sure how this connects to what's happening now," I admitted.

"I will get there," Ryeowon assured me. "There were rumors about Shin-Cho, nasty rumors of what he was doing in those places. I knew then I should have been harsher with him when he was younger. He looked up to his father. I did not do enough to stop him from following in his father's footsteps."

The expression on her face was the same look of disgust she'd gotten when Scarlet walked into the waiting room. It was hard not to react, especially when her lips curled with a sour revulsion.

"One night, two of our security men went out looking for him and found him with another man. He'd been... hurt. Shin-Cho's sins finally caught up with him. Our men brought him home, and I sent money to that man, so he would keep quiet about what he did to Shin-Cho, but it was already too late to stop the whispering." She sighed, playing with a ring on her finger.

"Hurt how?" I didn't like the sound of what she was saying. I liked it even less when she shrugged off Shin-Cho's trauma with a tiny quiver of her shoulders. "How bad?"

"He needed... time. We found him a retreat he could stay at until he felt better, but the damage was already done to the family. There was no way we could hide what he'd done. There were too many people talking about what might have happened." Another reproachful sigh, and my stomach gurgled from too much coffee and the acid burning up from my guts. "Our family'd already dealt with the scandal from Park Dae-Hoon. We couldn't have another incident, so our oldest brother, Min-Wu, arranged for Shin-Cho to enter the military. We thought that he would benefit from the structure, help him overcome his obsession with his father's ways."

I had never wanted to shake someone as badly as I did Seong Ryeowon. It burned in me, a bright want to wrap my hands around her shoulders and rock her until her head snapped off and rolled under the coffee table. Instead, I concentrated on gouging my pen into the notebook and reminding myself this was what faced Jae if ever his family found out about him. It was a sobering thought.

"Wait, he didn't stay in the military, right?" I looked up. "He left before his time was up?"

"Yes, unfortunately," Ryeowon said. "We'd enlisted Shin-Cho to get him away from the scandal. Our purpose was, when he came back from the military, he could enroll in a university and then work in the company. He was doing well then he was transferred to Choi Yong-Kun's command."

"I know he'd been found in a compromising situation," I hedged in. "Was it with this Choi Yong-Kun?"

"No, Choi Yong-Kun was his officer," she said tightly. "His other command was more thoughtful to what the family needed. I hold Choi Yong-Kun responsible for Shin-Cho's involvement with Li Mun-Hee. *That* man was known to have perversions. He'd been moved from four commands before serving under Choi Yong-Kun. Choi Yong-Kun neglected to protect my son from Li Mun-Hee. I blame him for Shin-Cho's dismissal."

I was going to piss her off. I knew it before I said what was on my mind, but I tried to be as delicate as I could. "Don't you think Shin-Cho knew what he was doing?"

"How could he?" Ryeowon asked, her eyes round with shock. "Shin-Cho was to be given time to right himself, and Choi Yong-Kun deliberately refused to help someone he was responsible for. Yong-Kun *knew* Shin-Cho was susceptible. My son is *not* gay, Mr. McGinnis. He needs time to see that. I need my family to understand that. Instead, my brother sends him here… to *Min-Ho*."

I'd thought I'd reached the bottom of her loathing barrel, but apparently I was wrong. She put a dose of venom on Seong's name that could have stopped a herd of elephants.

"Okay, but what does Choi Yong-Kun have to do with this now?" I asked. "Has he threatened him in some way? Demanded money to keep quiet?"

"He has disappeared," she responded curtly. "Along with Li Mun-Hee. Both of them… gone."

"So it was a plot to sabotage Shin-Cho's reputation?" My notes were beginning to look like a Venn diagram explosion. "Did they purposely set things up so Shin-Cho would be compromised, and then ask for money?"

Compromised. Like he was a heroine from one of the old romance novels from the fifties.

"I don't know. I wouldn't put it past Li Mun-Hee," Ryeowon sniffed. "He came looking for Shin-Cho. *To our house.* As if he had a claim to my son. My brother chased him off and told him never to come back."

"Did your brother tell him Shin-Cho was in LA?"

"I don't know. I wasn't listening," she admitted. "I was upset. David was getting married, and the Kwon family already was wary of the match because of Dae-Hoon. Shin-Cho's behavior nearly broke the engagement. We agreed that Shin-Cho would not be there, for appearance's sake, but David refused to honor the agreement between our families. It was very unsettling."

"How did Helena feel about Shin-Cho's involvement in the wedding?"

Ryeowon looked at me like I'd grabbed her for a romp on the coffee table. "What would she say? It was David's decision."

Not sure if she meant it as a *the wife has no say over the husband's declarations* thing, or if it didn't concern Helena because it wasn't her family's issue. Either way, I was already treading on thin ice with Ryeowon. I'd pushed her buttons as little as possible, but it was obvious we didn't agree about Shin-Cho's miraculous healing from being gay ever happening. I wasn't going to throw kerosene on the fire by bringing women's rights into the mix.

"How did you find out they, Choi and Li, were missing?" I couldn't imagine a suicide pact, especially not one involving Shin-Cho. For one thing, Choi was the one who outed the other two. Unless they'd set it up to extort money from the Seongs, he'd gained nothing. If anything, he ended up paying the price for pissing off a pretty powerful family.

"The police came to our house. One of them knew of Shin-Cho's... relationship with Mun-Hee. A neighbor heard a loud fight at Mun-Hee's apartment and called the authorities. When no one came to the door, the police went in and found blood on the floor," Ryeowon replied. "Choi Yoon-Kun's brother said he'd gone to confront Mun-Hee over something. When the police went to Yoon-Kun's home, he wasn't there, and it looked as if he'd packed to leave."

"Did you tell the American cops this?" I sat back, exhaling hard. "Has someone checked to see if Yoon-Kun's left South Korea? Did he have a passport?"

"I don't know. There are ways for people to leave without being tracked. He could have done it," she admitted slowly. "I didn't think Yoon-Kun would come here to hurt Shin-Cho. He is the one who failed Shin-Cho, not the other way around."

I wasn't sure how to handle the conflict inside of me. There was no religious fervor or gleam in her eyes. Seong Ryeowon truly believed her son could be cured of his homosexuality and that she'd failed him by allowing him to continue to think fondly of his father. I wanted to hate Ryeowon, or pity her.

I just didn't know how.

"Okay, let me see if we can't track down someone who can check on Yoon-Kun," I said. "But you should talk to the police. There's a Detective Wong on the case. He's probably a good place to start."

"Wong?" She sounded thoughtful. "He is Chinese?"

"Yeah." Jae'd told me a lot of Koreans had issues with the Japanese, for one reason or another. I wasn't sure how they felt about their neighbors from China. "Does that matter?"

"No, no, that is fine." She dismissed my caution with a wave of her hand. Ryeowon stood, then paused at the meeting room door. "May I ask you one thing, Mr. McGinnis?"

"Sure," I replied, picking up my notes and pen.

"You are gay, yes? Like Min-Ho?"

No *hyung* for her older brother, that was certain. I nodded. "Yes."

"Does your mother know?" Ryeowon's concern was visible, either sympathy for me or a woman she imagined was going through the same emotions she'd been through.

"No," I said softly. "She died when I was born."

"Ah." Her smile was wide, brightening up her face. It chased the years away, even softening the dark circles under her eyes she'd hidden with a thick layer of makeup. "That's good, then. She never knew you were like this. I am so glad for her. So much better for her. Have a good day, Mr. McGinnis, and thank you again."

CHAPTER SEVENTEEN

"SHIT, that's a cold woman," Bobby swore under his breath to Seong Ryeowon's back as she left.

We abandoned the porch for the office when a swarm of gnats decided our mouths looked like glory holes in need of business. Jae'd shown up a few minutes later with a few orders of carne asada fries and spicy carrots. Bobby took them off his hands as soon as he walked through the door, kissing Jae on the cheek in thanks. He was insulted when Jae recoiled in horror.

"Yeah, he only likes men, Bobby," I teased. My supposed best friend flipped me off and took a bag out of Jae's hands.

"Mmmmm. Mexican." Bobby ignored me in favor of opening the Styrofoam container and inhaling the intoxicating scent of charbroiled meat, cheese, and fries. "It's good to have a Korean boyfriend. They bring take-out."

"You don't have one now," Jae muttered. "Cole does, but I don't mind feeding you too. It's like he owns a dog I pick up hamburgers for."

"And Cole is happy about his Korean boyfriend. Be nice to Bobby. He's had a mouthful of gnat and spent the afternoon watching hippies commune with their extra-virgin spring water tea." I tugged on the hem of his T-shirt. Jae leaned over and gave me a kiss, then stepped back to unpack the food.

Perched up on the edge of my desk, he handed me a laden container, opened his food, and promptly poured Sriracha over his fries. My guts winced in sympathy. His probably snickered at me, mocking my tender intestines. He offered me the bottle, and I must have given him the same look he'd given Bobby, because he laughed hard enough to need a drink of water. Patting him on the back, I told them about my meeting with Ryeowon.

"Wow." Bobby whistled in disbelief when I got to the part about my mother. "That's... some kind of fucked up."

"We would think so," I said. "But, for her... for their family, I think she's doing more than most. Sounds like she pulled some strings to keep Shin-Cho under the Seong umbrella."

"He's not going to go off and get married, pop out kids, and forget about being gay." Bobby shoveled a fry into his mouth. "She should accept that and move on."

"Why not?" Jae cocked his head at Bobby. "*Hyung* did. Others do. He's her oldest son. She wants him to have... she wants him to continue the family."

"He's a Park," I pointed out. "They don't have something to say about it?"

"No, they lost the family connection to Shin-Cho and David after Dae-Hoon." Picking at the carrots, Jae found a red pepper and bit into it. I made a mental note to kiss him only after he'd rinsed out his mouth. "The scandal was too much. Luckily, it happened here, so they could—"

"Cover it up?" Bobby interrupted.

"Yes," Jae agreed. He was matter-of-fact. I'd gone down this road with him before, but Bobby was new to the journey, and probably wouldn't like where it was going to leave him. "The Seongs are more powerful than the Parks. It makes sense for Ryeowon to align her sons with the Seongs. It offers them more protection, especially after Shin-Cho was caught with that other man. The *chaebol* take care of their own."

"I can't believe I'm sitting here listening to you excuse this shit." He pushed his fries across Claudia's desk in disgust. "You're gay. Tell me this doesn't piss you off!"

"What is supposed to piss me off? Being gay is different when you're Korean," Jae replied calmly. "It *is* different. Do I wish I could love a man and still have my family? Yes, but I can't. Not until my sisters are out of the house, and my mother can be taken care of. When I tell her, I won't have a family left. Shin-Cho is lucky. His mother is forcing the family to provide for him. She loves him. She's fighting for him. She's risking her own family status when she tries to protect him."

"Bullshit," Bobby spat.

"Because it's not what you know? Because it's easy for you to walk away?" Jae's voice dropped to nearly a whisper, but the heat in his tone was growing. "Some families ignore what their sons do if they get married and have children, like *hyung*. Others cut them off like they weren't ever born. Korea isn't big. Your family's reputation and situation determines everything in your life: your work, your school… everything. Even here, we're caught between being Korean and wanting what's in our hearts. Don't tell me it's bullshit if you don't live like we do."

"Hey, both of you," I cut in. I was trying not to get up and dance around the desks. Not because I couldn't dance… although apparently there was a general consensus that I was lacking in that department, but because Jae said *when* not *if* he told his family. I wanted to savor the moment, and the two of them arguing would put a damper on that. "Pull it back a bit. Bobby, you know how crappy it can be to hide who you are. Shit's different for everybody. You know that."

"Yeah," he grunted in agreement, but he tackled his fries again. "That's why it pisses me off to see people shoved into hiding. We've worked so fucking hard to open shit up here. Hell, it was so fucking hard for me to do it."

"*Here*," Jae said. "The world is not *here*. I wish it were because… change is easier. In South Korea, not so much."

"Okay," Bobby capitulated. "Just don't expect me to like it."

"I don't," Jae responded gently. "I didn't say I liked it either. It just is."

For the next hour the only sounds in the office were us eating and the tap-tap of my fingers on the keyboard. Every once in a while Bobby would swear when he hit a dead end. Little by little our list of arrested blackmail victims dwindled. By the end of the afternoon, we'd discovered one moved back to South Korea while two others took their own lives. Of the two remaining in America, only one was still in Los Angeles. The other appeared to live in New York with his wife and daughter.

"I'll see if I can get a hold of Brandon Yeu. Maybe he'll be willing to talk about that night." I printed his information out of the contact database I subscribed to.

"Do it tomorrow, kid," Bobby suggested. "It's going to be visiting time over at the hospital. You'll be kicking yourself in the ass if you don't go."

"Fuck." I checked the time. "I've got to grab some flowers too."

"Don't forget the balloon," Jae teased. "It just won't be the same without the balloon."

IN THE end, we got the balloons.

Wrestling with the Mylar apocalypse I'd summoned to the hospital, I followed Jae as he carried in the large bouquet of roses and carnations we'd finally settled on. He liked the spray of white lilies which I vetoed for being used at funerals. I then chose an ornate chrysanthemum arrangement which apparently were death flowers for Koreans.

It was good to find out we were both morbidly compatible.

The hospital room looked like the botanical gardens vomited up its stomach after a hard night's drinking. There were at least two large wreaths with *hangul* written on banners across them, but it was difficult to see around the sheer number of bodies in the room. Martin spotted me through the herd, and took control.

"Okay, everyone out." He didn't speak loudly, but apparently there was some kind of vibration sensor among the Claudia brood, because within seconds the room was clear, a few stopping to kiss her on the cheek before they left. The door closed behind me, and I was left alone with the woman who should have had more common sense than to come work for me.

"Did you think you were going to tie those to me, so I'd float away like that house?" she rasped from her hospital bed. "Come here, boy."

I let go of the balloons. I didn't give a shit if they tangled up on the ceiling or popped when they hit the florescent lights. A few steps and I had Claudia's arms around me, squeezing the air from my lungs.

She smelled of antiseptic and the sour-skin powder scent of someone who'd been in surgery, but under it was warm vanilla and lavender soap and the steady thump of her heart pouring life through her soft, round body. The collar of the purple velvet robe I'd given her for Christmas tickled my nose when I buried my face into her shoulder, and something crinkled when I shifted against her side. Sheepishly, I let go and pulled out a stack of crayon drawings from under my hip, trying to smooth them out on my leg.

"Sorry," I mumbled, and put them on the table next to the bed. My face was wet, and I wiped at my cheeks, hoping Claudia hadn't seen me lose my shit.

"Don't be ashamed to cry, Cole." She patted my hand, tangling me into the tubing coming out of her arm. I undid myself and went to grab a chair, but she held onto my shirt. "Stay here. Sit on the edge of the bed, and talk to me."

I did as she told me. I usually did. I took a moment to study her. Her cheeks glowed pink, and her skin was back to its rich café shade, not a hint of the sickly gray haunting my dreams. There was a small handprint of glitter on her left cheek and some plastic barrettes stuck in odd angles in her hair. She'd obviously been subjected to some sort of little girl makeover, but it looked nice on her. It felt damned good to feel her warmth against me, and I didn't even mind when she smacked me on the side of my head.

"You will *not* apologize for me being here," Claudia scolded. "If anything, I got a free tummy tuck and all the Jell-O I can eat. I will not hear any of your crap about being the reason I'm here."

"I didn't say anything!" I rubbed at the spot, mostly for effect. "I am sorry—"

She smacked harder this time and grunted slightly in pain. Waving me off when I reached for the nurse's button, Claudia rearranged her robe so she was more comfortable and gave me an ogle. "Did they catch who did it? I heard about that boy. He was an idiot, but he didn't deserve that."

"No, he didn't," I agreed. "And no, they haven't caught the guy yet. The cops found the car, but that's about it. I probably shouldn't stay long. The doctors will want you to rest."

"I'll rest when I'm dead," she pronounced. "How are you? Where were you hurt?"

"Just on my back. Only a scratch." Tugging up my shirt, I showed her the bandage. "I've had worse."

"I don't see why you keep getting shot up, son," Claudia tsked. "It's like you go asking for it."

"This time I can say I don't have a clue." I told her about Wong's theory about the shootings being related, and then my visit with Seong Ryeowon. She was thoughtful when I was done. "Honestly, I wish all mothers were like you. Marcus is lucky to have you."

Claudia studied me for a long moment, then reached for my hand. Wrapping her fingers in mine, she sighed and squeezed hard. "Is that what you think? That it was easy for me when Marcus told me?"

"Maybe not... easy," I stammered. "Sure as hell better than Barbara and my dad."

"I threw him out," Claudia said quietly. "My boy... the son I'd fed from my breast and rocked when he was sick... and I threw him from the house like he was rubbish."

"You never told me that." Shock rippled through me. Of all of Claudia's sons, Marcus was the one she seemed to have the most *fun* with. "I didn't know."

"He was a boy, not even fourteen," she murmured. "And he came to me with full faith, and I cast him out. What does that say about me? What does that say about my heart that I'd do that to my son?"

"Why?" I was confused. "Why would you do that?"

"Because I'd been raised that it was a sin, and nothing Marcus did would save his soul," Claudia responded. "I left the house to go find my pastor because I was so angry and hurt. I needed to find something to hold on to. I needed someone to tell me I'd done the right thing and that it would all be okay."

"Did you find him?" I'd never been one for church, but Claudia and her family went every weekend. From what I've heard, they had a great time. I preferred sleeping in and having sex, but everyone communes with God in different ways.

"No, I never made it to church," she admitted. "I drove around, and somehow ended up at those gardens at the Huntington. My car ran out of gas. Right there. So I got out, and it was free to get into the Japanese place that day, so I went in. I found some rock where it was quiet, sat down, and cried my eyes out."

"I'm sorry…."

"No. Don't be sorry for me. See, I'd beaten my son, Cole," Claudia murmured. "I'd smacked their butts for misbehaving before, but this was the first time I'd raised my hand to him in anger. In hatred. My own son. And God, if I didn't sit there in some strange place when I was going to head to church because I was so lost."

"He'd come to me in faith and love, and I turned him away." She shook her head. "I'd lost faith, not in God or Marcus, but in myself. I'd let someone tell me what was right and wrong. All of these years, I've listened to preachers and people around me saying that someone like Marcus was wicked and evil."

"Not Marcus." I chuckled.

"No, not my Marcus. I *raised* that boy. I knew who he was. I'd seen him share with others who had nothing. I've listened as he worked out his brothers' disagreements, because they knew he was fair. I spat on him because he knew himself? Because he knew how to love? Because he was honest with himself and me? He came to me, knowing I would love him and hold him when the world would tear him apart, and I crucified him for his love," Claudia said with another squeeze of my hand. "There, *that's* when I finally heard God laughing at me. I'd been given a son who had flaws, yes, but who was a good man with a good heart, and I'd fucked it up."

"Claudia!" I mocked her. "Language. So you guys are okay? I mean now?"

"Now, yes, but he was a teenager eventually. I straightened him, okay," she laughed. "Of all of them, he and Martin gave me the least worries. But, do you know what I think Marcus was really sent to me for? Other than to teach me humility?"

"Nope," I said, shaking my head. "Not a clue."

"I think God knew that I'd one day get bored with retirement and go looking for something to do," Claudia said softly. "He knew that there was a broken gay boy who'd been treated with such little care that he'd need someone like me in his life. I just had to know how to love him. And if I couldn't find it in my heart to love the son I already had, how could I learn to love the one I would find?"

She held me again, tighter than she'd done before, and I fought not to fall, but wasn't very successful. Wrapped in her strong arms, I let the pain inside of me surface until I cracked open. It hurt. My throat turned raw, and I gripped Claudia's shoulders like I was drowning. She let me silently drench her, rubbing at my back until I couldn't breathe and finally had to come up for air.

Cupping my face, she held me fast and forced me to look at her. "There is nothing wrong with you that some good food and love can't fix. You just have to eat well and open your heart up. Despite those people who have tried to make you less than who you are, Cole McGinnis, you are a good boy. You deserve everything good that comes your way. Remember that."

"Okay," I murmured, and kissed her palm. Chuckling, I asked, "Did you *ever* make it to church that day?"

"No." She barked a laugh. "I called my friend to come bring me some gas, and then I went to find a church that didn't tell me it was okay to hate. Just because God smacks me on the head once, doesn't mean he calls me up to chat."

"True," I agreed. "'Course if God starts talking to you on a regular basis, you let me know. We'll get you a robe with the arms that wrap around your back."

She was tired. I'd worn her out, and now Claudia was sagging in her bed. Gathering up the balloons, I righted them as much as I could, and tied them to one of the chairs. We both waited a moment, expecting the chair to take flight, but it was made of sterner stuff and remained grounded. Jae knocked on the door, and they visited for a few minutes, long enough for Claudia's eyes to flutter and Jae to kiss her on the cheek. We let ourselves out of the room, holding the door open for a couple of the women to go in.

The hallway was remarkably clear of the horde, with the exception of a few of the sons hovering near the vending machines. Martin was waiting for us a few feet away and waved us over to where he stood. He gave me a quick hug and slapped me on the back. It was like being smote by a lightning bolt.

"I'm glad you came. Momma was asking about you. I told her you'd be in today." He took a Coke one of his brothers handed him, urging me to take a can from the stack they'd purchased.

"Wild horses couldn't have kept me away," I said. Jae'd refused a can, but took mine from me after I'd opened it, sipping it before handing it back.

"Jae-Min here says there's something we should talk about," Martin said. "Something about one of the flower arrangements. The ones with the Korean on them."

I looked at Jae. "What about them? They're not from Scarlet?"

"One of them is," Jae replied. "The other one isn't. A man dropped them off and asked to talk to the head of the family."

"I told him she was inside that room," Martin responded. "But he could talk to me if he wanted. He was Korean. Kind of spoke the same way Hyunae's mom does, like English was really hard."

"Hyunae?" I asked.

"Marcel's girlfriend," Jae and Martin said at the same time.

"She's Korean," Jae interjected. "Martin, tell Cole what he said to you."

"He said he was sorry about Momma," Martin replied. "I thought maybe he was someone Momma knew, but when I asked her, she said she really only knew Scarlet and her boyfriend. We'd already gotten flowers from them, and Hyunae's family sent fruit."

"Did he tell you his name?" I asked. "Shit, do you have a card or something from the flowers?"

"No name," Martin said. "But Jae-Min's got the florist card."

"I got it when I saw the wreath. It says *I'm sorry for causing you pain. I beg your forgiveness.*" Jae yelped when I grabbed him into a hard hug. "*Aish*, let go."

"God, I love you." He stiffened in my arms, but I refused to let him go, hugging him tighter. Kissing his ear, I whispered, "I told you I'm going to love you. Let me at least be fucking happy you read the wreath, okay?"

"Okay," he said grudgingly as I let him go. "For that."

"Thanks, Martin." I shook his hand and let him pound on my back again. My shoulder wound disagreed with me and sent a warning twinge down my spine. I told it to fuck off and take it like a man. My ribs disagreed and cramped up, showing an uncharacteristic solidarity with my shoulder. "I'll get a hold of Wong and see if he'll chase it down."

"Not a problem. If that's the guy that shot her, then I'm sorry I let him get out of here." He smiled, and it was not a pretty sight. "Next time I see him, he and I will have some words."

"Let me know if he comes back," I said. "Okay?"

"Sure," Martin replied softly. "I just can't promise you he'll be in any shape when you get here, but I'll let you know."

"Good enough," I agreed. "All he needs is his tongue so he can talk. Anything else… that's fair game."

"Man can talk with a stump," Martin disagreed. "But I'll do my best, Cole. I'll definitely do my best."

CHAPTER EIGHTEEN

I DUG through my notes for Brandon Yeu's number after offering to help Jae with dinner and getting rebuffed by a derisive snort. From the noise he'd made, one would think I'd lived on steak and frozen pizzas before he'd come along. If I didn't have a large chest freezer with half a cow and a stack of extra pepperoni and cheese pies in it, I could almost say he'd be telling the truth.

It took a few deep breaths before I dialed the phone. I was willingly going to break into a man's life and open up a wound he'd thought long healed. And I was going to do it with a rusty, dull fork only so I could find out what happened to a dead man.

"Hello?" The man sounded young. I wasn't sure what I was expecting, but a soft lilting voice wasn't it.

"Brandon Yeu?" I broached.

"No, hold on." The voice muted a bit, and I heard him ask someone else something. "May I ask who's calling?"

"Cole McGinnis. I'm a private investigator," I replied. "I need to ask him questions about a man he knew a long time ago."

There was a bit of a wait, only a few moments, but it was enough to make my stomach curl. When someone else picked up, my intestines decided my stomach had the right idea, and began crawling up my throat.

"Hello? This is Yeu." I introduced myself first then laid out what I'd been asked to do. There was a dead silence on the other end, and then a shuddering sigh. "It's been a long time since I've heard that name."

"I can imagine," I replied. "I'm not looking to make trouble for you. I'm only trying to find out what happened to Park Dae-Hoon, so his sons have some closure. If it's any consolation, they've decided to return the money he'd taken, along with any interest. I'd like to arrange that at least."

"I don't... know," he stammered, and in the background someone asked him if he was okay. Yeu murmured something in response, then came back to me. "What do you need?"

"Mostly, to find out if you'd seen anything that night. Anything would be helpful. I'm trying to recreate what happened at Bi Mil. I'm hoping to find something to lead me to where Dae-Hoon went after that."

"Let me think about it," Yeu said. "My life is different now. I don't... hide anymore, but you're asking me to think about a time of my life I'd much rather forget about."

"I know," I said. "It took me a bit to call you. I didn't want to intrude, but...."

"You've been paid to," he laughed.

"It's kind of not about the money," I replied. "One of his sons came to me because he felt like I would understand what his father went through being gay... what he's going through now. It's kind of personal. If you want, we can meet someplace other than my office. Maybe even a restaurant? I'll buy."

I let Yeu think about it, and by the long hissing sigh I heard over the phone, he was torn. Jae-Min came into the living room with a couple of beer bottles and a small bowl of arare. Neko followed close on his heels, obviously hoping the bowl contained something more cat-palatable. He set the bowl down, then chased her off the storage chest. Flopping on the couch next to me, he rolled his shoulders to work the kinks from his body, and I got lost in the movement of his hard nipples under his T-shirt.

"Okay," Yeu finally said. "Let's meet up."

He named a place in Koreatown I'd eaten at before, and asked if I was free for a late lunch. I noted the time in my calendar, then sifted through my notes until I found the column of transactions from Dae-Hoon's account. Verifying the amount of money he'd initially given Dae-Hoon, I calculated the interest and named a final amount. He whistled under his breath.

"God, that much?" He sounded blown away. "That's insane. And they want to give it back to me?"

"I'll need you to sign a receipt for it," I said. "But yeah, they want to give it back to you."

He signed off, and I tossed my phone on the crate, where it apparently offended Neko, because she batted at it from her stalking place on the floor. With her tiny black paw reaching up over the edge, she struck at the phone until she was satisfied it'd been beaten into submission. Her fluffy black tail bobbed along the chest edge. Then she took off, bouncing out of the room with a chirruping song.

"That cat is all kinds of fucked up," I said, watching her exit. "Where the hell did you find her? Silent Hill?"

"She belonged to a friend of mine," Jae murmured, looking up from his tablet screen. "He found her outside in a dumpster. Someone'd tossed her in and closed the lid. I think she was only a couple of weeks old. He already had two cats, and they weren't too happy about having a kitten around. He gave her to me after he got her weaned."

"What was his name? Moreau?" I took a piece of arare and picked at the seaweed wrapped around it. Jae gave me a look, and I nibbled on the black square I'd peeled off. "What?"

"You're supposed to eat it all together," he pointed out.

"I'm also supposed to love women," I murmured. "Look how well I follow the rules there. How long do we have until dinner?"

Korean food went two ways. Either it took forever to get stuff together, or it was instant. Since I had more than one appetite whetted, I thought it would be in my best interests to find out which one I could sate first.

"About an hour." He went back to tapping at the screen, then looked at me from under his lashes. "Why?"

"Put that down," I said, nodding toward the tablet. "And I'll show you."

He took his time, deliberately taunting me by turning off the tablet then securing it back into its case. When he bent over to put it on the other couch, I grabbed him by the hips and pulled him back onto my lap. He landed with a grunt and braced himself against the storage chest, glaring at me.

"You could have broken something," Jae growled. "You could have broken me."

"I'd have kissed and made it better," I promised. "In fact, let me try to do that now."

It was a cliché. I knew it, but Jae's mouth always had a hint of spice to it. Either a fragrant tinge of cloves or a more powerful smack of a pepper he'd chewed on. There was always a bite to kissing him.

Of course, there was always a risk of a bite when kissing him too, but it was a chance I was willing to take.

I turned him over, laying him back onto the couch. It was long, and wide enough for me to stretch out over him and still have room to maneuver my hands around him. Jae squirmed under me, laughing when I gnawed on his nipple through his shirt, but eventually I got my fingers under the fabric and up to where the tight nubs pearled on his chest. Lightly pinching at them, I played with his nipples and hooked his shirt up over the back of his neck, exposing his belly and chest. Jae reached for me, but I shook my head.

"Let me taste you for a bit," I murmured into the hollow of his throat. "I don't spend enough time doing this."

"You only have an hour," he reminded me with a low chuckle.

"Baby, I can have you screaming in less than an hour," I said against his chest. "How long do you think it'll take me to make you come in my mouth?"

"Suppose I don't want to," Jae said, wrapping his fingers into my hair. Tugging sharply, he pulled until I raised my head and looked at him. "Suppose I want you inside of me instead?"

"Then maybe," I whispered back. "Maybe I can try to catch a few drops on my tongue when I make you lose—"

I never found out what his opinion on my idea was, because his hands were down the front of my jeans before I could finish my thought. He found my cock quickly, squeezing it hard enough to curl my balls up, and I gasped, lifting my hips instinctively. His grip was firm, refusing to let go of me, and I came back down, pressing my mouth on his until I stole the air from his lungs.

Yanking his pants and underwear down, I tugged them off his legs and ran my hands back up, reveling in the feel of his hard muscles jumping under his skin when I got to his thighs. Sinking my teeth into the long stretch of muscle near my fingertips, I grinned up at him when he yelped in surprise.

"Mine," I growled. "Stupid thing to say. Very old-school, but fuck it. Mine."

The storage chest was good for several things. First, it made a good place to put our dinner. Secondly, it had handy drawers I could stash things like pens or condoms in. After having Jae over for more than a week, I nearly filled the damn thing with enough condoms to make balloon animals for every drag queen within a five-mile radius.

Which was a hell of a lot since a cabaret show opened up down the block, and most of the women tottering in that place had more hair on their chest than Neko did.

"Help me get undressed, babe," I asked, raking my teeth over Jae's throat.

"No," he replied with a wicked smile. "But I'll get you going."

He'd already popped the top button of my jeans when he first grabbed me, so it was a fairly easy trick for him to slide down the metal zipper. My cock was already too hard to be touched, and I hissed when he slid his fingers underneath my shaft. Tugging me free of my underwear, Jae stroked at my length, easing the sting where my zipper bit me when he pulled my cock free.

"Let me get these off before my dick gets chewed through," I muttered, but his hand kept moving. "You're not helping there, dude."

"I think I'm helping just fine," Jae replied, and snagged my earlobe with his teeth. Worrying at the bit of flesh he'd captured, he stroked me at the same time. My brain fought with the idea of getting the rest of my clothes off and the all-consuming need to bury myself in Jae's hot body.

Need always trumped thought. Especially when my brain unplugs at the merest hint of Jae's mouth on my body.

"You are going to fucking kill me," I growled. "Turn over. I want to fuck you through the damned couch."

I got my shirt off quickly and shoved it under Jae's crotch, milking him as I fumbled with the condom wrapper. Tearing off the end with my teeth, I slid the latex down over my shaft and pulled off some of the lube from the foil. Jae's back begged to be kissed, and I consented, suckling and nibbling along his spine and rib cage until he writhed under my mouth. His hips canted up, and Jae shifted on the couch, his ass spreading slightly when he bent forward and dropped his head down.

Jae rolled his shoulders forward, jutting his blades out like wings. I took the bait, and bit down hard between them while I slid my lubed fingers into his heat. His entrance coyly closed over my intrusion, kissing my fingertips as I toyed with him. Instead of pushing through his resistance, I ran my touch around him, slowly coaxing his body into accepting me.

"Cole-ah," Jae gasped when I slid all of my fingertips right past the edge of his entrance, breaching him momentarily before withdrawing again to caress his pout. He swore when I did it again, his back and legs tensing hard enough to make him tremble. He arched, opening himself up further, and moaned, resting his cheek against the arm of the couch. "Please."

"Yeah, baby?" I kissed the small of his back. Then I went back to teasing him open.

He mewled, a soft keening sound rumbling up from the back of his throat, and he thrust back, impaling himself on my fingers. Chuckling, I drew back, then dipped in again, enough to spread apart his entrance for me. Jae hissed, and his hips twitched, undulating with need.

I was already milking, the tip of the condom damp with my seed. My cock ached, bouncing between Jae's thighs as I kneeled to press into him. Leaving my thumb hooked into him, I eased in, taking my time as he adjusted to being spread apart so much his skin was taut around the head of my dick. He tightened around me, trying to push back, but my hand against the inside of his ass kept him from moving too much. I flexed my thumb, stretching him a bit from the inside out, then inched in further, massaging his entrance as I went.

Jae whimpered, making huffing kitten cries, and gripped the end of the couch, dimpling the fabric. His knuckles were white, the skin bare of blood across the bone. I pulled out, and he keened, hunching his shoulders in protest. Teasing him with the tip of my cock at his entrance, I moved my hips and pressed in, burying myself deep inside of him.

I moved my hand out of the way, letting the rocking of his body drink me in. The muscles of his ass tightened, firming the round mounds I loved to knead. Resting on my knees, I dug my hands into his creamy skin, filling my palms with the meat of his ass. Pushing his cheeks apart enough for me to see my cock sliding into his entrance, I rocked in, spreading him thin around me.

Jae gripped the couch arm and shoved back, getting up on his hands and knees. My chest struck his back with a smack, and I reached up to lock my arms around his slender waist. Sliding my cheek against his shoulders, I opened my mouth and licked at the salty dew forming over his pale skin. He moaned and cried out my name, moving one of his hands down to cup himself.

We moved together, unwilling to break apart for long. I kissed his shoulders, muttering some nonsensical sounds. He responded passionately, hooking me in then drawing himself off my cock until only the tip remained kissed by his heat. I let him ride me, holding myself still as Jae impaled himself on my shaft. With my hands on his hips, I guided him along my length, slowing him down when he staggered off rhythm.

He growled at me, impatient and needy, so I bit the space between his shoulder blades, and slammed into him.

The couch creaked under us, the springs taking as much of a beating as Jae was under my cock, but I had faith it would survive the assault. Much like Jae-Min, it was stronger than it looked.

"Now, *agi*," Jae hissed between his clenched teeth. "Harder. Please."

I picked up the pace, spreading my hands across the small of his back to hold him still. I didn't want him moving. I wanted him to take each thrust I gave him as much as he could… until he felt like he was breaking apart under the shock waves coursing through his gut. Dragging my dick over his core, I worked him hard, running my fingers through the sheen I'd drawn up from his skin. Our legs and balls slapped hard together, our skin meeting with fierce sound. His skin was turning rosy where my hands grabbed, and I clenched his ass, kneading at the muscled roundness until he cried out.

His hair was plastered to his cheeks when I broke my pace and slowed down to a near crawl. Jae protested, crying out and panting, but I was firm. I'd bring him to his release, but I wanted him to feel me do it. I reached under his belly and lightly gripped his slim, hard cock. Rocking into his hot core, I stroked him off, keeping my fingers off his overly sensitive head until I was ready to come myself.

I felt his passage spiral around me, and his balls drew up to mine. The rush of his sac on my skin was a molten pour of heat on my already hot body. He came into my hand, filling the cup of my fingers, and it overflowed, a torrential tide of seed and satiation. His spicy scent drove me wild, and I lost myself in Jae's body, rocking hard as he twisted tight around me.

My climax hit with a force that dropped me. My lungs were taut, depleted of everything except the heat of Jae's skin, and my mouth was filled with his taste, a salty sweetness he only shared with me. I could barely bring my fingers up to my lips when the first wave of my release hit, and my body jerked uncontrollably when I swallowed Jae into my throat, spilling myself into him until I was afraid I would black out over his back.

His spasms slowed, and his breathing faltered, picking up when I slid back onto my knees to give him some air. Gathering Jae up, I pulled him back against me, sliding him into my lap until he sat sideways across my legs. He was lethargic, his eyes sleepy and hooded, the perfect time to cuddle him against me. Wiping him off with the other side of my shirt, I spread his legs wide enough for me to get the condom off, and rolled it up in the shirt, tossing it out of the way.

Jae leaned on my shoulder, unable to do more than draw his knees up and breathe. We struggled to gain our composure, unable to look each other in the eye without chuckling. I brushed the stray strands out of his eyes and kissed his temple, running my fingers through his damp black hair. His breath was hot on my neck, and he surprised me with a lick of his tongue against my collarbone.

"You taste good," he murmured softly. My hand rested on his thigh, and he played with my fingers, drawing on my palm. Relaxed and warm, he sighed and said, "You make me feel safe."

"I'd do anything to make you feel safe, babe," I replied. "You know that."

"Now," Jae whispered. "I know that now. I like feeling... safe. Like I can fall, and you'll... be there. Even if you don't catch me, you'll be there to help me get back up."

"Do you mind if I try to catch you?" I cocked an eyebrow at him. "I've fallen from some pretty high fucking places. It really hurts."

"No, I don't mind," he sighed again. "But, sometimes Cole-ah, I will fall, and you won't be able to catch me. It's just something I'll have to do by myself, but it will be okay if you help pick me up. I don't mind falling. I just... don't want to open my eyes and find I'm alone."

I pulled my fingers from his and cupped his chin, forcing him to look at me. "I will *always* be there to pick you up, Kim Jae-Min. Whether you want me to catch you or not, I'll be there to kiss and make it better. Okay?"

"Okay," Jae nodded, solemn, and quiet. There were so many words left unspoken between us, and they hung there, heavy and silent, like teardrops needing to be kissed away. He murmured something, but I didn't catch it.

Frowning, I kissed his full mouth. "What did you say?"

"*Kamsamida.*" He looked away, ducking his head so I couldn't see his face. "*Saranghae.*"

I grumbled and drew him closer, wrapping my arms tight around his waist. "I am *really* going to have to learn Korean."

"Not yet, *agi*," Jae teased. "Not until I'm ready to have you hear what I say."

"God, you drive me fucking nuts." I shook him lightly, enough to make him laugh. My cell phone started crooning something about bad boys. I frowned at Jae. "Did you change my ringtone?"

"I thought it matched you," he admitted, reaching for the phone and handing it to me.

"We were having a moment there," I grumbled as he slid off me. Grabbing his pants, he tugged them on and padded off to the kitchen. I watched his ass, then slid my phone on to answer it. "Hello?"

"Cole-sshi?" The man on the phone was either drunk or having a stroke. From the sounds of conversation and clinking glass coming from the speaker, I was betting on drunk. "It's David Park."

"Hi," I replied, frowning when I looked at the clock. It was way too early to be drunk dialing someone. "What's up? Where are you?"

"At a place," he mumbled something else, but it was in Korean and I was lost.

"Hold on." I stood up and went into the kitchen. Holding the phone out to Jae, I said, "It's David. He's fucked up, and I can't understand what he's saying."

Jae listened to David for a few moments, then cradled the phone against his shoulder so he could turn off the oven. He nodded and said *de* a few times, agreeing with whatever David was selling him. After a minute, he said something firmly and turned the phone off, then rubbed at his face.

"What?" I asked, taking the phone from him. "What's going on? Why's he drunk? It's not even eight o'clock. I thought you guys were supposed to be hardcore drinkers."

"You guys meaning Koreans? Even we have our limits." He snorted and slapped my arm. "We should go get him. He's down at a club on Wilshire."

"Tell me he didn't drive." My stomach growled, but I ignored it.

"I don't know," Jae said, grabbing his keys. "But I told him to wait. Come on, before he changes his mind."

I closed the door behind me, then realized I was barefoot. The cement was rough on the bottom of my feet, and I grabbed Jae's keys so I could get a pair of Vans from the foyer. Slipping them on, I commandeered his Explorer. "You tell me where to go. I'll drive, and you can get him into the car."

"Okay," Jae said, sliding into the passenger seat.

"Did he tell you why he's sloshed off his ass?" I asked, backing the SUV out.

"Yeah, tomorrow's Helena's service. Kwon told him he's not welcome." Jae shrugged when I shot him an incredulous look. "It's complicated. The family blames the Seongs."

"Okay, I can see that," I said, coming to a stop sign. "So how come he called me instead of having someone from his family pick him up?"

"Because someone snuck into Shin-Cho's hospital room and tried to shoot him again," Jae replied calmly, as if it were as common as finding a penny on the street. Giving it a moment's thought, I had to give him that it was getting way too familiar an event in our lives, something that had to be rectified as soon as possible. "They chased the guy, but he got away."

"Did anyone see who it was?" I asked. "Wait, let me guess: some Asian guy with black hair."

"Doesn't matter," Jae replied, running his hand over my thigh. "They found a Korean man in a rental car about three blocks away. He was shot in the head. David says they think it's Choi Yong-Kun."

"So it's over, then?" I almost sighed in relief. "Fuck me."

"It might be, but I don't know," Jae said grimly. "Unless Choi Yong-Kun somehow could shoot himself in the back of the head, then I'd say no."

CHAPTER NINETEEN

IT LOOKED like every cop in Greater Los Angeles showed up for free donuts and coffee at a strip club and got the address wrong. Throw in some dance kids, some blinking LED pacifiers, and someone scratching some beats, and it would be a full-blown rave.

Seong Ryeowon, however, didn't look like she was in much of a mood for a party.

We'd hunted David down at the bar. It cost me a bit to get him liberated since he ran a tab, and the large Korean man at the door had explicit instructions not to let him wander off without paying up. I forked over my card and made them give me a receipt. After a few seconds of glaring at me, he shambled off and came back with a strip of paper written in hangul and a total that would have paid my electric bill for a few months.

It took me nearly twenty minutes to get David down from the fourth-floor club and into the car. Pouring him into the back seat, Jae strapped him down with both belts, hoping to keep him from sliding around in the SUV, then we drove to the house Seong Ryeowon rented.

The same house where we found the outdoor rave being thrown by the men and women of the Los Angeles Police Department.

Scarlet spotted us first and hurried over to where we parked. With the cops blocking off the cul-de-sac, I had to find a space a few hundred yards away, and by the time I got the back door open, Scarlet was by the car.

She was dressed the most masculine I'd ever seen her in Converse sneakers, a white T, and jeans. Her face was bare of makeup, and her long black hair was pulled back at the nape of her neck. She looked young, an androgynous man who made heads turn in both admiration and confusion.

The kind of guy who'd get his face kicked in if he was in the wrong neighborhood.

"Hello, *musang*." She kissed Jae's cheek and slid her arm around my waist. "I'm glad you're both here…. Is that David? Oh God, it's David! We thought he was missing. Is he okay? What happened?"

"Yeah, no. Not missing. Just really fricking drunk." I'd gotten the belts off him, and had my hands around his upper thighs to yank him toward me. "Stand back. I think he drank his bones loose. He's kind of liquid."

David proved he had more liquid in him than his bones. I'd almost gotten him clear of Jae's car when he sat up and horfed all over my back. The hot, steaming fluid coursed down my spine and right into the gap between my waist and my jeans. It hit me, the side of the car, some of the seat, and the back seat floor mats. Its reek, however, was as pervasive as a London fog.

Two things happened simultaneously. I screamed blue bloody murder and let loose every fucking swear word I'd ever heard in my lifetime. The second, and more potentially dangerous thing, was my bellowing got the attention of the armed police officers barricading the house.

About half of the horde broke off and headed toward Jae's car, weapons drawn and shouting for us to drop to the ground. Jae backed away from the car, and Scarlet held her hands up, alarmed at the amount of guns pointing her way. David chose to ignore my shouting, the cops, and the guns, and instead, decided to hose down the front of my jeans before I could get clear of the splash zone.

"Oh, fuck you, you fucking son of a bitch." I was grabbed from behind and yanked hard. The cop holding me caught one whiff of what I was covered in and gulped, twisting quickly to get away from me. I had a stronger stomach than he did, but he threw me off balance, and I stumbled back. Nearly sliding off the curb, I got clear of the SUV and shook off what I could from my jeans, breathing through my mouth to avoid the fumes.

Most of what David threw up was booze, if not all of it. Judging from the amount he came up with, I'd say the bar pretty much earned what they'd charged him. If someone came near me with a match, I'd probably burst into flames.

I put my hands up, but the cops were much less interested in me now. Scarlet took over, sliding around me in as wide a circle so she could to talk to one of the older policemen. The one who'd grabbed me let Jae and I put our hands down, and grunted either an apology or an order for me to go bathe. I'd have liked the first one, but wouldn't have said no to a bath.

"Let's see if we can get the boy into the house," I muttered, making my second attempt at corralling David. Hooked over my shoulder, he started waving his hand around, and jabbered to everyone around us in Korean. Jae took one look at the inside of his car and sighed heavily, shutting the door on the mess.

"Give me the keys." Jae held out his hand. "I have a gym bag in the back. There's a pair of sweats you can wear. Maybe a T-shirt."

"I'd kiss you, but...." I shrugged as best I could with over a hundred and fifty pounds of drunken David over my shoulders. "Actually, the keys are in my pocket. Can you grab them?"

He gave me a skeptical look. I returned it with a wide-eyed innocent one.

"I can't reach." I jiggled David a bit. "You're going to have to grab them."

"Pfah," Jae grumbled, and turned his head to avoid getting close to me.

"Oh, so it's not that you don't want to feel me up? It's that you don't want to smell me?" His fingers dug into my front pocket and snagged the ring on his keys. He shook himself when he got clear of me. I'd have taken offense, but at that point, I wanted to be as far from me as possible.

"Cole, come." Scarlet hurried me along. "Let's get him in the house."

A portion of the lawn was cordoned off, and I had to make a wide circle to get to the front door. Something dark was on the lawn, but I didn't stop to take a look. I should have foisted David on one of the many black-suited guys standing near the house, but I was already soaked to the skin in soju and whiskey, so it made little sense to share the misery. Nearby, someone must have had an out of control fireplace flue, because a faint trail of smoke lingered around us, and closer to the house, there was an odd scent to the air, a sour, burnt chemical flavor that stuck to my tongue. I wasn't sure what was worse: the evening air or David.

A soft-voiced woman greeted me at the door, giving me a deep bow as she asked me to enter. I took a second to kick my Vans off, juggling David as best I could. He moaned and made an urping sound, threatening to douse me again.

"I swear to God, you hairball on me again," I growled. "I'll drop you. Right here. Right now."

I dumped David onto a bed the staff led me to, and asked the officious woman if there was somewhere I could shower and change. Ten minutes later, I emerged from the hot water smelling of citrus soap with a faint undertone of booze. Jae was waiting for me in the guest bedroom where they'd stashed me, perched on a wide, comfortable looking chair. I'd put on the sweat pants and shirt Jae had on him. The pants were a bit short, and the thin cotton T-shirt was ridiculously tight across my chest and back. I felt like I was a twink trolling for a good time. My own clothes were nowhere to be seen.

"Where's my stuff?" I looked around, and he handed me a pair of fluffy house slippers. "What's this?"

"Put them on. It's considered polite to provide guests with footwear for the house. And your stuff's in the wash." Jae sniffed at me experimentally. "You still smell a bit... alcoholy... but not a lot."

"Yeah, I smell like a Harvey Wallbanger."

"That sounds... dirty." Jae eyed me. "Did you make that up? What is that?"

"It's a drink. Do enough of them, and you'll be banging the walls, trying to walk," I replied, sliding my feet into the slippers. They strained to accommodate my feet, but surrendered admirably. My heels stuck out over the end of them. "If I trip in these, don't try to catch me. Save yourself."

"Are you done?" He shook his head and headed to the door. "One of the detectives wants to talk to us about David."

The detective in question was Wong, whom I'd already spoken to. He was a pleasant-faced Chinese man who looked like he could break a tree in half with his bare hands. This theory was confirmed when we shook hands, and I was left with the feeling he was being careful with my wee, delicate little body. Like my brother, his barber set the haircut razor for Hedgehog #4. Unlike Mike, he was quite concerned about my adventures in carrying David back to his lair.

"Please, sit down," Wong said, gesturing to one of the many chairs in the long formal parlor. "I feel like I'm going to break someone or something if I move around too much."

There was a coffee set on the heavily carved wooden table set up near a pair of French looking davenports. A silver urn steamed a fragrant promise of nicely roasted and brewed beans, while a tempting array of dainty cakes glistened on a plate nearby.

Poking at one of the frothy concoctions with a fork, I asked, "If I eat one of these, I won't suddenly shoot up into the chimney, and have to kick a lizard named Bill to get out of here, right?"

"Please excuse Cole. He's missed dinner. It makes him cranky." Jae gave Wong a look that would have done a basset hound proud, and sat down. He poured a cup of coffee for himself and lifted the urn slightly toward Wong. "Coffee?"

"Please," he smiled. "Thanks."

I didn't like his smile.

To be fair, I'd had great sex with my lover, then gone to rescue the Seong Prince errant only to have him chuck up his drinking binge down my boxers, and now a Chinese guy with a wedding ring was smiling at my boyfriend. And yes, I'd missed dinner. That tended to make me cranky, but I was mollified when Jae passed the full coffee cup over to me, then poured himself and Wong one.

I was easily mollified. Jae's wicked side smirk at me didn't hurt.

"What was all the police action for? David wasn't gone twenty-four hours yet." I picked at a piece of cake. It was green and had some sort of nut shaving on top. I waited until Wong was taking a sip of his coffee before I pecked at a bit of it and put it on my tongue. It was not too sweet, and kind of creamy.

I had no fucking clue what flavor it was supposed to be. So I handed it to Jae and went for something brown. In most worlds, brown meant chocolate. Maybe coffee. So my odds were good it was something I'd recognize.

"Mrs. Seong informed me you know about her son's relationship with a South Korean officer named Choi." Wong flipped through his notepad.

"Choi Yong-Kun," I confirmed. "David told Jae-Min... that's a lot of hearsay. He should probably tell you himself."

"Why don't you both start with where you were from about three this afternoon to when you arrived here at eight?" Wong suggested.

"Um, we were at the office running down some contacts," I started, tracing our movements from the florist to the hospital and then back home. Jae frowned a little when I said we were hanging out while he was making dinner, but I kept it clean enough for Wong's purposes.

"That's when Park called you?" he asked. "You, specifically, Mr. McGinnis?"

"Yeah," I replied. "But he sounded drunk, and I don't speak Korean, so I handed the phone to Jae."

Jae relayed what David told him over the phone about being forbidden to attend his fiancée's funeral service, and then the discovery of Choi's body. Jae looked perplexed. "He seemed to think that everything was over now, but it didn't make sense, because from what David-sshi told me, it sounded like Choi Yoon-Kun was murdered."

"He was," Wong confirmed. "A patrolman was alerted to the presence of Choi's body and immediately shut down the area where his car was found. I don't have anyone able to place David Park in the area, but four hours ago, his family contacted us with concerns about his safety following a conversation he had with a Mr. Sang-Min Kwon, his fiancée's father."

"Yeah, I know Kwon." I rumbled. "Kind of an asshole."

"Unfortunately, that isn't enough of a reason to kill someone these days." Wong clucked in concern as I choked on the piece of cake in my mouth.

"What about Kwon?" Jae sat forward, cocking his head at Wong. "What happened to Kwon?"

"Around two hours ago, Sang-Min Kwon was found staked to the front lawn of this residence. At the time of discovery, he was still mostly engulfed in flames, most likely fueled by an accelerant of some sort. So I'm going to have to ask both of you, where were you two hours ago, and can you help confirm David Park's whereabouts for that time? Or are we going to all be taking a trip down to the station?"

"FUCK me," I whispered under my breath, and Jae sighed, resigned to my coarse, uncouth ways. He pursed his lips when I looked his way. "What?"

"I forgot to feed the cat," Jae grumbled at me. "And it's stupid that I'm worried about that right now."

"It's not stupid," I argued. "The cat's evil. She could be having Thai food delivered right now and charging it to my card. Kwon's dead, and so is Choi. Who the hell are we going to blame this crap on now?"

"I don't know," Scarlet replied softly. "I just want this all to stop."

We'd been moved from the overly pretentious formal room to a more breathable family space. Scarlet joined us, and the cakes were replaced with a heartier offering of sandwich triangles. They were only heartier if someone were Scarlet's size. Even in Jae's long fingered, slender hands, they looked like play food made by a three-year-old.

I ate four of them and tried not to look like I wanted to graze over the rest like some mad cow.

Scarlet picked up another two and put them on my plate, and patted my knee consolingly. "Eat. You're starting to lose your color."

I took my time chewing, trying to make the tidbits last longer. Jae sacrificed two of his triangles to me, and I tried to be manly, refusing them with a shake of my head. He leaned over to kiss me and shoved them into my mouth.

"What happened to being careful about someone seeing us?" I mumbled through the crumbly cheddar.

"No one's here," Jae said, but he and Scarlet exchanged a look. "And right now, I'm too tired to care."

I slid over to his side of the couch, reaching behind him to rub between his shoulders. "Hey, they'll let us out of here soon. We'll go home. I'll get us some real food, and we can just chill."

"Someone set him on fucking fire, Cole," he ground out. "The same guy who probably shot at you set Kwon on fire. What the hell am I supposed to do with that?"

"I'm going to leave you two to talk this out." Scarlet was a master at subtle exits. Picking up the dirty dishes, she was out of the room before either one of us could blink. She shut the door behind her, and we were alone.

"Great, now I've chased *nuna* away. Fuck," Jae swore, and threw himself back into the couch. Grabbing a small bolster, he winged it full force into the wall, saying something in Korean that needed very little translating.

"You didn't chase her away," I said. "She loves you."

The room faced the backyard, a gloomy affair of hedges, classic marble statues, and overgrown roses. There was no light on outside, and the soft illumination from the lamp on the table next to us gave us enough light to see one another. I pulled myself closer, mindful of any more flying pillows. I reached for his hand, but he wavered, refusing to let me touch him. Finally, I grabbed him, wrapping fingers around his.

"I'm not going anywhere," I said slowly. "I'm not going to let myself be set on fire, and I'm not going to let myself get shot to death."

"Yeah, like you've been good at that so far?" he snapped back. "You've been shot more times than anyone else I know. *Aish!* Can't you dodge at least *one* of them? How many more people need to die around us? Who's next? Scarlet? Bobby? Mike?"

"Hey, that's not fair," I countered. "We didn't cause *any* of this, and I sure as hell didn't *ask* to get shot."

"Cole, you can't even avoid vomit," Jae sighed.

"Babe, if I'd known he was going to throw up, I'd have tossed him right out of the car before we even got here. We're going to have to ride home in that car. Did you think I wanted to smell that all the way back?"

"When is this going to stop?" He didn't sound angry, more resigned to the nonsense around us.

"I don't know," I admitted. "Soon? Maybe? I don't know, Jae."

"Is it always like this around you?" He waved his hand in the air. I could have pretended not to understand him, but I knew he meant the chaos that seemed to follow me everywhere I went. "Does it have to be so crazy?"

"Yeah, pretty much. Life gets shitty sometimes." Pressing in, I maneuvered him against the couch arm, reminding him of the hour we'd spent before David imploded our evening. He shifted a bit, uncomfortably so, and I grinned, knowing he could still feel the stretch of me on his body. Leaning forward, I ghosted a kiss over his lips. "But it's good too, right?"

He returned my kiss with a hotter intent, sucking my lower lip into his mouth and tugging on it. Taking one last nibble, he whispered, "Sometimes."

I carded my fingers through his soft hair and pulled his head closer until our foreheads touched. "I'll take care of this, Jae. We'll see this through, and it'll be fine. It's just... a bit crazy right now, but it can't be this way forever."

"What happens when the crazy stops, and all you're left with is me?" His tongue darted across his upper lip, and I chased it with my mouth, catching the tip before it disappeared again.

"If all I'm left with is you," I murmured. "Then I'm going to die a happy man."

"Just die an old, happy man," he grumbled, and bit the end of my nose. "Or I'm just going to finish you off myself with a pillow."

"Ah, you frighten me," I teased.

"You should be scared." Jae smirked. "I'm going to fill your mouth with kim chee paste and duct tape it shut, *then* smother you with a pillow."

"So you've thought about this?"

"No, that's off the top of my head," Jae replied airily. "Imagine what I could come up with if I had time to think about it."

"Very frightening," I asserted. I slid my hand down to the back of his neck, cupping him lightly. "Bring it, baby."

We kissed.

It was sweet and slow. In the dark of a single light with the world raining down around us, it was a promise of a starry night once the clouds cleared.

Damn, I wanted a lifetime of those kisses.

"I'll wait for this, you know," I whispered when we came up for air. My mouth was barely on his, and our lips touched then broke apart as I spoke. "For this. For you."

"Suppose it's too long?" He closed his eyes and turned his head, resting his temple on my forehead. "Suppose...."

"I intend to die a happy old man, remember." I stroked at his nape, making him sigh. "I'm not sure I'm going to be as happy waiting for you as I'm going to be actually having you, but I'm willing to find out, *jagiya*."

His eyes flew open, and he stared at me in mild shock. "Who taught you that word?"

"Huh." I pursed my lips and stood, pulling him up with me. "Guess I know a little bit more Korean than you thought."

CHAPTER TWENTY

LOS ANGELES in the pouring rain is a miserable place.

People forget how to drive, someone at Metro arbitrarily decides to send out only the buses that break down in the middle of the street, and more importantly, the city apparently bought its traffic lights at a garage sale, because as soon as there is the slightest hint of moisture in the air, they start blinking purple.

Goddamn light trees don't even *have* a purple, but they were certainly doing their fucking best to blink it.

When I'd agreed to meet Yeu in Koreatown, there hadn't been a whisper of an incoming storm. If I'd known, I'd have suggested we drive up to San Francisco to have dim sum at Hang Ah. It would have taken me less time to drive there than it did to get down Wilshire.

Parking was crap. I finally gave up looking for something on the street and went into the four-story garage across the street from the restaurant. The light on Sixth and Kenmore was out, so it was a quick game of *Frogger* through the crowd and the rain to reach the hole-in-the-wall eatery. I'd been there before with Jae. They made a pancake with kim chee I used to be suspicious of, but now it was something I looked forward to.

Jae also picked out any eyeballs from my food before I looked at it.

I was man enough to know my limitations. Eyeballs, when not attached to a human being, and staring back up at me from my food, counted as a limitation. I also didn't like tongues, but on a shrimp those were harder to see. When one restaurant gave me a whole fish as panchan, Jae just took the head while I pretended to study the décor.

The décor sucked. The fish, however, was great.

I realized when I got to the restaurant tucked into the corner of the strip mall, I had *no* idea what Brandon Yeu looked like. The place was half-empty, caught between the lunch and dinner crowds, and the storm probably kept everyone but the die-hard eaters away. When I entered, a trim, distinguished Korean man stood up at one of the back tables and waved me over.

He didn't look like the type of guy people imagined at a gay bathhouse raid, but then those kinds of guys also usually found their jollies elsewhere. Attractive and fit, Yeu was a little shorter than me with wiry, muscular arms. He had a natural tan, and laugh lines around his brown eyes. He'd come to our meeting in slacks and a button-up shirt, rolling the sleeves back to expose a thick leather-banded watch on his wrist. The gold band on his ring finger was scuffed a bit, definitely not a new piece of jewelry, but it still glinted when he extended his hand.

"McGinnis? I'm Brandon Yeu." He shook my hand when I offered it. He must have read the slight confusion on my face. "I looked you up. There's a picture of you on your website."

"Hi. Please, just call me Cole." I'd forgotten about the site. Mike'd put it up for me when he had his security firm's redone. For all I knew, he could have plastered on pictures of me when I was three, riding the furry pony I'd gotten for Christmas butt naked except for a cowboy hat and a gun belt.

"I have to admit, I was kind of surprised to hear from you," he said as an older woman set glasses of barley tea in front of us.

I ordered *bulgogi*, hoping it was the one without bones, and Yeu ordered something with a lot of *D*s and *K*s in it. It sounded like the rice cylinder bobbles and ramen dish Jae liked, but I'd have to wait to see if I was right.

Opening the portfolio I'd brought with me, I extracted the check David had the bank cut for me a few hours ago. Passing the envelope over to Yeu, I said, "The Parks would like to extend their apologies about this. Shin-Cho and David would have come, but there's been a few tragic events in the family. They send their regrets."

Events seemed to be too small of a word for Helena's death, Shin-Cho's injuries, and the terror that seemed to follow the Park brothers, but it was the best I could come up with. Yeu didn't need to be burdened with details, and from the relief on his face, I guessed he was glad to keep our meeting short and concise. Formal family apologies seemed to run for hours and did nothing but make people uncomfortable.

He opened the envelope and took the check out, staring at it for a few seconds. Tapping it against the table, Yeu grinned up at me sheepishly. "To be honest, I wanted to tear it up into little pieces and fling it back in their faces."

I shrugged and said, "They were kids when this all happened. They're just trying to make things right."

"I know. It was a moment of pride and outrage that lasted as long as my husband reminding me our son's going to be in college soon." He put the check back into the envelope and grinned at me. His front tooth had a chip in it, an endearing flaw in his smile. "He's still a freshman, but I might as well worry about it now."

"Is your husband Korean? 'Cause I've got to admit, it seems like most of the Korean guys I meet are gay." I took a sip of the cold barley tea. "Could just be who I'm hanging out with. My boyfriend's Korean."

"Probably because it's easier to be gay and Korean here than in Korea," Yeu replied. "There, you don't even say the word, or they look at you funny. But no, my husband's Chinese. Same problem, though. His family's kicked him out of the registry. My father was the same way until my son was born, and my brothers' wives only had girls. Now I'm the favorite."

He did what all parents do, producing a photo from his phone with seeming ease. A cute pre-teen boy with Yeu's nose and smile stared out at me from the screen, his arm around a fierce looking Korean patriarch whose eyes shone with pride.

"Dean's a smart kid. I want the best for him." Yeu put his phone away. "My father's offered to pay for his college, but… it's important for me to get him through it."

"Yeah, I know how that is."

"Doesn't stop my father from trying to buy him a car, but I've stalled him at least until Dean's got a license." He chuckled. The meal arrived, and we thanked the woman, tucking into our food. A few seconds later, she came back with a small cast iron pot of steamed egg froth, urging me to eat more, then patting me on the back as she left.

Yeu laughed. "Guess you've been here before."

"Yeah, Jae likes it here," I replied. "*He* gets spoiled rotten. Probably because he's prettier than I am."

We ate in silence for a bit. The bulgolgi was perfect, and I'd been right about the D-K dish. Yeu picked out pieces of noodle with his chopsticks, and ate without slurping the red sauce across the table. Lacking that skill, I kept fighting with my rice until I gave up and reached for the spoon.

"I'm not really sure what I can tell you about that night." Yeu finally broached the topic I'd come for. "Yes, I did see him, but I was pissed off at him so I didn't stop to talk. When the cops came through the door, I'd just arrived."

"Dae-Hoon was upstairs with someone else. That person went out the back, but she didn't see Dae-Hoon leave that way. Were you in the front?"

"Yeah, I wasn't fighting them. They put cuffs on me and had me sit against the wall outside. They were bringing one of those trucks to take us to the station," Yeu recalled. "The cops were pulling people down the stairs. Dae-Hoon was one of them, but so were a lot of other men."

"Do you remember anything about the person he was with? Anything?"

"Just a cop. He was wearing a uniform, I think." Yeu looked away, frowning as he tried to dredge up memories of that night. "He was white… and big, but that was pretty much every cop there. Dae-

Hoon wasn't put at the wall like the rest of us. The cop took him outside and put him in a black sedan. It could have been an unmarked car. I don't know. I didn't really think about it. I had other things on my mind at the time."

"Anything else?" My notes were lean. I needed to find the cop that escorted Dae-Hoon out of the building. He was the next step in the chain to Dae-Hoon's disappearance.

"Not that I can think of. The cop put Dae-Hoon in the car and drove off." Yeu shrugged. "I was put into one of those paddy trucks. Went down to the station, got arrested, and left the next morning to tell my father I was gay. I'd spent the night in jail because of it. I guess I was just tired of getting pushed around. That's the last time I saw Dae-Hoon."

We lingered a bit over the food, mostly talking about football, and disparaging Los Angeles' inability to get a team, much less keep one. I refused a third helping of the steamed egg but ate the rest of the fishcake. Yeu polished off the rest of the panchan and declared it was time for him to head home.

With Jae on an engagement party shoot until ten, I'd have the house to myself, not something I actually wanted. Crossing the street, I climbed the stairs to the third level of the parking structure where I'd left the Rover. Dialing up Bobby to see if he wanted to watch a game, I'd just exited the stairwell when the lights went out.

The structure's walls were high, barely letting in the watery outside light. The cold storm front doused nearly all of the sunlight, hanging a dark gray veil over the area. Lightning crackled across the sky to the west, a brief scatter of forks followed by an earthshaking rumble. Another boom followed, this one close enough to make me miss hearing Bobby's machine pick up on the other end. I blinked, trying to get my eyes adjusted to the lack of light, when another flash went off right over me, filling my eyes with a painful white-blue wash.

"Son of a bitch," I swore into the phone as Bobby's voice mail wound down. My eyes were watering, and the blinking only seemed to make it worse. The Rover was a large gray mass at the other end, and I crossed over toward it, avoiding the lakes pooling up from the rain as it came in from the sides. "Yeah, ignore that, Bobby. Sorry, lights are off down in Ktown. Hey, if you want to catch a game tonight, let me—"

The first shot went wide, hitting the car parked a few spaces from where I was standing. Startled, I twisted to get down, flinging myself to the concrete, and my phone skittered out of my hand, landing somewhere in the dark recesses between a car and the containment wall. I saw a bit of a flash coming from the right, but other than that, I could barely see in front of me. I ducked down and tried to look for some cover. The level hadn't had many cars on it when I'd parked, and there seemed to be even less from what I could make out from the fuzzy blurs swimming in front of me.

I ran, slamming my hip into the shot-up car. My foot splashed through a stream pouring out of the front of the compact, the oddly metallic smell of radiator fluid hitting me in the face. Wiping the damp off my lashes, I let my eyes adjust to the dim light while I huddled at the rear of the backed-in tiny car. I couldn't see my phone, but there was little chance of it surviving hitting the concrete. They seemed to break with only a sharp look and a scolding. I didn't think smacking into congealed rock would do it any good.

"Bad place to be, McGinnis," I muttered. "And why the hell don't you carry a fucking gun?"

It was a moot point. Said gun was safely snoozing in a lock box at the top of my armoire, probably dreaming of electric pigeons. I poked my head out a bit, jerking back when another bullet whizzed past my head and slammed into the high concrete barrier behind me.

Of course I'd parked the Rover at the far end of the level, but even if I reached it, it was still only made of steel and glass. I was fond of the new Rover. I'd just gotten the seat to where I wanted it, and the mirrors were adjusted perfectly for me to see out the back window and sides. I'd be damned if I was going to turn it over for target practice. If anything happened to it, my insurance company would insist my next car be a tank.

I decided to try reason.

Shouting over the edge of the car, I kept an eye out for any movement. "Look, I'm guessing you're the asshole that's been trying to kill me lately. Want to tell me why?"

Having only been targeted for death twice in my life, I had a fifty-fifty chance of whoever was shooting at me giving me a reason. Jae's cousin had been more than happy to bare her soul, while Ben went to his self-inflicted grave with all of his grudges against Rick and I buried with him.

"Where's Shin-Cho?" The voice echoing through the structure was male, and definitely Korean. His English was a marbled blend of vowels and slurring hisses. Choi was dead, and I tried the only other person I could imagine would be wondering where Shin-Cho was.

"Li Mun-Hee?"

That earned me another bullet.

It blew out a couple of the windows, going through the driver's side and out the rear glass. A pebbled rain poured down on me, and I used the sound to cover my scuttling over to a Honda a few spaces away. A second later, another round popped off, and a chunk of concrete flew off the wall, smacking the ground between the cars. Hovering at the front of the car, I was thankful the owner'd pulled in and left me with a lot of room to maneuver.

"Look, Mun-Hee," I shouted again, fighting a roll of thunder passing over. "You might be pissed off at Shin-Cho, but everyone else is innocent in this!"

"Why would I be mad at Shin-Cho? I love him. He's mine."

I heard a scuttling sound and peered under the car. Li was closer to the side of the structure facing the street where the walls were lower. I could see his boots as he walked around by the stairwell. Even if I made it to the ramp, he was between me and the exit. I only had the top level as a choice, and that would leave me fully exposed.

"You shot him," I reminded Li. "At the bar. Remember?"

"I shot that man! The one talking to him!" Li's frustration was growing, and he paused in midstep. I was guessing he was checking behind every vehicle when he hurried over and stopped in the shadows behind a lowered sports car. "I wasn't trying to hit Shin-Cho."

"And Helena? What the hell did she do?" I had no idea how many bullets he had, or how many he shot. Those cool scenes where the good guy counts off the rounds then jumps the bad guy were full of shit. I had no idea if he had a full magazine or was using a Colt Revolver, and there was no way in hell I was going to risk my head to find out.

"I was aiming for Kwon," Li yelled back. "That...." I didn't know the word he used. It didn't matter. It was pretty obvious Kwon hadn't been one of Li's favorite people. "He's the one who took Shin-Cho. Waiting for Shin-Cho to come to America, so he could have him again. He needed to die."

I could argue that very few people actually *needed* to die, but I didn't think Mun-Hee was willing to listen to any arguments I might make on the subject. He proved that by shooting out another window, startling a bird that apparently had taken refuge from the rain under it.

"Great, now he's shooting at anything that moves," I grumbled, and checked to see where his boots were. If I'd been smart, I'd have brought my gun and shot under the cars to hit his feet. But then if I'd been smart, I'd also have taken a high-powered flashlight so I could see better.

Mun-Hee hadn't moved, probably listening for the sound of my voice before he pounced. A flash of lightning hit, and I yelled at him, hoping to keep him talking and distracted. "What about Choi? What is it? One big conspiracy to keep Shin-Cho from being with you?"

I'd timed it pretty well. The thunder masked any sound I made scrambling across the floor, and at the same time, Mun-Hee emptied a couple of rounds into the car I'd been hiding behind. Alarms started going off, blaring and chirping in a hideous symphony when another wave of thunder and lightning, closer and louder than the others, hit. The noise was deafening, and I chanced looking to see where Mun-Hee'd gone.

I'd blinked, and like some damned stone angel, he was now only a few feet away, standing still and cautious as he looked around for his prey.

The weapon he had in his hand was a dark, wicked thing. I hadn't seen the type of gun it was, but that really wasn't going to help me. Even though he seemed like a shitty shot, he could still get lucky. I didn't need to know the type of gun being used to kill me. Dead was dead. There wasn't going to be a test later.

"Choi was trying to stop me," Mun-Hee muttered loudly. He was only a car length away from me, and he shuffled around the floor, unsure if I'd made it across to the other side or was still bunny-hopping down the row. "He followed me here. He didn't think I saw him, but I did. He wanted Shin-Cho too. I could see it."

"Shin-Cho's not that hot," I mumbled.

Li was obviously off his nut. For all I knew, Choi'd been the man-whore of Seoul with the ladies, and Shin-Cho's stalker was right about his seductive ways, but I doubted it. I shifted as I crouched, and bit my lip when my elbow struck the wheel of the car I'd made it to. A creeping numbness hit my nerves, and I clenched my mouth shut, ignoring the sensation of my funny bone's complaints.

The wheel rattled a bit when I'd hit it, and a chunk of mud fell off the hubcap, landing near my feet. Resting my hand against the tire, I pressed on the outer rim again, and was rewarded with a tell-tale rattle. I took a quick peek under the car's bumper to see if Li was where I'd left him. He hadn't moved an inch.

I'd actually formulated a plan. Sitting complacent and drowsy near one of the support columns was an old Lincoln Continental. It was an aging monster, tired and worn after years of battling Los Angeles traffic and the hot California sun. Its sides were battered, scarred from daily combat. A long red mark ran along its powdery, faded lime green, a coup counted against a lesser opponent.

It was a glorious beast, and I thanked it and God for its sacrifice.

Having an older brother who pretty much sucked at any sport involving throwing a ball, I spent a lot of my childhood playing odd games as Mike struggled to find something he was good at. He'd finally grown old enough to handle a weapon, so the weekends of mind-numbing faux-sports thankfully came to an end when my father pitied him enough to take him to the gun range. Still, I had Mike to thank for my rusty disc-golf skills when I yanked off the Continental's hubcap, stood up, and aimed for the back of Li's head.

Hubcaps are dangerous things, especially ones made from Detroit steel. Retention notches over time fray, breaking off into dozens of corroded tiny knives, and more importantly, the outer ring could slice through a chunk of soft meat like nobody's business.

The old monster's tire covering flew, cutting through the air as if it were an original pie plate made in Bridgeport. Its sharp crenulated edges made a whistling sound as it flew, startled Li, and he turned, his eyes going wide when he saw the spinning metal disc. His mouth slack, he took a step back, but the hubcap merrily whistled on. Tilting slightly, it struck Li hard, snapping his head back. Blood gushed from the gaping wound running down his throat and soaking his shirt in a torrent of red.

I sprang forward, slamming into him with my shoulder. Pain shot down my arm, and my chest cramped under my scarring when his torso folded in half and smashed over my bent-over body. Twisting up, I grabbed his wrist to yank the gun away, and he wheeled away, unsteadily flailing about for balance.

The sparse years of boxing with Bobby taught me a lot about inertia and momentum. My childhood with Mike, however, taught me that when an opponent went down, that was the time to kick the shit out of him... no matter what good sportsmanship said about the matter. Seeing as Li had a death-grip on his gun, I opted for the older brother school of warfare.

I clenched my hands together, brought them up over my head, and brought them down on Li's face. Repeatedly.

He lost a tooth first. The gun came next, quickly followed by his consciousness.

Standing, I kicked the gun away and shook out my hands. Blood dripped from cuts on my knuckles, and my palm stung where the air struck skin I'd abraded when throwing the hubcap. My knee ached a bit, and I belatedly realized I'd struck the Continental's fender when I'd attacked Li.

"Sorry, old man, but I really needed to hand Li his ass. I didn't have any other choice." I saluted the car before bending over to rest my hands on my knees to catch my breath. "I'll buy you a car wash. Looks like you need one."

Boots echoed from the stairwell, and a small phalanx of blue uniformed men poured out into the garage. Weapons drawn, the one in front shouted for me to let go of my weapon and get down on the ground. Sighing, I held up my empty, bloody hands for them to see and nodded to the prone, gasping man lying like a tribute in front of the Lincoln.

"Where the hell have all of *you* been?" I asked tiredly. One of the cops twitched nervously, and I frowned at him, nodding at his drawn gun. "And I swear to God, if you shoot me, you better fucking kill me, because if you don't, my boyfriend sure as hell will."

CHAPTER TWENTY-ONE

"I HAVE hunted and gathered for you, my love," I announced as I came through the front door with two hefty orders of *bún thịt nướng*. "It's not wooly mammoth, but I think we'll be okay."

Jae didn't even look up when I came into the living room and gave him a kiss on the cheek. He did, however, look more interested in the kiss than the food. At least I had that going for me.

It was noon on the day after Li decided it was a good day for me to die, and I'd spent a few hours in the office doing invoicing and trying to track down more gay Korean men to give money to. I was going to hand the list off to a Seoul investigator Seong hired to discreetly contact the men living there.

Putting the food down on the no-sex-zone storage chest, I nudged Neko out of the way so I could sit down next to Jae. He'd taken over the room to work in, something I liked him doing on the days he didn't have shoots. It was kind of nice to know Jae was in the back while I worked in the office out front.

It was very domestic, and not something I was going to share with anyone, especially not Bobby or Mike.

Jae's laptop was open and on the crate, with black wires crawling across the floor to connect it to a server box. The television I'd wanted to watch the game on last night was playing what looked like the news with a placid, pretty young woman speaking very seriously about what looked like the grand opening of a restaurant. A bright red and yellow banner scrolled on the bottom of the screen, white hangul flashing about something important. Of course, from what I'd seen of Korean television, a sale on cabbage was sometimes considered to be the most vital piece of information anyone needed. They also had the weirdest commercials I'd ever seen.

"What're you watching?" It was out of my mouth before I even thought about it. "Sorry, stupid question. Let's try, how was your day?"

"Okay," he murmured, setting down his tablet.

I hooked my arm around his waist, and Jae moved over, lifting up to straddle my thighs. Resting his arms on my shoulders, he hooked his hands behind my head and sighed, touching my forehead with his lips. He didn't sound fine. He didn't sound bad, but fine definitely wasn't on the menu.

"What's up?" I'd say I stole a kiss, but one cannot steal what is freely given. "Hey, I didn't get shot."

"About time," he grumbled at me. "And nothing, really. Spoke to my mother. I sent her what I could from the Kwon party. They paid me anyway, even though I told them not to. *Hyung* insisted I keep it."

"That was nice of them," I said. "Especially considering all the shit they've been through."

"Yeah, David's mother also sent over a fruit basket and a check. She wants to pay for getting the car cleaned." Jae shrugged. "I feel bad about taking it. I already steamed the carpets. It wasn't that bad."

"Keep it," I insisted. "He threw up down the back of my pants. I had recycled soju in the crack of my ass. I demand you be compensated for the lack of freshness of my butt."

His smile was bright enough to chase away the gloom lurking outside, and his soft, low chuckle was molten chocolate on my tongue when I kissed him.

"You're crazy." Jae hugged me, pressing himself tightly against my chest. I wrapped my arms around his waist, holding him there, enjoying the feel of him on me.

The news woman cycled away from the restaurant, and was now focused on an array of enormous chrysanthemum wreaths lined up in front of a glass building. Kwon's face appeared on the screen, followed by a smaller picture of Helena, smiling as she'd been the last time I'd seen her.

"Hey, what's going on?" I loosened my hold on Jae so he could slide across my lap and look at the television. "Is that about Kwon?"

"Yeah, he's *chaebol*, remember? That's his family's company headquarters. They're showing the memorial wreaths coming in from other families and companies. He was the oldest son. It's kind of a big deal he died."

I was sorry Kwon died. Even an asshole like him shouldn't have had his life end the way it did. Even more so, Helena's passing was senseless. Their family now had a gaping wound where two people existed, because Li Mun-Hee was obsessed with a man he couldn't have.

"What's she saying?" I leaned forward, keeping a hold on Jae's waist so he didn't slide off my lap.

"I thought you spoke Korean now." He smirked at me.

"Only the words I want to know," I replied smoothly. "Actually, only the words I can use. The rest, I have you for."

"Huh." Skeptical didn't begin to describe the look on his face.

"Answer the question. What's she saying?" I grabbed a pinch of his ribs through his shirt where he was ticklish. "Who's that putting the flowers down?"

"Um, Park Dae-Su," Jae replied. "That's Shin-Cho and David's uncle. The Parks are showing good face."

The camera zoomed in on Dae-Su as he straightened the banners on the standing wreath, and he spoke softly to the cameraman, obviously expressing condolences to the Kwon family. Someone off camera asked him a question, and he turned his head slightly, answering them in the same steady voice that reminded me so much of David.

"Fucking hell." It was a strong reaction to a brief bit on a memorial service, but the resemblance between David and his uncle was pretty remarkable. Looking at the elder Park, I could clearly see what David would look like in twenty or so years. "I've got a question."

"Okay." Jae disentangled himself from my hold and migrated over to poking at the cold noodle dishes I'd brought home. "Pork and shrimp?"

"I don't know. I just pointed to the menu and grunted. She speaks fluent McGinnis."

"So it's probably those microwave pizza rolls on rice noodles, then?"

"It's like living on the edge with me," I proclaimed proudly. "Every day is an adventure."

"Pork," Jae announced. He plucked one of the fried spring rolls out of a smaller bag, offering me the open end after he bit into it. "What's your question?"

"When Koreans name their kids, they follow, like, a formula, right?"

"A formula?" He raised his eyebrows.

"I mean like you and your brother," I said. "Both of your names begin with Jae. The Park boys are Shin."

"Yeah, most families use a generation name, so everyone in your... group...." Jae made a face at the word he chose. "They'd all have the same first sound. Not everyone does it, but almost all do, especially if the family's old."

"So Dae-Su." I gestured to the television, but the broadcast had already moved away from the Kwons. "His brothers would all be named Dae-something?"

"Like Dae-Hoon?" Jae poked me in the stomach in mock disgust and went back to digging through the food. "*Aish*, Dae-Su's Dae-Hoon's brother, remember?"

"Yeah, that's what I thought." I gave him a big kiss and stood up, almost stepping on the cat begging by my feet. "Leave me some noodles. I'll be back soon."

"Don't forget we've got dinner with Tasha at Mike's tonight," Jae called out after me.

"Won't forget!" I shouted back as I grabbed my keys. "I even got a cake."

A SILVER two-seater convertible sat in the garage, its top pulled up in preparation for more rain. The washer and dryer next to the closed back door were churning away, and a plastic basket of crumpled towels and linens sat waiting for their turn in the cycle.

I dodged the light smatter of raindrops as best I could, after I parked the Rover at the curb. Shaking off what I could, I rang the doorbell and waited. The middle-aged Korean man who opened the door was hauntingly familiar to me, and not just because I'd seen him in photos with his husband, William. Funny thing about genetics, sometimes brothers really looked alike, even when seen on a Korean broadcast.

Smiling, I said gently, "Hello, Dae-Hoon."

I'd taken a chance that he'd be home, after checking his schedule on the college's website, but sometimes students sucked up more time than expected. I imagined my Ancient History professor still had nightmares about me. God knows, I still had them about *her*.

His reactions were liquid, emotional, and clearly written on his face. There was no denial there. Not even a hint of repudiation. He finally settled on resignation and opened the screen door to let me in. I introduced myself, then followed him to the living area I'd sat in when I'd first visited. Sitting down on the couch, I waited for him to find a place to land, but he wandered a bit, then stared out the picture window at the backyard. A moment later, he seemed to shake himself back to the present and slowly lowered himself into a chair.

"Have you told them?" He spoke in a gentle, encouraging voice, and it was easy to imagine him as a professor. "Do they know... I'm here?"

"No," I reassured him. "I thought about it on the way over here, but I don't think I should be the one to talk to them. That's kind of on you."

"How are they?" Dae-Hoon leaned forward. "Are they okay?"

I told him about what happened to his sons over the past few days, including Shin-Cho's dismissal from the military. He sagged back into the chair as I told him about his oldest son's fall from grace and his subsequent banishment to the badlands of Los Angeles. Explaining the bank glitch, he frowned, hissing in frustration.

"They intend to give the money back," I informed him. "Both of your sons don't want it."

"It was always for them," Dae-Hoon said. "I never expected it to get so out of hand. I truly didn't. It was supposed to be only a little bit to help them with schooling if they needed it, but one person told another, and soon, men were giving me money so I wouldn't tell anyone."

"You could have always said no," I broached. "It's a pretty common word."

"What are you going to do now?" He flinched when I shrugged. "Are you going to tell them?"

"I think they'd rather have you than the money." I dug out my notebook and jotted down David's local phone number. Tearing off the page, I handed it to Dae-Hoon. "They'd probably at least like to know you're alive. Shin-Cho could use some support, being gay and everything, and David's grieving. Call them, Dae-Hoon. They're your sons. Now, if you'll excuse me, I'm taking my boyfriend to a dinner at my brother's."

He led me to the door, still clutching the paper in his hand. Nodding numbly at me, Dae-Hoon closed the screen door behind me. Clearing his throat, he called my name. "McGinnis?"

"Yeah?" I turned, digging my keys out of my front pocket.

"I don't know what to say," he murmured. "It's been so long."

"Start with *hello*," I suggested. "Then work your way to *I'm sorry*. After that, there's nowhere to go but up."

I'D PICKED up the cake before grabbing Jae from the house. He held it in his lap, picking at the tape keeping the pink box closed until I scolded him. Pouting, he made a face at me and sniffed at the cardboard, his frown growing deeper.

"This smells like box," he complained under his breath.

"That's because I know you," I said. "There's a plastic container in there holding the cake. I didn't want you picking the maraschino cherry off the top before we got there."

Maddy opened the door for us, giving me a huge hug before taking the cake from Jae. He leaned over to slip his shoes off, and she was waiting for him, laughing when he squirmed in her arms and glared at me. I saluted him with the cake box Maddy'd given me, and headed toward the kitchen.

"Where's Mike?" I asked her.

"He went with Tasha to get ice cream," she said, rolling her eyes. "Apparently one can only get a certain brand of mint chocolate chip, but no one told me what that was."

The mats were still in place, and the room smelled of orange sauce and meat. A variety of vegetables in different stages of being sliced were laid out on the counter, and a bag of corn ears waited to be divested of their silk. I set the cake down on the counter and undid the tape. Pulling out the container inside, I turned it so Jae could see it.

"It's a chocolate cake." He examined it, then gave me a skeptical look.

"No, not just chocolate," I corrected smugly. "This is a *dobash* cake. See that half cherry on the top? That's mine."

"It's a chocolate cake," Jae repeated.

"*Dobash*." Kissing the corner of his mouth, I shooed him away from the counter. "We lived in Hawai'i for about six months when I was a kid. I don't remember a lot about it… mostly sand and getting sunburned, but I *did* remember this cake. It's not just chocolate. It's like milky cream chocolate orgasm. A very big difference."

"Don't get him started on that cake." Maddy dismissed my treasure with a wave of her knife. "And if you want a zombie cherry, Jae, there's a jar in the fridge. Don't let Cole tease you with it."

"Trust me, Mad Dog," I smirked at her. "When I tease Jae, it's not about cherries."

I was saved from her snappy rejoinder by the house phone going off. She slapped my hand from the carrots and reached for the handset. With her back turned, I raided the carrots, offering one to Jae. He turned his nose up at it, choosing a fresh pepper instead. Biting into it, he grinned and kissed my mouth, leaving a burning tingle on my lips.

"No, he's not home. Can I take a message?" Maddy motioned for me to pass her a pen from the cup on the counter. She froze in place, listening carefully to what the caller was saying. "Wait, hold on. Please... just hold on."

"What?" My stomach dropped. I came up behind Maddy, touching her side. "What's wrong? Is it Mike?"

"It's a man from Tokyo calling about your mother," she said haltingly. Maddy was pale as she handed me the phone. "You need... to talk to him. He... Cole... he says he's your brother."

Don't miss the beginning of the story in

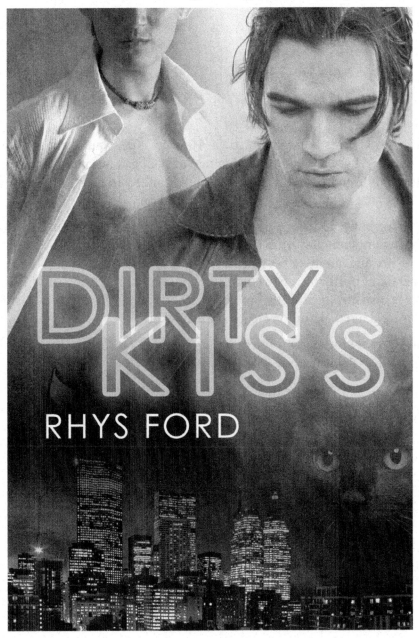

http://www.dreamspinnerpress.com

RHYS FORD was born and raised in Hawai'i, then wandered off to see the world. After chewing through a pile of books, a lot of odd food, and a stray boyfriend or two, Rhys eventually landed in San Diego, which is a very nice place but seriously needs more rain.

Rhys currently has a day job herding graphics pixels at an asset management company with a fantastic view of the seashore from many floors up and admits to sharing the house with three cats, a black Pomeranian puffball, a bonsai wolfhound, and a ginger cairn terrorist. Rhys is also enslaved to the upkeep a 1979 Pontiac Firebird, a Qosmio laptop, and a red Hamilton Beach coffeemaker.

Visit Rhys's blog at http://rhysford.wordpress.com/ or e-mail Rhys at rhys_ford@vitaenoir.com.

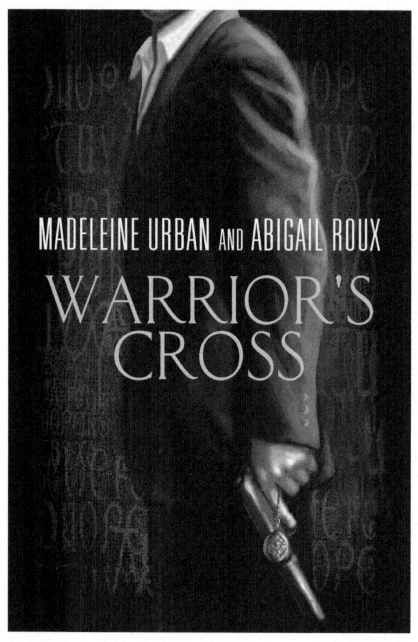

CPSIA information can be obtained
at www.ICGtesting.com
Printed in the USA
LVOW13s1211190617
538605LV00006B/803/P